Leg Up

Enjoy the ride!
Sue

Susan Archer

Copyright © 2020 by Susan Archer
All rights reserved under International and Pan-American
copyright conventions

The cover photograph was taken by Brooke Jacobs
(www.JacobsPhotography.com, used with permission) of the
fabulously talented WCC CH The Daily Lottery. Brooke took
this photograph during his victory pass under the spotlight for the
Five-Gaited Stake at the 2019 World Championship Horse Show.
Danny Lockhart is in the irons.

FOREWORD

Leg Up is the fourth book in a series that began with *Stake Night* and continued with *Show Time* and *Victory Pass*. I recommend that you read those books first to become familiar with the horse and human characters, many of whom reappear as they continue their quests to win the most coveted prize in the Saddlebred show horse industry, a World Championship.

Leg Up takes place five years after the end of *Victory Pass*, in which our villain, Johnnie Stuart, has self-destructed at the World Championships when he is disqualified during the workout of the Five-Gaited Stake. His behavior earns him a life-time ban from the industry, and Missy Phillips goes on to win the World Championship for the second year in a row on Toreador, a horse bred and originally trained by Johnnie.

In this book, we find out who fills the void left by Johnnie and whether a new generation of Saddlebreds emerges from the promise of the stallions and mares highlighted in earlier stories.

ACKNOWLEDGEMENTS

I thank all the readers of this story's predecessors, *Stake Night, Show Time* and *Victory Pass*. I continue to be amazed that so many enjoyed the stories and I sincerely appreciate the kind comments I've received in person and on social media. Your encouragement has made this next story possible.

In addition to the readers, I have many people to thank for helping me with this fourth story. This last year, I've been lucky to be a part Rose Stables, a fun, lively barn in Shelbyville KY filled with supportive stablemates. While we will always miss the training and coaching of Jerry Hutson, Gerhardt Roos' and Cobi van den Berg's talent, energy, work ethic, and ability to communicate (sometimes at full voice), have taught me that horse shows really can be fun. I also very much appreciate Renee' Biggins' instruction and her ability to patiently explain the same concept in different ways until I fully understand it.

As with the first three books, my friend Lori Weis helped with editing. She is a wise counselor and a careful reader, helping me ensure the story is interesting, even to a non-rider. I especially appreciate her sense of humor, her amazing memory, and her attention to detail. My friend Cindy Sherman was also a pre-reader, and answered many questions throughout this process.

I thank the supportive Saddlebred and Morgan communities, many members of which I've only met on-line. These kind people have helped me understand topics like transitioning from gaited riding to driving. Ya'll know who you are!

Finally, and most importantly, I want to thank my wonderful, supportive, loving husband Rick. He is always at the rail, reminding me to focus and "stick with it!" These are words that apply to life as well as to the show ring and I try to take them to heart. I love you, sweetie.

And before you ask, the human and equine characters in the stories are fictional. Any resemblance to the characters we see in real life barns and at shows is purely coincidental.

TABLE OF CONTENTS

CHAPTER 1

Helen Stanton hears her husband Matthew coming through the door from the garage and she glances up from her laptop computer. "You got home just in time. They've already started the live feed and the first class is about to start."

He kisses her on the cheek and then heads to the kitchen with his shopping bag. "I got a rotisserie chicken and a salad. I knew we wouldn't want to mess around in the kitchen tonight."

"Sounds good," she says absently, tucking her frizzy red hair behind her ears. "I'm trying to get the TV to display what's on the computer screen. We won't be able to see much if we're both watching the show on my laptop." After a few more key presses, she smiles in relief. "Ah, there it is! Look Matthew! It's the green shavings!"

He joins her in front of the large screen. "Yes. There's no other show like it, is there? Are you sorry to be missing it this year? We could have gone just to watch."

"I know, but I didn't want to spend all of our vacation time going to Louisville for the World Championship when we didn't have a horse to take. It'll be okay watching it from here." Her voice sounds artificially cheerful, even to her own ears, so she quickly changes the subject. "Why don't you pour us some sort of bourbon drink so we can get in the Kentucky mood?"

She waits for him to leave the room before blinking back the tears that are threatening to run down her cheeks. She takes a couple of deep breaths and studies the information she has printed out about the entries in each of tonight's classes. When Matthew returns with the drinks and settles in next to her on the couch, she hands him the papers. "To make this more fun, I think we should see which one of us is the best judge. Let's try to guess who will be in the top three of every class. Whoever has the most right at the end of the night gets to choose what they want for dinner tomorrow night and the other one has to make it."

"Well, I may not be much of a judge, but I think that I can make pretty good guesses by just reading the names in the entries."

1

She snorts, "Maybe so, but I doubt anyone would have ever picked my name out using that method. And I did get a third-place ribbon last year on Glitter Girl."

Matthew raises his glass in a salute. "That's true. And it only took us four trips to Louisville to get in the top three on Saturday night."

"I still can't believe it. Some people that show Saddlebreds never even get to show there once." She sips her drink, "Remember our first trip there with Happy Dance six years ago? We got a sixth-place ribbon in the qualifier and I was so happy with it that I decided not to show in the championship."

"I remember. That joy was every bit as good as last year's Saturday night ribbon. Maybe we should have found a catch rider this year, or let Melody show Glitter Girl in the Ladies Division."

"Maybe. But it would have been hard for me to watch someone else show her, and I know how selfish that sounds. It is so disappointing to know that I'll probably never get to ride a horse like her again." Despite her efforts to stop them, the tears that have been threatening all day now spill down her cheeks and she starts to sob.

Matthew pulls her into a hug and says consolingly, "Now honey, that might not be true. You never know. They might find a treatment for neuropathy that would allow you to ride again."

Helen's shoulders shake as she struggles to control her sobs. "My doctors haven't given me any reason to believe that could happen. And everything I read says nerve damage like mine is permanent and progressive. Maybe I could ride a trail horse, but I don't think I could ever ride a world class gaited horse again. I can't even balance well enough to swing my leg over her back, much less rack around a corner. It's embarrassing. I'd end up as a smoking pile of rubble in the dirt."

Matthew continues to hold her as the National Anthem plays on the live feed from Louisville. "You don't have anything to be embarrassed about. I wish the doctors could be more helpful, but I've never known you to be someone who gives up easily. And this is an important part of your life. Being around horses makes you happy. So we're just going to have to figure out how to make it happen."

2

Helen sniffles and quickly changes the subject. "The first class is the Ladies Three Gaited Championship, so pay attention and pick out the horses you think will be in the top three."

They are silent as they watch most of the first class and then Helen says, "I don't think I know anyone in this class, but I noticed from the program that there are a lot of Spy Master foals in it. And so many of them have clever names, like Bond Girl, Super Sleuth, Spy Runner, Private Eye, and Jack Ryan. People are so clever naming foals."

"Who's Spy Master?"

"He's a stallion that was bred and trained in California. I think he's about 10 or so years old now. He won the reserve world championship in the Five-Gaited stake when he was young. That was before we bought Happy Dance." She pauses to take another sip of her drink and to make a note. "I'm not sure why he retired, but I seem to remember hearing that he colicked at the Kansas City Royal and almost died. He kind of disappeared from sight for a while, but then his foals started showing up at horse shows a couple of years ago. And they're winning."

"But he was a gaited horse, wouldn't you expect to see them in the gaited classes?"

"Oh, the night has just begun. From what I saw in the program and the on-line ads, we're going to see several of them in the gaited classes, too. They've been doing really well during the entire show. On-line, everyone is talking about what a huge influence he is having on the breed. And there's a lot of grousing about needing more diversity in the blood lines."

She stops and listens carefully as the ring announcer reads the numbers and names of the winning horses and riders. Helen cheers up when she finds out she has identified two of the top three.

"Maybe you could become a judge," Matthew complains. "I didn't pick any of them."

"Well, I've been paying attention this week to who won the qualifying classes so I've got an advantage," she admits. "The harness ponies are next and your guess is definitely as good as mine in that class."

3

"I don't even know what I'm supposed to be looking for in a good harness pony, so I'll go put dinner together while you watch. Let me know when something interesting happens."

She laughs, despite her low mood. "It's a horse show, honey. It's all interesting."

Matthew returns to the family room with loaded dinner plates just as the Fine Harness World Grand Championship class is entering the ring. He watches carefully as the well-dressed drivers maneuver their elegant, four-wheeled buggies around the ring behind gorgeous, high-trotting Saddlebreds. "So, tell me about this class."

"I actually don't know much about any of the driving classes. I've never tried to drive a horse and they don't show in harness much at our barn. In fact, they don't even have harness classes at some of the Denver shows. But it's a performance class where the horses enter the ring at a park trot."

"Remind me again what a park trot is," he interrupts.

"A park trot is square and animated. They aren't supposed to go too fast and the gait should be powerful and collected. It is supposed to show off a horse's motion in all four legs and it takes a special horse to get a lot of motion without going too fast. That's what makes it so challenging. I've read that it is difficult to train a horse to have a great park trot. Rather, it's a result of good breeding and conformation. I read that a horse's front leg has to sit up at the point of the shoulder to allow the forearm to come up really high."

"They're beautiful," he takes his seat beside her, watching the screen intently.

The announcer tells the drivers to show their horse, and Matthew asks, "What does that mean? Aren't they already showing their horse?"

"It means that the driver can pick the trotting speed that they think their horse is best at. Typically, it will be faster than the park trot."

"Is that for the reason you said? Because they can usually get more motion at a higher speed?"

"I guess so. I don't really know much about it."

4

"Look at how beautiful they are." He watches for several minutes and says, "I think you should do that."

She looks at him, "Do what?"

"Get a harness horse. You wouldn't have to worry about mounting. And you'd be able to get back into showing horses. Why couldn't you try that?"

She looks at him in astonishment. "I don't think I'd like driving at all."

"Why not?"

"Just the thought of sitting behind a horse and being so close to their hind feet intimidates me. I don't even know how those drivers see around them to figure out where they're going. And I don't know how they connect with the horse when they can't feel or influence the horse with their seat and legs. I think it's a lot harder than it looks."

"Harder than riding a gaited horse in a big amateur class at Louisville? You learned how to do that."

"As you know, it took a lot of years."

"So what? You have time." He takes a sip of his drink, "As added incentive, just look at the beautiful gowns the women are wearing."

"But Glitter Girl isn't a harness horse. And this body doesn't look great in those form-fitting sequined gowns," she says, motioning at her slightly chubby frame.

"Honey, don't put yourself down like that. You're gorgeous no matter what you wear. But I'm serious. Let's sell her and get a harness horse," he suggests reasonably. "I just think it would be a shame to give up on your passion when we might just need to adjust to a new reality. I think you should at least consider it."

Helen listens to the announcer and deliberately changes the subject. "Look at that. A horse named Sneaky Suspicion just won the class! That's another Spy Master foal. See what I mean about how they're dominating this year? Now we need to start paying close attention. The next class is the Ladies Five-Gaited Championship."

"Do you know anyone in this class?"

Helen is watching the gaited horses enter the ring, "Yes! There's Missy Phillips now. She's riding Texas Beauty Queen."

"I remember that horse from last year."

"Yes, she's had her quite a while, at least six years." Helen taps some keys on her phone. "Texas Beauty Queen is 12 years old. And she has some foals. They must have done embryo transplants."

"Are you saying that because she's still showing?"

"Yeah. I don't remember her ever skipping a season and if she had carried a foal, she wouldn't have shown."

"Have you thought about trying to get an embryo out of Glitter Girl?"

"We've talked about that before, but it's expensive to get into the breeding business. It's hard enough for us to support a show horse, much less a mare and foal. There's too much risk that we wouldn't get a good one and too much money required while we're waiting for it to grow up enough to even know whether it's going to be any good. And what if it isn't? We can't exactly keep it in our front yard as a lawn ornament."

"Yes, but wouldn't you like to have a Glitter Girl baby? She's been such a wonderful horse."

"Yes, but the financial risk is too much for me." She glances back at the screen, "It doesn't look like Texas Beauty Queen has lost a step, even though she's 12. Look at her rack!"

They watch the remainder of the class quietly and are unsurprised when Missy Phillips is named the winner. They watch two more classes until the bugler summons the Amateur Five-Gaited class to the ring. Helen leans forward, watching carefully as the gaited horses trot into the ring. "Look, there's Blair Durant on Vendome Copper. He won it the last two years in a row." She watches as several other horses trot in. "And there's Missy on War Paint."

"Isn't that the horse that bucked in the line up last year?"

Helen laughs, "Yes. And she still got a ribbon. If it had been me riding, they'd have kicked me out of the ring. That mare is either brilliant or she's a disaster. She's a full sister to a horse named Night Train. Do you remember him?"

"Isn't he the horse that the trainer was riding when he lost his cool in the Championship several years ago?"

"Yes, that was Johnnie Stuart. I'll never forget that night. He threw a shoe in the workout and was disqualified because he'd already had one time out. He threw a tantrum over it and got a lifetime ban."

"Yeah. Now I remember. It was dramatic."

"It was. I remember watching it on-line and not really understanding what was going on at the time. They didn't do a good job of explaining it and the cameras didn't show what was going on in the ring. But I learned later that he deliberately trampled one of the ring stewards."

"That's inexcusable. Where is he now?"

"I have no idea. But he bred some good horses. War Paint, Toreador, and Night Train all came from his breeding program."

"Whatever happened to Toreador? He won the World Championship, didn't he?"

"Yes. He's famous. He actually won it four years in a row with three different owners. Johnnie Stuart bred and trained him and won on him the first time. Then Blair Durant's mother bought him. That was the year that his trainer got hurt when she was leaving the ring after the qualifier, so his groom actually showed him in the championship and won. And then Missy Phillips bought him and won twice with him. He was a gelding and I think he's retired now. I haven't heard much about him in the last couple of years."

They watch as the class reverses and begins trotting the second direction. Matthew asks, "So who do you think is going to win this class?"

"Missy. My money is always on Missy."

"You're just playing the odds," he scoffs.

"I am. She has lots of nice horses and can ride as well as anyone in the ring. I met her the very first time I went to that adult riding camp in Kentucky and she's always been really nice to me, so I like to see her do well."

"I'm getting them all confused. I can only tell them apart by what the rider is wearing. Is that one Vendome Copper?" Matthew asks as the camera picks up a chestnut gelding with a thin white strip on his face.

"Yes! Good eye!"

7

"He's been around a long time, hasn't he?"

"Yes, he has. He must be 12 or 13 years old by now."

"She looks so calm."

"Yes. I don't think that woman ever sweats or shows any emotion. I was lined up next to her last year and she didn't even crack a smile when she won. I would have been whooping and hollering." She sips her drink, "Actually, come to think of it, I was whooping and hollering when I got third."

"So was I! That was an awesome moment."

They watch the rest of the class and are unsurprised when Blair Durant is announced as the winner with Missy Phillips as the reserve champion.

"Look! She's still not smiling," Helen says in disbelief as the camera follows Blair's path to the end of the ring where the trophy is presented. "I think that's crazy! And the first and second place horses are in the same barn. Those trainers must be really good."

"Who are they?"

"It's Beech Tree Farm. We got to tour it once when I was in Kentucky for camp. The trainers are a young couple named Bobby and Jennifer Acton. They have lots of nice horses there."

"Probably because they have lots of clients with plenty of money. The two things usually go hand-in-hand, I've learned."

"They do," she admits. "Although I'm certainly not complaining about the results we've had. I never would have thought that we'd be fortunate enough to be competitive at the world championship. It was fun."

"Don't use the past tense," Matthew admonishes. "We'll be back there again."

CHAPTER 2

"Emily! This is the last time I'm going to call you. If you don't get in here this minute, your brother is going to eat every last pancake." Angela Rivers refills the platter of pancakes as she shouts, then fastens her bright blue eyes on her tall, dark-haired 16-year-old son. "Jeremy, go make sure your sister is out of bed. We'll be late for church if we don't get a move on."

Kenny refills his wife's coffee cup, moves her blond ponytail to kiss her neck, and then pulls out a chair at the kitchen table. "If she misses breakfast, it will be her loss. Come sit down and eat while the food is still hot."

"She's only 12. It is my motherly duty to make sure she eats something besides cereal."

He helps himself to the heaping platter of steaming food. "You're right that she's 12. If she would rather eat cereal for breakfast than your wonderful blueberry pancakes, it's her loss."

"She's coming," Jeremy mimics his sister's voice and her recognizable eye roll as he rejoins them at the table.

Kenny smiles and hands the platter to Angela. "So other than church, what's on your agenda today?"

"School starts tomorrow, so I'm going to run to Gillette and do a little shopping to make sure these kids have something decent to wear. What about you?"

"I'm going to bring the yearling colts in and get started on them. Watching the show from Louisville on the live feed last night inspired me. A lot of Spy Master's foals earned big ribbons, so I think these youngsters we have will be in high demand and I want to be ready when people come to buy. Can you believe that it's been seven years since we had Spy Master in our barn before he competed at Louisville?"

"That's crazy," Angela replies. "That was a whole year before we moved out here from Kentucky to help your aunt and uncle with the ranch. I had never even been to Wyoming before. I'll never forget the night we arrived when the wind was howling and the snow was drifting. I thought we'd come to the end of the earth."

9

"And the wind hasn't quit blowing for more than two days in a row since then," Kenny jokes. "I still miss Aunt Marie and Uncle Jim. I can't believe they've been gone for almost five years. We were so fortunate to inherit this beautiful ranch from them, even if it is a never-ending pile of work."

Jeremy looks up from a bite that is dripping with syrup. "Speaking of work, I've got the new stalls ready for the young horses and I've checked them for nails and everything. I've even got them bedded. I was hoping we'd have time to go over to the Sellers' place this afternoon. Levi and his dad are going to work some cattle and I wanted to take Ninja over and see if he's learning anything."

"Why don't you take one of the three-year-olds instead? Since Ninja's first show is next week, I want to keep him focused on harness. He certainly doesn't need to be doing any cantering."

"He's afraid to get dumped." Emily says with a laugh, joining the family at the table and tossing a blond ponytail that matches her mom's behind her shoulder. "Those three-year-olds are spicy."

"I'm not afraid to get dumped," Jeremy retorts, his dark eyes flashing. "I just like riding Ninja."

"Yeah, but the younger horses need some work around cattle. I think it keeps them from getting too bored with their training," Kenny interjects. "I'm going to start gaiting Ninja's little brother tomorrow, so an outing today would be good for him. After today, we'll take his shoes off and we won't want to let him trot again until his slow gait is solid."

"But he's so hot-headed compared to Levi's quarter horse. It's hard to get him to calm down and watch a cow, especially when we're just starting and he isn't tired yet."

"You could put him on a lunge line and work him in the round pen before we leave just to take the edge off. The only way he'll get better is to just keep doing it, son. I think he's going to make a great show horse, but I want to make sure that his mind stays healthy. Giving him work outside of the show ring and the round pen will make him a more sensible show horse."

"Speaking of new homes, have you gotten any bites on Ninja?" Angela asks.

"Not yet, but no one has seen him show yet. If he has a good show at the Colorado Fall Classic, we'll get a nice picture of him and advertise him. I think that will help."

"Did you decide whether I can skip school on Friday and go to Denver with you for the show?" Jeremy asks.

"I could really use your help, but I don't want you to miss school during the very first week, especially now that you're a Junior in High School and taking all those honors classes. You'll need to keep your grades up if you want to be a veterinarian someday. So I'm going to go down on my own. I'm only going to take the two four-year-olds, so I don't need you to show anything in the Juvenile division. I'll get someone down there to help me get into the ring with Ninja in his harness class. I need you to hold down the fort here and make sure the yearlings are doing okay. You know how wild they can be their very first week in the barn. I'll be back late Saturday night."

Jeremy's disappointment is obvious but before he can respond, Emily chimes in. "Dad? Do you think I could get a gaited horse to show?"

Everyone at the table looks at her in surprise and Angela reacts first. "What? I thought you were all about barrel racing and rodeo. Since when did you want to show Saddlebreds?"

"I've been thinking about it for a while now. It looks like a lot of fun. And why couldn't I do both?" She widens her blue eyes and looks at her dad, "Please?"

He laughs at her obvious attempts to charm him, "Every horse we have here is for sale. And the shows are so far away that I don't think you'd have much of an opportunity to show. Colorado only has four shows a year."

"But will you think about it?"

"Let's talk about it another time. Maybe if you keep your grades up and you step up to help Jeremy with some of his chores in the barn, we can talk about it. But right now, you need to hurry and finish your breakfast and get ready for church."

CHAPTER 3

"This party gets bigger every year." Bobby Acton comes into the kitchen and hands his wife an empty platter. "I hope you bought a lot of burger patties because they're going really fast."

Jennifer laughs as she reaches into the refrigerator to remove another platter of meat. "I'm pretty sure that I have plenty. How many people are here?"

"It seems like everyone in the industry."

"But no clients, I hope."

"Right, no clients. Just horse trainers, farriers, vets, and grooms and their families."

"Well you'd better get back out to the grill so we get them fed before they drink too much beer. I'd hate to have to drive everyone home. It isn't like we can call an Uber out here in rural Shelby County."

Bobby leans down and plants a kiss on the top of her head, returning to the pool deck just in time to see his mentor, Clark Benton, arriving at the party. "Hey Clark! Welcome! I'm so glad you could make it this year."

"Thanks for inviting me," the older trainer drawls, peering out from under his cap embossed with the recognizable Kiplenan Saddlebreds logo. "It looks like you've got the party of the century going on here. Cars are parked all the way down your driveway, nearly to Shelbyville Road."

"This party gets bigger every year. I think everyone is anxious to let their hair down after the Louisville show."

"If I had any hair, I'd probably fit in better with this young crowd," Clark laughs, watching several people splashing in the pool. "And from the look of things, it's good that almost everyone is taking tomorrow off. There will be more than a few headaches to go around."

Bobby puts more burger patties on the grill. "It looked like you had a great show. Was Mr. Kiplenan pleased?"

"I think so. You never know what you're going to get with the judging panels but he's been around the business long enough that he doesn't get too upset if the ribbons aren't what he thinks he deserves."

"You're lucky to have a customer that is so secure."

"Don't I know it! I've been with Mr. Kiplenan's barn for almost 20 years now. It's a real luxury to only have to please one person. I don't know how you trainers with a bunch of different amateurs stay sane."

"It does have its challenges," Bobby admits. "It's been especially tough to have Missy Phillips and Blair Durant in the same barn, much less having them compete head-to-head in the Amateur Gaited division."

"I always thought the problem was more Blair's mother Marianne, rather than Blair."

"You're right. Blair is a pretty nice gal. Her mother just wants to win. And if she doesn't win, there is always someone to blame. At least she wasn't complaining last night when Blair beat Missy in the Amateur Gaited Championship, but her smugness is harder to handle than her complaints. Especially since I didn't think the judges got it right. Vendome is starting to show his age a little and I thought War Paint was the better horse."

"I agree. I remember when they bought Vendome Copper from us. I think that's the reason you quit working for me and moved over here to Beech Tree."

"Yes," Bobby smiles at the memory. "That and the opportunity to join Jennifer over here at her Dad's old place. Vendome Copper has always been my favorite horse. I can't believe that he's 12 years old."

"And still racking up a storm. You must take good care of him."

"We do. And while I complain about how high maintenance Marianne is, she doesn't scrimp when it comes to caring for her horses. We use everything we can to make sure he is comfortable and happy, including chiropractors, acupuncture, magna wave, and preventive joint injections."

"I haven't used magna wave. Do you think it makes a difference?"

"I think it does, but we're only using it on horses that have some age on them. You're working young ones, so I don't know that it would help them as much."

"And it isn't cheap."

"No. It costs about $100 per treatment and I've got a couple horses that get two or three treatments before a show. But it's been proven to reduce inflammation and increase cell metabolism. It pushes fluid into the tissue and I just think the increased circulation helps my older horses stay sound."

"I've been doing some reading about it and it does seem to be a valuable therapy." Clark is watching the crowd, and changes the subject, "Isn't that Holly McNair?"

Bobby follows Clark's gaze to a pretty woman in her early forties with long, curly brunette hair just arriving at the party. "It is, although I don't know that I've ever seen her look like that." He admires the bikini top that displays the woman's perfectly toned stomach. "It looks like she's in a mood to celebrate her win with Sneaky Suspicion in the Fine Harness Stake last night."

"I heard she bought Johnnie Stuart's place and renamed it Spy Hill Barn, just in case there's any doubt which bloodline she favors," Clark mentions dryly. "I imagine every horse on the place is related to Spy Master. What do you know about her clients?"

"I heard that her California customer that owns the horse she won with is moving all of her horses from the west coast. Her name is Eileen Miller and she still owns Spy Master, too. I don't know how many other horses that lady has and I haven't heard about anyone else moving into the barn."

"That's a big place and I think it's got bad juju. I wonder if anyone did an exorcism to eradicate Johnnie's evil spirit?"

Bobby laughs. "Yeah. As awful as it was at the time, the best thing that ever happened to me was when he fired me a day or so before Christmas. I ended up selling used cars to pay my rent, and I was terrible at it. When you called and offered me a job, it changed my life." He flips several burgers. "Johnnie was a jerk but he taught me a lot about horses."

14

"I think Johnnie could be a little rough on a horse and we know that he could be rough on people. He couldn't keep anyone working for him for more than a year."

"He was a disciplinarian, for sure. And his bloodlines turned out horses with attitude. Some people might even call a couple of them criminals. As you know, there's a fine line between making sure a horse isn't allowed to have dangerous habits that will get someone killed and being too harsh. I won't argue that Johnnie didn't ever cross that line."

Clark nods. "Well even if that lady from California has half a dozen horses, there isn't any way that would be enough for her to keep a barn that big in the black."

"I did hear that she's going to stand Spy Master at the barn. She'll make money from the stud fees."

"True, but no one's been in that barn since Johnnie left the country. I imagine it needs maintenance and we both know that isn't cheap. Unless she wins the lottery, she'll have to get some more horses in that barn just to pay the bills."

"You're right, and we know that you can't pay the bills with just boarding and training horses and have competitive prices. Everyone needs a lesson program or a pretty brisk business of buying and selling to earn commissions in order to make it."

"Good customers in this business don't grow on trees, so she'll have to take them from someone else," Clark notes. "You've got the best customers around, so you might want to watch out."

Bobby laughs, "I've got a customer or two that I might pay her to take."

"Don't tell me. Those would be the ones that don't pay their bills on time and are always complaining about the farrier and vet costs."

"Yep."

CHAPTER 4

Annie Jessup spots Missy Phillips leaning on the rail of the practice ring at the Coliseum and takes a place next to her. "I'm so glad I ran into you. I wanted to congratulate you on your wins. Winning the ladies gaited class and taking reserve in the Amateur class on Saturday night at Louisville is an amazing accomplishment. It must be almost as good as the feeling you had several years ago when you won the Amateur class and the gaited stake on the same night. No one had ever done that before and no one has done it since."

Missy smiles and gives Annie a warm hug. "Thanks Annie. I'm a very lucky person to have had such great horses and trainers. Toreador gave me two World Championships, and now I have War Paint and Texas Beauty Queen, who are both amazing. But I think my favorite horse of all was Josephine's Dream, who you bred and trained. I heard that you got her back. How is she?"

"I did get her back. The young girl that you sold Josie to went off to college and her family gifted her back to me. I was thrilled and she's doing great. She's busy bossing the broodmare band around. As a matter of fact, I'm showing her first foal, Dream Weaver, in the three-year-old gaited class tonight."

"I saw that in the program and I'm looking forward to seeing her. What's she like?"

"She's a grand filly. She inherited Josie's huge engine, but her sire gave her a wonderful neck. She's going to be bigger than Josie."

"I always thought that Josie had no idea that she wasn't the biggest horse in the ring. She always had such a presence when she racked down a straight-away and she was a blast to ride. It was a real testament to that mare that she won the Amateur Stake at Louisville just a year after nearly being killed in that terrible trailer wreck."

"Yes, that still registers as the very worst night of my life," Annie admits. "I wasn't even sure that she would survive, much less go on to win a World Championship."

16

"So now that she's a full-time broodmare, are you taking embryos from her?"

"No, I'm having her carry every foal. I am probably just being a little old-fashioned about it, but I'm also getting to the age where I'm trying to limit the number of young horses I'm working each year. I'm focusing on quality rather than quantity. I did splurge and pay a huge stud fee for Spy Master and Josie has a two-year-old stud colt by him."

"Wow. That's a gaited match made in heaven. Both of them are tremendously athletic. What's the colt like?"

"He's beautiful, but he's been a little slow to mature and I'm really being careful not to rush him because he has Josie's temperament. I brought him into the training barn last Fall just to see if he might get ready for the two-year-old class at Louisville this year, but he just wasn't coming along like I wanted, so I kicked him back out into the field. I'm going to try him again this winter."

"Well, I'm going to be shopping for something young this winter, so keep me in mind."

"You've certainly got some good ones."

"I do, and I'm going to have to sell something before I buy something. My dad is generous, but he's limiting me to having just two in training at a time."

"And that's Texas Beauty Queen and War Paint?"

"Yes. Queen is a perfect Ladies horse. She's big and elegant and she's very particular about where she puts her feet. She's very precise about her gaits. But she's 12 and I think any good juvenile rider could handle her. She's the grand dame of the barn. She's in a stall where she can watch the younger horses work and we laugh that she's secretly sneering at the ones that are just figuring out how to slow gait and rack. When she gets to work, it's like she's saying 'Here! Hold my beer!' as she flies around the ring. I love how effortless it is for her. And she's at the point where she needs a young girl to take care of."

"And who will dote on her," Annie agrees. "What's War Paint like?"

"She's a different beast altogether," Missy shakes her head.

"Didn't she come from Johnnie Stuart's breeding and training program?"

"She did, and it shows. She's a wild thing even at nine years old. There is never a dull moment with her."

"I remember last year at Louisville when she bucked in the line-up."

"It was so embarrassing," Missy laughs. "She was completely undone by the grooms and trainers running in to strip the saddles for the conformation judging. When Jennifer gave me a leg up to remount, War Paint completely lost her cool. She went bucking and jumping across the ring. I have no idea how I managed to get my leg over her and stick with her."

Annie laughs, too. "We wouldn't be laughing if you hadn't succeeded."

"True. But I did get punished a bit with a sixth place. I guess they really do care about manners in an Amateur class." Missy rolls her eyes and shrugs her shoulders.

"She made up for it this year. Congratulations on the reserve championship."

"Thanks, we had a great ride. I would be lying though, if I didn't admit to being a little disappointed. Winning is a lot more fun than coming in second." Missy changes the topic. "Tell me a little bit about your three-year-old. What did you name her?"

"Dream Weaver, but I call her Dreamy. She thinks a lot of herself. This is her first show, though, so I'm not sure how it will go. She's got some snort in her."

"She wouldn't be Josie's foal if she didn't have some snort. You always coached me to have a strategy and a plan for every show. What's your strategy tonight?"

"To stay out of trouble and to come out of the ring without more dirt on my suit than when I went into it," Annie laughs. "Seriously, though, my plan is to stick to the rail the first direction to give her some security. If she's up to it, I'll get a little more creative the second direction. I've noticed that the judges are not paying much attention to the far end of the ring, so I'll use that area to correct her and set up her passes. I'd love to win some of the Sweepstakes money, but it's more important that she has a good experience."

"How much is in the pot this year?"

"It's big, nearly $50K." Annie glances at her watch, "I'd better get back to the stalls and start getting my filly ready to go."

Two hours later, Annie is trotting into the ring, adjusting her contact on the reins to keep her filly's attention. She lowers her post and gently tightens her legs to give her filly some extra security in the unfamiliar environment, reducing the likelihood that her horse will balk at the lights and the noise. Dreamy's head is so high that Annie can barely see over her ears and Annie can feel the filly's back end slide towards the center of the ring as the horse hesitates. Annie clucks softly to encourage her young horse and uses her left leg to straighten the horse's body and push her to the rail. Dreamy's right ear flicks back at Annie briefly before returning forward. When another three-year-old passes her on the left, almost close enough to touch, and Annie feels her horse flinch and then surge forward.

"Easy, girl." Annie uses her voice and body to steady her mount and even out her cadence. Once she feels Dreamy relax slightly and steady her trot, she glances at the judges to assess her ring position and the traffic around her. To avoid being covered up by the other horses, she guides her horse deep into the corner to let the crowd behind her go by, and slides the bit in Dreamy's mouth to make sure the mare is attentive and set up to make a good pass. Coming out of the corner, she raises her left hand slightly, giving a gentle tug on the inside rein. Dreamy responds by squaring her body and lightening up her front end, resulting in a very nice trotting pass. Annie begins to relax into the class, gaining confidence that her filly is listening and working well.

The first slow gait and rack go well, but Annie feels Dreamy gain strength and momentum with every pass and by the time the announcer asks the class to reverse, Dreamy is far less patient with her transitions, twitching her ears in frustration when Annie asks her to slow down. To keep her horse looking happy, Annie pushes her more aggressively with her seat and legs and begins working off the rail. She still goes deep in the corners whenever the traffic allows, using her double bridle to keep Dreamy's head in the ideal position by tweaking the snaffle rein to raise her head a fraction of an inch and then lightly adjusting the curb to keep

19

Dreamy's nose in. Simultaneously, she moves in her seat to correct any imbalance in the horse's body and gives a gentle cluck to generate impulsion out of each corner. She can feel her horse getting stronger in the mouth and more resistant to correction as the class proceeds, much like a locomotive running downhill.

When the announcer calls for the walk before the slow gait, Annie is just beginning a pass towards the far end of the ring, and when she is half way through the pass, she slows her post and contains Dreamy's trot, slowing her enough so that she is still trotting when the announcer tells the class to slow gait and avoiding the frustration her horse is likely to express during the walk.

Annie sits deep into her saddle, spreads her hands, applies a strong leg on each side and clucks. Dreamy hops once and then begins an elevated four-beat gait down the rail. Annie maneuvers her horse off the rail and is rewarded when Dreamy squats lower in her hind quarters. When the announcer tells the class to rack, Annie squeezes with her seat and legs and loosens her reins slightly, encouraging her horse to show off her speed. As she nears a corner, she speaks to her horse, "Easy girl," to slow her in the turn, enabling her to maintain a balanced four-beat cadence through the maneuver.

When the announcer finally tells the class to canter, Annie can tell that Dreamy is tired. So she focuses on keeping her horse on the rail, conserving her remaining energy and being careful to maintain her right lead as other horses gallop past.

As soon as the announcer calls for the walk and then for the young horses to line up, Annie says "Whoa," and halts Dreamy for ten seconds with her head facing the rail to give her a chance to catch her breath and to let them both refocus. Her horse's neck is glistening with sweat and is foamy where the reins have rubbed. Annie glances over her shoulder to time her final pass so that she catches the judges' attention, and then turns Dreamy and cues her to rack, widening and lifting her hands, providing light alternating cues on the snaffle rein to keep Dreamy's head up despite her tiredness. Her horse responds with energy, flying down the rail, causing Annie to smile widely as they sweep around the corner and into the line-up. Annie pats her heaving horse and smiles in satisfaction as she waits for the ribbon winners to be announced.

As is the tradition with the Sweepstakes at the All American Horse Classic, the winners are announced from the fifth place forward while all contestants are still in the ring. The young horses and riders mill around waiting for the announcer to make his introductory remarks, and Annie halts Dreamy on the rail near where Missy Phillips is standing.

"She looked wonderful," Missy says. "Have you put a price on her?"

Annie laughs along with several people who have heard the question, deliberately interpreting Missy's question as a joke. "I might just have to hang onto her. I'm really pleased with her. She was sensible tonight. I think I could have called on her a bit more going the first direction. For her first show, she was steadier than I expected."

"I agree. You certainly won the second direction. And that last pass was incredible!" Missy leans over the fence and says more quietly, "I'm serious about asking for a price."

"Let me think about it. I think this one is pretty special."

Before long, the announcer proves that the judges have agreed with Annie's assessment, awarding Dreamy the Reserve Championship ribbon and prize money.

CHAPTER 5

"It's weird being here just to watch," Helen remarks as she leads Matthew through the halls of the stabling area for the Colorado Fall Charity Horse Show, using her cane to carefully maneuver across the uneven footing.

"Yeah. It's a lot less exciting but at least we didn't have to show up two hours early" he teases, stepping to the side of the aisle to let a groom lead a huge black Friesian horse by him.

"Ah! There are the Mountain Ridge stalls," Helen points to the bright red curtains at the end of the next aisle. "The Kentucky Saddlebred people are always so surprised at the variety of classes at our shows and that we have so many different breeds. I always tell them that it would be a pretty short show if it was only Saddlebreds and Saddleseat."

"I like the different classes, although I could do without all the western pleasure classes. It takes me a solid week to get the lyrics of that Roy Rogers Tumbling Tumbleweeds song out of my head. That should be used as a torture device. It's as bad as water-boarding, I'm sure. My favorite class is the ranch riding class where they have to go over obstacles and open gates and stuff."

"I like that too, and every year there are more Saddlebreds entering it. But it does make for a long show. Another difference between here and Kentucky is that we always show on Sundays, and there are always morning and afternoon sessions.

"Yes, it's grueling. We hardly ever got out of here before 10 PM on nights when you showed."

"Showing here is the horse trainer's equivalent of a marathon. Those pansies in Kentucky have no idea what we go through," Roger Jeffers has obviously overheard their conversation, coming forward with his hand extended to Matthew and giving Helen a quick hug of greeting and calling over his shoulder, "Melody? Matthew and Helen are here."

His wife and training partner emerges from the dressing room, tightening her tie. "You're just in time. Glitter Girl's class is coming up."

22

"How many are in her class, do you know?" Helen asks, glancing into the stall where the groom is putting the final touches on her mare's tail.

"Only six, I think. It's an open class, so you never really know what will be in there. Could be some young horses that trainers just want to get in the ring to see what they've got."

"We'll get out of your hair and go watch a couple classes. Good luck!" Matthew and Helen leave to find seats in the stands and arrive just as the Open Harness class enters the ring. "Look! There's Kenny Rivers," Matthew points out. "I didn't realize he would be here."

Helen leans forward in her seat. "I didn't either. We need to stop and say hello to him. I'm still so grateful that he sold Glitter Girl to us."

"Even though I don't know anything about harness horses, that one he's got looks pretty nice," Matthew remarks as the chestnut gelding marches around the ring. They watch the rest of the class in silence, and applaud loudly when it is announced that Kenny's horse, Nile Ninja, has won the class.

Two classes later, Melody rides Glitter Girl into the ring in the Open Five-Gaited class. Helen watches carefully as her mare executes each gait flawlessly, even flat walking during the transitions.

"She looks a little out of place in this class," Helen tells Matthew.

"What do you mean?"

"She's a little too well-behaved. She doesn't look exciting enough."

"I don't think you're being fair. I think she looks great."

"I'm not saying she doesn't look great. I'm only saying that she doesn't look like an open horse. She isn't wild enough."

Helen is unsurprised when Glitter Girl is awarded a third-place ribbon. Back at the stalls, Helen unwraps a peppermint for her mare and pats her neck while Roger begins toweling off the sweaty horse. "What did you think, Roger?"

"I think the judge was a little hard on her, but it was probably because she just doesn't fit in an open class. She's nine years old and solid as a rock. I think she could have won the Amateur class last night."

"I probably should have let you find a juvenile or amateur to show her. I wasn't ready to watch someone else ride her in my class."

"I understand that. She's got such beautiful manners that she'd be a lot better fit in a Ladies class rather than the Open class, if you still want Melody to show her. Unfortunately, we don't have enough gaited horses at this show for them to offer a Ladies class."

"Matthew thinks I should try harness," Helen says carefully, glancing over her shoulder to make sure her husband isn't within earshot. "What do you think?"

Roger pauses in his task to look his client in the eye. "I take it that the doctors said your balance and pain won't improve?" He leaves that last word as a question, and when she nods, tears filling her eyes, "Well, I think it's a brilliant idea. There isn't any reason why we couldn't do that. You've learned a lot about a horse's mouth and how to generate impulsion from the hind end. We'll just have to translate those skills to a cart."

"It hasn't ever appealed to me. It doesn't seem like you'd have the same level of communication with the horse that you get from sitting on them."

"It's just different," Roger says. "I really enjoy working a good harness horse. Their elegance and power epitomize the Saddlebred show horse reputation. In fact, I'd argue that the most famous show horse of all was The Lemon Drop Kid. He won four world championships in the 1950's and was on the cover of Sports Illustrated."

"We'd have to sell Glitter Girl before we got another horse. We need the money to buy a new one and we can't afford to have two horses in training."

"I understand. Before you pull the trigger on that, why don't you come out to the barn sometime over the next couple of weeks and we'll put you in a cart and see how you like it?"

CHAPTER 6

When Holly's phone rings, she checks the caller ID and rolls her eyes, preparing herself for another conversation with the man whose ego is even bigger than the barn he built. "Hi Johnnie!"

"Good morning little lady," the older trainer's Kentucky drawl is still thick, despite having spent the last five years in Canada. "I thought I'd call and check on my investment since your payment is late."

"It's not due until the end of the day, Johnnie. I just sent the electronic instructions a few minutes ago." Holly quickly makes herself a note to call her bank.

"I'm mighty happy to hear that. I'd hate to have to repossess it now that you've moved in. How are things going?"

"They're great, but I'm really glad you called. I haven't figured out how to turn on the sprinkler system in the indoor ring."

They talk for several minutes about the facilities and then Johnnie asks, "So have you met any of your neighbors yet?"

"I have. I went to the annual post-Louisville bash over at Beech Tree. It was a wild time."

"Those kids over there have no idea what they're doing. They have no business calling themselves trainers. Hell, I fired Bobby Acton for incompetence seven or eight years ago."

"I don't know that they're incompetent. They did well enough at Louisville. They won the first two prizes in the Amateur Gaited class and they won the Ladies Gaited class."

"All that means is that they have the clients with the most money in the business, like Missy Phillips. Did they win any young horse classes?"

"I'm not sure."

"Well, just maintaining a horse that was taught their ABC's by someone else doesn't make you a trainer. I bred, raised, and trained SS Toreador, which was the first nice horse that Missy Phillips ever owned."

Holly grits her teeth and compliments him, "I think everyone realizes that you're responsible for Toreador's success."

25

"You mean SS Toreador" He is clearly irritated with her lapse. "Every horse I bred had an SS on the front of their name to remind people they came from Stuart Stables."

Holly wonders if her efforts to be nice to this man so that she can get his help with issues such as the sprinkler system are worth the effort. "Of course, Johnnie. The SS is one of the most recognized brands in our industry."

"You're damn right it is. I sold SS Toreador to Marianne Smithson and she moved him to Beech Tree because she's a diva and I didn't kowtow enough to suit her. Jennifer Hornig was in way over her head and nearly ruined that horse and I had to fix him. Missy Phillips won the Gaited Stake on him and they took all the credit. I should have filed an ethics complaint, but I let it go because that's the kind of guy I am."

"It sounds to me like you let them off the hook," Holly leans back in the chair in her office and encourages him to go on. "How did they end up with War Paint? You bred and raised her, too, right?"

"You mean SS War Paint?" he reminds her, but doesn't wait for her response. "If I'd been training that mare, she damn well would have won this year. Missy bought that filly from me when the association kicked me out. I spoke truth to power about the piss-poor judging at Louisville that year and the Saddlebred Association didn't like it. But I made that lady pay through the nose for SS War Paint. That mare is a full sister to SS Night Train, who is still the best breeding stallion in the industry."

Holly considers refuting that statement and defending Spy Master's record, but decides to keep him talking instead. "What's the connection between Missy and Jennifer and Bobby? She's been there for a long time, now."

"She's been there six or seven years," he admits, "and as long as they keep her happy, they'll be successful. She has money to burn and likes nice horses. It also doesn't hurt that she can ride a little."

"Where'd she get her money?"

"Her daddy is a Senator and I think they own an oil field or two."

"Ah. That's nice for her."

26

"Yeah. If I were you, I'd cozy up to her. She's about your age. You're both single ladies. Who knows, maybe you can sell her a horse or two. Better yet, maybe you can get her to leave those people at Beech Tree. She'd be a pretty valuable client."

Holly realizes that Johnnie might have just made the time she spent on this call worth it. "That's a very good idea. I just might have to get to know Missy Phillips."

CHAPTER 7

"Are you ready for something new?" Melody Jeffers greets Helen when she enters the barn on a bright Saturday morning.

"I am. I hope I don't make a fool of myself."

"Don't worry about that. We're just going to have a little fun today. I thought we'd start by going through the parts of the harness and showing you how it goes on. That will make it easier for you to understand how to communicate with the horse when you're driving him." Melody leads Helen up the stall aisle, stopping in front of an open stall.

"I know this horse," Helen exclaims. "This is Buddy. My old favorite lesson horse."

"Yes. We don't use Buddy for riding anymore except for the tiny kids because he gets a sore back. But he drives well, so he'll be perfect for today. I thought you could help me put his tack on."

"That pile of leather looks complicated," Helen laughs, pointing at the harness that is laying on a towel by the stall door.

"There are a lot of pieces, but it's actually pretty simple. This piece is a breast collar," Melody says, picking a lightly padded, roughly triangular piece from the top of the pile. "The first thing we do is put it over Buddy's head. The strap goes across his chest. The breast collar should be level across the point of the horse's shoulder and should allow for a little bit of room in the front. We don't want it to be tight." Once they've finished that, Melody reaches for a set of leather straps.

"That looks like a martingale."

"It is. Obviously, we can't fully attach it yet, but it will run from the girth up through the slots at the front of the breast collar." Melody demonstrates how to thread the martingale through the breast collar. "I just tie the two martingale straps together so they don't fall down before I'm ready to connect them."

"What do you need next?"

"Grab the surcingle for me. That's the big piece that goes around the girth."

Helen easily identifies this large piece and hands it to Melody. "It looks like it has a tail piece on it."

"Yes. That's called a crupper. The first thing we do is undo the crupper to make it easier to put on. Then we gently place it under his tail, making sure that all the hair is fitting smoothly over it." Melody demonstrates by lifting Buddy's tail and sliding the crupper under it. "It's really important to make sure none of the tail hair is wrapped around it in a weird way before we reattach it. That will cause a soreness and we really need to avoid that."

"Is that hard to do on a young horse?"

"It is, but we just take our time and it doesn't take long at all for them to realize that it doesn't hurt or feel uncomfortable. But it is really important to move slowly and gently. That's particularly true if the harness is cold and a little stiff." Working as she talks, she continues, "Then we slide the surcingle forward, and you'll notice it raises the tail slightly as the strap to the crupper tightens a little."

"Is it hard to fit a harness to a horse?"

"I wouldn't say that it's hard, but it does take time and patience. Once you figure out how all the pieces fit together and how loosening one strap impacts where everything else sits on the horse, it isn't too bad." As she talks, Melody reaches up on Buddy's back to make sure the surcingle is fitting flatly and comfortably across his back and that the ring on the top is centered. "We actually use the same show harness on multiple horses and we keep a cheat sheet of the hole numbers we use on each piece for each horse. That's really important when the classes are close together and the horses are young, as we want to make sure it fits like it did at home so that it feels familiar and comfortable."

"What's next?"

"This D ring at the top of the surcingle is where the breast collar attaches," Melody reaches for the clip at the top of the breast collar and snaps it into the ring. "On a show harness, that's a water hook instead of a D ring, but it serves the same purpose. Then we thread the martingale through the girth strap and gently tighten the girth, much like we would on a saddle."

"It seems like it sits a bit further back than a saddle girth does."

"Yes. The important thing is that it doesn't need to be as tight as a saddle girth. It just needs to be snug. The back pad is designed so that the strap moves freely and independently around the pad to allow the cart to move slightly independently of the horse. The pad should have contact all the way around Buddy except for some space in the gullet to allow for airflow and comfort, and it should fit in the flat spot just below his withers." Melody demonstrates as she goes along. "The breast collar and the crupper work with the surcingle to keep it in place. We just don't want to have it slipping back and forth as he works. Now, go ahead and feel how much tension is on the tail back strap. That's the name of the strap that goes to the crupper," Melody says, standing back.

Helen moves forward, patting Buddy, and puts her hand under the strap. "It's not as tight as I thought it would be."

"That's why I wanted you to feel it. There shouldn't be a lot of tension on it, but it can't be floppy and loose, either. As a rule of thumb, it should be fitted so there is about a hand, or four inches, between the horse's back and the strap."

"What's next?"

"The lines are next. That's what we call the reins and sometimes they're called traces. I always start from the back. Notice that these reins have stops on them," she says, showing Helen the hard leather pieces that are threaded onto the long leather reins. We thread the lines from the back through the terrets on the surcingle, and then through the martingale rings. Notice that there are right and left lines. The tab on the buckle that is up near your hand should go on the side of the buckle that is closest to the horse's bit. Also, make sure the rein stops are on the side of the martingale closest to the bit."

"What's the purpose of those?"

"It keeps the bit from getting stuck behind the martingale ring when you pull on the line. We definitely want to avoid that." Melody helps Helen thread the line on the other side of Buddy, as she talks.

"Next, we work on the head. I like to use a separate caveson for my harness horses because it is easier to adjust. The caveson should fit about a finger width below the cheek bones. I think that makes it look better. Then we slip the bridle on, by slipping the snaffle bit into his mouth, just like we would on Glitter Girl."

"I see that it only has one bit. That should make things easier. But the bridle looks different and has blinkers."

"Right. The blinkers prevent the horse from being distracted by the cart and other horses. Buddy's eyes need to be right in the middle of the blinkers. The blinker should be cupped around his eye and should not touch his eyelashes."

"I see. What's this piece that runs down the center of his face?"

"That's called a check piece. It connects to the overcheck and maintains his head position." Melody continues pointing to the harness elements as she talks. "And also notice there is a gullet strap that runs from the throat latch to the nose band under his nose. That is optional, but we like it because it is an extra safety feature and it keeps the bridle from coming off if you have a big wreck."

Helen laughs nervously. "That sounds like a good idea."

"You tighten the throat latch about like we would on your gaited horse. Not too tight. We want to make sure he can flex comfortably." She then moves to the caveson, "And we tighten the caveson like we would on any bridle. Not too tight. We want to be able to slide a finger or two between the leather and his face." She adjusts the curb chain, "I'm going to put the curb chain in the last hole so he'll be especially forgiving today. Finally, we connect the reins to the bit."

Melody stands back from Buddy and then picks up the ring of the martingale. "I like to have the martingale adjusted so that the rings are slightly below the rings on the surcingle that the reins go through," demonstrating the correct fit to Helen.

"What's next?"

"Now we connect him to the jog cart." Melody makes sure the stall door is fully open and that the latch is fully retracted, saying, "Be careful not to snag any of his harness pieces on the

31

door when you take him out of the stall" as she gently leads him into the barn aisle and down to the ring.

Once in the ring, she positions Buddy in front of a jog cart. "This step usually takes two people. Bring the cart shafts up high and pull the cart forward, and then lower them into place on his sides, being careful not to bump him or move too suddenly. Insert the shafts into the leather loops that are attached to the surcingle, and make sure they're all the way up past the tug stops on the shafts."

"Got it," Helen says from Buddy's other side.

"Now connect the shafts into the breast collar."

"Done."

"Now snugly connect the leather strap that anchors the shaft into the surcingle."

"I'm not sure I did that right," Helen says uncertainly, standing back for Melody to check her work.

"That's perfect."

"Can you tell me about the overcheck?."

"As you know, the overcheck goes from the middle terret on the surcingle, up the neck, between the ears, down the front, splits at the bridge of the nose, and goes to the rings of a bridoon bit." Melody traces the overcheck with her finger as she talks. "It is actually a piece of safety equipment. It keeps a horse from lowering his head too far and catching the bridle on the shafts. Adjustment of the overcheck can be tricky. It needs to be tight enough to keep his head up so that it is hard for him to canter or buck, but it has to be loose enough to let him raise his back to pull the cart. The overcheck can impair bending, so we have to make sure the horse stays balanced. If it is too tight, it will strain his neck muscles and ligaments and can even cause sore backs that show up as lameness. I like it to be pretty loose while I'm warming up. Once he's warmed up, I tighten it. If you start off with it tight, you risk making your horse uncomfortable and irritated right off the bat."

"We definitely want to avoid that," Helen agrees.

"Yeah. I'll get in the cart and demonstrate how to hold the reins and handle the whip and then we'll put you in." Melody makes sure the reins are untangled, "Never wrap the lines around

32

your arm and be careful you aren't standing on the lines because that would be dangerous if he were to startle and jump. Just loop them around your arm." She clucks at Buddy, sits backwards on the cart seat when it starts to move, and effortlessly swings her legs around to the front.

"That's my biggest anxiety," Helen admits out loud. "I'm not nearly that graceful, and my lack of balance and short, stubby legs will make it hard to get in."

"Don't worry about that at all," Melody says over her shoulder. "He'll stand and I'll help you get in the cart. I just use this cart every day and I've developed some short cuts for getting in and out of it." She clucks at Buddy to coax him into a jog. "Now the only thing you really have to worry about is not running into the wall. Remember that these lines are a lot longer than reins, so you have to think ahead a bit and use your hands and your voice to telegraph your intent to Buddy. Just keep in mind that it's like riding in that the impulsion comes from the back, but it is much harder to create when your legs and seat aren't in contact with the horse. Use your hands, voice, and whip to tell him when and where to go."

Melody makes two complete circuits around the ring, talking through her movements while Helen watches. Finally, she cues Buddy to halt and asks, "Ready?"

"As I'll ever be," Helen jokes, walking to the cart.

"We'll just go nice and slow," Melody reassures her as she helps her into the cart. "Bring the rein into your hand between your fourth and fifth finger, and then the rein exits the top of your hand. Yes, like that! Now put the whip in your right hand and hold it up." After making sure Helen is secure, she continues, "Use your voice a lot. Buddy isn't going to do anything stupid, so you can be pretty gentle with his mouth. Just cluck at him and let him walk off."

"Oh! It's bumpier and jerkier than I thought it would be!"

"You'll get used to it, just cluck and let him trot."

Helen follows instructions and Buddy is soon trotting slowly around the ring.

"See? That's pretty easy, right?"

Helen laughs, "It's actually pretty fun."

"Keep his head straight. Buddy likes to rubberneck to the outside, so use your inside rein to straighten his head. There! That's it!" Melody coaches, "Think ahead when you come to a corner. You need to use some outside rein too, or he'll overbend. Don't worry, he's sensible and won't run into the wall, but give him plenty of signals that you want to turn."

She watches Helen make several circuits. "Cut across the middle and try the other direction. It's like driving a car in that you have to look ahead a bit in order to get a straight line." As she watches, "Now touch him very lightly with the whip and get him to step up a bit."

"Ooh! Even bumpier," Helen says gleefully, as Buddy trots around the ring. After several more rounds, she turns Buddy towards the center of the ring and says, "Whoa."

As they are leading Buddy back to his stall, Helen asks, "If I had a harness horse, I'd need to buy a harness, right?"

"Yes. Much like you had to buy a saddle to show your gaited horse."

"What do they cost?"

"You can get a nice used show harness for about $2,500. A new one from Freedman, which would be my first choice, is going to run $4,500 or more. Even a simple jog harness can run about $1,500."

"Do I need a cart, too?"

"It depends on the trainer. In our barn, we let clients use our carts and buggies, but if their horse busts them up, the client has to pay for the repairs. In other barns, trainers let clients show with their buggies, but charge them a usage fee at shows. Still other trainers require their clients to buy their own buggies. From my point of view, that would cause a logistical nightmare if you had several clients that needed to have several buggies transported to every show."

"Geez."

"But we're getting ahead of ourselves. We don't even know yet whether this is something you really want to do. And if it is, whether you'll want to go for a pleasure driving horse or a fine harness horse."

"True. And I already know the carts are different."

34

"Everything is different, even the lengths of the reins. They're 75 inches for fine harness and 83 inches if you're driving a pleasure cart."

"So that means we need to make a decision about what division we want, pleasure or fine harness?"

"Eventually, yes. But if you want to transition to driving, you could just go find a horse that is the best athlete you can afford and then adjust everything else to fit the horse."

"That makes a lot of sense to me. Can we schedule another lesson for next week?" When Melody agrees, she says, "I'll see if Matthew can come so we can talk about what we should do with Glitter Girl."

CHAPTER 8

4:00 PM September 30, Beech Tree Farm, KY

Jennifer is just finishing the next day's training schedule when Marianne Smithson opens the office door. "I'm glad I found you working," she says. "I was afraid you'd already be done for the day."

Jennifer stands to meet her client, "You can almost always find me here for another hour. Can I get you a cup of coffee or a water? How are you?"

"Never mind that. I don't have time for niceties. I'm here to talk about Vendome Copper."

Jennifer is puzzled. "Is there a problem? He just won another World Championship and the Royal is only 45 days away."

"I was at the Old Stone Inn for lunch today and some people at the next table said they thought War Paint should have won. They said Vendome Copper should be showing in the Juvenile division."

Jennifer laughs.

"Why are you laughing? It isn't funny."

"But Marianne, you've been in this business for a long time. You know as well as anyone that everyone is entitled to their own opinion, but not to their own facts. The fact is that Vendome Copper won. War Paint made mistakes and Vendome was perfect."

"Be that as it may, I think it is time to find Blair a new horse. She's a beautiful rider and shouldn't be riding a horse that everyone thinks a little kid could ride."

"We can certainly start looking for a new horse for Blair. Alternatively, we could move her to the Ladies division. We could also put him in Gaited Pleasure. He will flat walk and would dominate that division."

"I don't know why I have to keep repeating myself with you. Blair is a top rider and I want her to show in the top division."

Jennifer hesitates only a moment, "You're the boss. I'll start looking."

"Thank you," Marianne says tightly. "And I'd like it to be a Christmas surprise for her, so make sure you keep it quiet."

36

As soon as Marianne has left, Bobby pokes his head around into the office. "What was that about?"

"You chicken!" Jennifer teases. "You knew she was here and didn't help me handle her?"

"But honey, you're so much better at handling her than I am. What did she want?"

"She overheard some hens at the Old Stone Inn talking about Vendome Copper. She got the impression that they didn't think he should have won and that he belongs in the Juvenile division."

Bobby helps himself to a soda from the refrigerator. "I'm sure you told her that opinions aren't the same as reality."

"I said something like that, but you know how defensive she gets when she thinks someone is dissing Blair."

In unison they recite, "Blair is a beautiful rider," in a tone that is remarkably close to Marianne's and then they laugh.

Jennifer continues, "Seriously, though, I think she probably is right and it is time to find a new horse for Blair. She wants it to be a Christmas surprise, so we'll have to get busy."

"But what does she want to do with Vendome?"

"We didn't talk about that. I assume she'll sell him."

Bobby is quiet. "That will hurt."

"Honey, I know he's your favorite. Maybe we can find someone in this barn to buy him. Don't panic yet."

CHAPTER 9

When Kenny answers his phone, Roger Jeffers says, "I was a little afraid that you'd see my name on your caller ID and not answer."

Kenny laughs, "You're one of my only connections with the outside world. It's been almost a month since I've been off the ranch other than to run to town for feed or parts."

"Yeah, I figured you'd be a little lonely up there, listening to the wind howl."

"I am! So tell me what's new in the world of Saddlebred horse trainers."

"I figured you would know more than I do. I've been hearing that your friend Holly McNair picked up and moved her operation from California to Kentucky."

"She did. She bought Johnnie Stuart's old place."

"That's a big decision. Why did she do that?"

"It's not really clear to me. I think that she wanted to grow her business and thought that she'd do better if she moved her barn to a part of the country where everyone already knew what a Saddlebred was. In California, Saddlebreds are a minority."

"Did her customers let her take their horses?"

"I think the only customer she held on to is Eileen Miller, the lady that owns Spy Master and Sneaky Suspicion."

"I don't envy someone trying to fill a barn in Kentucky. There's a Saddlebred barn every mile or so all the way down Shelbyville Road from Louisville to past Shelbyville. And that's not even counting all the barns in the Versailles and Lawrenceburg areas. Does she appreciate how difficult that will be?"

"I honestly don't understand it myself," Kenny agrees. "So how is everything at your barn? I noticed that Melody showed Glitter Girl at the Fall show in Denver. I didn't get to see her go because I was unharnessing my mare. But I was curious why the lady that bought her wasn't riding her."

"It's a sad story, actually, and is the real reason I called you," Roger admits. "Helen Stanton still owns Glitter Girl, but has been diagnosed with peripheral neuropathy."

"That's a shame. My aunt had that and it is tremendously painful."

"That's what I understand. She has it mostly in her feet, so her balance isn't very good on some days. She just doesn't feel comfortable or safe sitting on a horse, particularly one with the kind of gas that Glitter Girl has."

"I'm sorry to hear that. When I sold that mare to her, I thought it was a perfect match and they've done really well for several years," Kenny says, waiting for Roger to get to the point of the call.

"Helen loves that mare, so it has been a tough decision but I think she's considering trying to get a harness horse rather than throw in the towel on horses altogether."

"That's a great idea."

"I know you've been breeding to Spy Master and it isn't a secret that they've been dominating the top ribbons at all the big shows, but I've never had a Spy Master-bred horse myself. What can you tell me about them?"

"I like them. He stamps his foals with a great neck and their front legs are set forward on their chest so that they typically have great motion on the front end. I like training them. They're pretty sensible." Kenny pauses, "The one thing I've noticed is that some of them are a little slow to mature. I've had to kick them back out into the field more often than I can remember doing when I had more diversity in my breeding stock. I don't know if it's the Wyoming lifestyle or our weather or maybe just random chance, but they also seem to take a long time to warm up. I can feel their joints loosen when other horses are probably finished with their workouts."

"So you need to breed to a game mare, otherwise they're tired before they even hit the ring?" Roger's tone is joking, but Kenny recognizes the seriousness of the question.

"As I said, it might be my imagination. I don't know whether others have noticed this. My mares are hot-blooded, so it isn't really a problem for me. And all in all, I like Spy Master's foals.

I'm going to keep using him in my program, unless he gets too expensive. I just wanted to mention what I had noticed."

"Thanks. I appreciate it. Have you put a price on Nile Ninja?"

"No, I haven't. He's a little green still. Denver was his first show."

"I didn't get to see him go, but I heard he was very nice."

"I'm glad he got some attention. I was really proud of him."

After more small talk, they disconnect. Angela has overheard the call and asks, "How's everything with Roger?"

"It sounds like it's good. I got the feeling that I might be able to interest him in buying Nile Ninja for that lady who bought Glitter Girl from us. But he was also asking about Spy Master's foals and how we liked them."

"I picked up on that. I knew that they were a year or so behind our other foals but I hadn't heard you mention that you thought they were slow to warm up."

"Like I told Roger, it might be my imagination and it might just be coincidence, but they actually seem stiff and sore when they first get going. Especially on Mondays and cold days. The old-timers used to call it Monday Morning Disease, but I read in school that it is actually a real thing."

"Is it something to worry about?"

"I don't think so. They work through it eventually, and I've been trying some dietary changes that seem to be helping."

"You downplayed it with Roger."

"I did. I'm not really sure there is anything actually going on. If I was sure, I'd have been honest with him about it."

CHAPTER 10

The first person that Holly sees when she approaches the show ring at the Alltech Arena is Missy Phillips, who is watching a class from the rail. She finds a place next to her, "You're Missy Phillips, right? I've been looking forward to meeting you! I'm Holly McNair."

Missy turns with a friendly smile, "I know who you are! You're the brave soul that bought Johnnie Stuart's place. And, more importantly, you won the fine harness class at Louisville."

Holly smiles, pleased to be recognized. "Well, you know all about winning at Louisville. Congratulations on your phenomenal year. You must not be showing here," she adds, motioning towards Missy's summer dress and sandals.

"No, we decided to give the horses a bit of a rest to refresh them. It's been a busy season and I'm hoping to go to the Kansas City Royal."

The announcer is calling the Amateur Gaited class to the ring so both women turn their attention to the horses trotting through the gate. "Who do you like in this class?" Holly asks.

"I'm actually here to watch one of my mare's foals. There she is now," Missy says as a striking bay mare with four white feet and a white blaze trots through the gate.

"Did you breed her?"

"No. Right before I bought Texas Beauty Queen, they harvested an embryo for Louise Clancy-Mellon. This stunner is the result."

"Who's riding her?"

"That's Amber Gianelli. She's an Amateur Owner Trainer."

"I've heard her name before. She's the queen of all catch riders, as I understand it."

"She is very talented. Underfunded, but talented."

"What do you mean?"

"I've been told that she struggles to make ends meet. Louise had a soft spot for Amber because she rode Louise's filly Emoticon when she won the 3-year-old gaited class at Louisville

41

a few years ago. As a result, I think Louise gave her a good deal on this mare just before she died."

"I think I remember Emoticon winning."

"Yes. Amber beat some big names in that class and Louise kind of took her under her wing as a result."

"I see." Holly watches the class for a moment. "What's this mare's name?"

"Texas Debutaunt. Louise had a sense of humor," Missy explains, pointing out the spelling of the mare's name.

"This class hasn't even reversed yet and she's already got it won unless she screws up the second direction."

"She won't screw up. Amber never screws up."

"So are you looking to buy a new horse?" Holly asks, curiously. "You've got some pretty nice ones already."

"I do, but I like to keep my eyes open. I told my trainers I'd come watch this one. I don't ride against Amber very often because she tends to stick to the local, smaller shows, so I haven't had a chance to see this mare go."

"The mare looks capable of doing well at a large show. Why doesn't she go to them?"

"Probably time and money. Amber rents a stall in a Morgan barn in the Louisville area and does all the work herself. Plus, she has a 9-to-5 job. I think it's too hard for her to haul long distances and spend several days at a show. When Louise was still alive, I think Louise made it possible for her, but she probably has trouble managing it by herself."

"Well, she's doing a good job," Holly says admiringly as Amber racks past them. "That mare's rack is slick. Do you know that she's for sale?"

"I've learned that everything is for sale. It's really just a matter of establishing a price."

Holly laughs, "That is the truth. You sound like my kind of gal."

Missy joins in the laugh and changes the subject, "How are you liking Kentucky?"

"I'm still settling in and figuring everything out. It's a lot different than California. The feed is different, the weather is different, and the people are all new. I'm still hiring staff, fixing up the place, and figuring out where the spigots are around the barn!"

"Johnnie moved out a long time ago. I imagine it needs some maintenance."

"It does. I've been recruiting barn cats to get rid of some unwanted residents, so if you know of any hungry cats, I'll give them a good home."

"Why did you decide to move?"

"Lots of reasons, but mostly because I saw the advantage of being in the heart of Saddlebred country. All of our shows were overnight stays and the fires caused the price of hay to skyrocket last year. When the barn I was in changed owners and they nearly doubled the price of my lease, I decided to get out."

"Wow. That's crazy. Did many of your California clients make the move?"

"I'm happy with how that worked out," Holly says non-committedly. "Eileen Miller brought all her horses out."

"I haven't met her. She owns Sneaky Suspicion, right?"

"Yes, and Spy Master, and a few others. I'll be standing Spy Master as a stud at the farm."

"Oh? That's big news. His foals sure made a splash at the championships."

"They did and I'm excited about promoting him. In fact, he's got a coming four-year-old gaited filly named Secret Agent that you might want to look at."

"I'd like that. I'll jump at any opportunity to go see nice horses." They watch Amber collect the first-place ribbon and complete her victory pass. Before turning to go, Missy says, "I was planning on stopping at the Old Stone Inn in Simpsonville on my way home. They have a great patio. Do you want to meet me there for drinks?"

"I'd love that!"

CHAPTER 11

"How was school today?" Kenny asks Jeremy and Emily the same question every evening when the family sits down for dinner.

"Good!" Emily says. "Mrs. Sieler is showing us how to write a play."

"That sounds fun. Can we look forward to a performance?"

"Probably," she sighs dramatically and rolls her eyes. "But I think Ashley will get to be the star."

Kenny switches his attention to his son, "Jeremy? How was your day?"

"It was fine. I have to do a project in honors biology and need to figure out a topic."

Angela puts the meatloaf on the table and sits down. "Do you have any ideas?"

"I want to do something related to horses. We've been studying genetics." He helps himself to the food on the table and then looks at Kenny. "They do DNA testing at the Saddlebred registry, right? Maybe I could do a project about that?"

"Yes, they do. But only as a means to identify a horse."

"Why wouldn't you know who a horse is?" Emily asks.

"Sometimes a horse gets sold and separated from his papers. It happens for lots of reasons. Sometimes an owner might die and a Saddlebred gets sold by people that don't realize it's registered. And sometimes horses end up in auctions and no one cares enough to keep their identity straight." Kenny pauses, "There are some breeders who might not be happy with how a foal turned out and they might send a horse to an auction without identifying it so that it won't reflect poorly on the quality of the breeding program."

Jeremy looks up from his plate, "But that seems dishonest."

"It is, but it does happen."

"It's like losing your name," Emily remarks.

"Exactly. And the registry has a program where they use DNA to help a horse be reunited with its name." Kenny reaches for more potatoes, "There are some pretty interesting genetic diseases you might write about. Lordosis is an example."

"That's when they have sway back, right?" Jeremy asks. "We've been learning about dominant and recessive traits."

"Lordosis is associated with a recessive gene, so both parents must pass on the gene for it to show up in the foal."

"It seems like it would be easy to wipe it out then," Angela interjects. "Just test the mares and studs in a breeding program and don't breed those that have the gene."

"As I remember, researchers had identified the chromosome sequence but not every horse with the genetic marker had a swayback. It was only a strong likelihood, something like 80%."

"That's pretty high," Jeremy says. "But I still don't know how I'd turn that into a project. Although I'd like to do something related to animal genetics. I don't think anyone else in my class will do that."

"I don't know very much about this area," Kenny remarks. "But maybe there is something interesting about different genetically-caused diseases or traits that are breed-specific. Like Appaloosas are predisposed to eye problems and there are some orthopedic diseases in race horses that have been shown to have a genetic component. There are even some behaviors that have been shown to have a genetic component."

"Maybe I could do some sort of project on how to breed a perfect horse."

"That's called genetic engineering." Angela says. "They use it to do things like breed naked chickens."

"Naked chickens?" Emily giggles. "Who would want that?"

"Well, just imagine how much time and money it would save if you didn't have to pluck a chicken once you butchered it."

"But it has ethical implications," Kenny points out. "It's easy to understand why you would want to manipulate genes to get rid of a horrible disease. But is it right to manipulate genes to unnaturally build a new creature? Or to change a cosmetic detail, like the color of a horse? There's a big difference between breeding to get what you want and taking some chances and deliberately manipulating a cell's makeup to take the chance out of the equation."

"You've given me some ideas," Jeremy says. "Can I use the computer tonight?"

CHAPTER 12

When Bobby pulls his truck into the driveway of the boarding barn where Amber keeps Texas Debutaunt, Missy looks out the passenger window at the ramshackle barn and facilities, "We're not in Kansas anymore."

"Yes, it's a little rough. But I think that's fairly common at a boarding barn that isn't making any money from training or buying and selling. They're trying to keep their prices affordable."

"It's easy to forget how spoiled we are at places like Beech Tree. We don't even have to think about who is going to mow the weeds and fix the fences."

"My mom had horses in a boarding barn like this when I was a kid. I remember her saying how hard it is to train a horse. You're always working around a variety of other owners, some of whom know what they're doing and some of whom don't. Some keep their stalls clean, and some don't. Some steal tack or leave their own lying around, and some don't."

As they enter the barn with Missy's saddle, they see Amber Gianelli at the end of the aisle. Bobby greets her and after a little small talk asks, "How long have you had a horse here?"

"It's been a couple of years now. It's hard to find a place that is close to home and work. I spend a couple of hours here every day, so I don't have any extra time to spend driving."

"You've done all her training yourself, haven't you?" Bobby asks as he helps Amber put Missy's saddle on.

"I have. I get a lot of help and advice from Clark Benton, though. I still catch ride for him occasionally and he has been generous with his equipment and has even come over to watch me work her."

"They don't get any better than Clark," Bobby agrees.

"Is it hard to train in a barn like this?" Missy asks.

"I try to do it really early in the morning, before anyone else is here. I can usually get the round ring to myself that way, although I have to train before the horses are fed and she

47

sometimes gets a bit irritated when she sees the feed wagon and she's still working."

Bobby nods, "I can imagine. Are they mostly Saddlebreds here?"

"No. It's a real mix. And there aren't any other show horses. They're all pleasure and trail horses. That's another reason that I like to ride early. They get a little judgmental about traditional Saddlebred training techniques. I've had people here criticize me for putting quarter boots on Debutaunt's feet and for riding with a whip. Some of them even believe that using a bit is cruel."

"I see postings like that on social media, and it is all I can do to not engage," Missy admits.

"It just goes to show that there is plenty of room in the horse world for all kinds of horses and all kinds of owners," Bobby says diplomatically. "What would you like us to know about your mare before we ride her?"

"I haven't shown her much and I've been her only rider, so she's got a few more raw edges than most six-year-olds. It's hard for me to get to multi-day shows, and to show during the week, so we've mostly done county fairs."

"Is that why you didn't show her in Louisville?" Missy asks. "Because I saw you show her at the Fall Classic and she looked great."

"Entries were due on the first of July and I didn't think she was going to be good enough to win, so I couldn't justify spending all that money and taking all that time off work. I could have stabled with Clark, but I just wouldn't have felt right about using his grooms without being able to pay them." She redirects their attention back to her horse. "Debutaunt has a great work ethic. She's very earnest and serious. She doesn't play around in the ring. She is picky about how you tighten her girth." Amber makes this last comment to explain why the mare pins her ears back and threatens Amber with her teeth as the girth is pulled snug.

Thirty minutes later, in the truck on the way back to Beech Tree, Missy asks, "What did you think?"

"She's a very nice mare. Amber has done a great job with her."

"I really liked her. She's got a personality like her mother, Texas Beauty Queen, although she doesn't slow gait like her."

"I think that might be conditioning. I think that if we had her pull a jog cart for 30 minutes or so every few days, we could muscle up her hind end and it would make it easier for her to squat down and elevate her front end. What else did you notice?"

"She's very light in the bridle."

"Yes, she is. Almost too light. You can tell that she's used to a single rider and Amber has exceptionally good hands."

"I could tell that I irritated her a little when I bumped her."

"That will go away with time. I can fix that pretty easily."

Missy turns to him, "What were your impressions?"

"I liked her a lot. I see a lot of Texas Beauty Queen in her. She's beautiful and her neck hinges in exactly the right place. No amount of training can fix a bad neck. She's well-balanced and worked equally well both directions. I liked that she moved off my leg readily. I could move laterally at any gait. That was impressive."

"I like her, but I'm not sure that I'm ready to be done shopping."

"I think that if you're serious about her, we should ask Amber if we can take her over to Beech Tree and work her for a couple of weeks. That would be the best way to uncover any real holes or bad behaviors. She didn't strike me as a very sweet horse. I would want to make sure that she didn't have any evil habits."

"You mean like biting or kicking?"

"Yes. Having her around full time would make it easier to evaluate her."

"Maybe Amber would think it was a bit of a vacation," Missy suggests.

"Maybe. Ideally, we could wait until after we get back from the Kansas City show. That's only 10 days away. Why don't I call Amber and see if she'll go for that?"

CHAPTER 13

Holly sits alone at her desk in the cluttered office at Spy Hill and fans out the pile of past due bills that threatens to spill onto the floor. Who knew that opening a barn in the middle of Saddlebred country would be so hard? As the trainer with the reigning World Champion harness horse, clients should be beating a path to her door.

She leans toward the computer screen that shows a long list of financial transactions, all of which are written in red. Holly rubs her hands over her face, but the numbers remain red. She picks up her phone and dials a number, grimacing in disappointment when she has to leave a voicemail. "Hi Missy. This is Holly. I'm dying for some fun tonight and I hate drinking alone. Are you in town? If so, are you up for a party? Call me back."

Holly ends the call and tosses her phone onto the desk. After staring into space for a few minutes, she opens the bottom drawer of her desk, pulls out a half-empty bottle of bourbon, removes the top, and takes a long drink. She grimaces as the liquid burns and then enjoys the warmth and relaxation that slowly follow.

CHAPTER 14

6:30 PM November 13, American Royal Facility, Kansas City, MO

"Well that didn't go well," Bobby remarks to Jennifer when their clients have finally left for the evening after the Amateur Gaited Stake in Kansas City.

"The only way for Marianne to be happy is when Blair wins," Jennifer agrees. "Coming in second, especially to another horse in our barn, is not her idea of a good show. You'd think that being the reigning World Champion would buy us a little gratitude and breathing room."

"You were busy putting War Paint away, but she really let me have it."

"Let me guess. She threatened to leave the barn."

"Of course, but it was worse than that. Evidently she heard Missy talking about shopping for a new horse and she asked me what progress we'd made on looking for a new horse for Blair."

Jennifer sighs. "Blair doesn't want a new horse, but Marianne is right on that score. We haven't made any progress. There are very few horses available that have world-class quality, no matter how much Marianne is willing to spend. And having world-class quality isn't the only requirement we have. Whatever we find for Blair is going to have big shoes to fill. She's a timid rider and it takes her a long time to trust her horse. You should have been around when I first had Toreador and was trying to turn him into a horse that she could show. That was a nightmare. Vendome Copper has been the perfect horse for her."

"Yeah," Bobby says slowly. "Now don't freak out, but I told her that we had a horse coming into the barn next week that we were trying out."

"What?" Jennifer looks up at him in surprise. "But Texas Debutaunt is coming in for Missy to look at."

"I know. But I had to tell her something."

"But you've just set up a big conflict. What if they talk?"

"Come on, babe. They're not going to talk to each other. First of all, Blair isn't even going to know about it. And Marianne doesn't talk to Missy when she's standing right next to her. All

51

we have to do is make sure they're not both in the barn when we're working the mare. That'll be easy enough."

Jennifer goes back to packing the tack trunk next to her. "I don't blame you for trying to stall that woman, but what will we do if Missy buys that mare? Or worse yet, what if they both want her?"

"We'll cross that bridge when we come to it," Bobby snorts. "It's not the worst thing in the world to have two buyers with money going after the same horse."

"I don't know. It feels like a dangerous game to play."

"I had to tell her something to get her off my back," Bobby says defensively, handing Jennifer two bridles to place in the trunk she's packing. "I've been thinking about how perfect Vendome is for her and how hard it will be to replace him. Maybe we should be looking for a young horse that we can turn into a new version of him, rather than trying to find one that's already at that stage."

"Yes, I've thought of that. Even though I've been keeping my eyes open for a three- or four-year-old that looks steady but is also incredibly talented, I haven't seen much. It's a risky thing to go after something young. And it often surprises me that they're not always a very good value. The sky is still the limit and the owners haven't had the reality that comes with a few shows set in yet. We both know horses that were great at three or four, and completely unimpressive when they were seven. We definitely don't want that to happen. Marianne would lose her mind. Getting beat once, like Blair did tonight, is more than enough for her mother."

"It is possible that Texas Debutaunt might be a better match for Blair than for what Missy wants or needs."

"I'm sorry that I didn't get to go with you when you took Missy over to see her. When does the mare show up at Beech Tree?"

"I'm going to go get her next Tuesday evening."

"We'll just have to wait and see what happens, then. One thing that I know for certain is that Marianne can't feel like she's getting Missy's leftovers."

Bobby snorts, "Yeah. You're right that it will take our very best diplomatic skills to manage this. I think that the only reason Marianne wants a new horse for Blair is that Missy is shopping."

"I'm sure you're right. Sometimes I wonder how awful it would be if Marianne got mad and left the barn."

"It isn't like it hasn't happened before. Twice, in fact. Somehow we always let her come back."

"We do that because you love Vendome Copper."

"And I like Blair. It's only her mother that causes the trouble. And I don't think we're successful enough to have the luxury of running off a client with her resources."

"Yeah. She does pay her bills on time. It's hard to decide whether it's better to have a nice client that doesn't have much money or a bitchy client with money to burn."

CHAPTER 15

"I'm so glad you could meet me at such short notice," Eileen Miller greets her best friend Karen Shields at their favorite wine bar in La Jolla. "I needed a friend to vent to and I was certain you'd understand."

"I watched Sneaky's class on the live feed last night and I knew you would be disappointed. You sure got out of Kansas City fast, though. I didn't expect you to get home until later today."

"I moved my flight up because I needed to avoid seeing Holly. I thought that I might say too much in the heat of the moment and I needed to put some time and distance between us."

"Tell me what happened," Karen demands while flagging down a waiter to order wine for them both. "Start at the beginning and don't leave anything out."

"You know when Holly moved her business to Kentucky, I was the only client from Morning Star Barns that moved my horses with her."

"Yes, the rest of us just couldn't imagine having to travel all the way to Kentucky to ride or see our horses. We're more into trail riding than showing, anyway."

"True. It didn't make sense for anyone else, but I thought it made sense for me. Now I'm not so sure." Eileen pauses to sip from the wine glass the waiter has just placed in front of her. "When Holly moved, I'm pretty sure she told me that she had a lot of clients lined up and it sounded like she thought her business would really take off. But it is now clear to me that my horses might be the only ones in the barn."

"Is that necessarily a bad thing?"

"It's a terrible thing. She appears to be completely out of money. Sneaky looked underfed and Holly's only groom quit in the middle of the show! She told me that it was because he demanded a raise and she stood up to him, but he told another trainer that she hadn't paid him for almost a month!"

"Oh no."

54

"To top that off, Sneaky looked terrible in her class. She was low on energy, her coat is dull, and I bet she's lost 50 pounds since the Louisville show."

"I know you well enough to know that you would confront Holly about Sneaky's condition. What did she say?"

"She was full of excuses. She said that she couldn't get good help and that she got a bad load of hay and that some potential clients bailed out and that the barn she bought needed more maintenance than she expected and that she had to replace all the footing in every ring and that someone…"

Karen holds up her hand, "I get the picture."

"The weird thing is that she showed up with brand new stall curtains and a new gown and all new tack trunks."

"It sounds like she's making some poor financial decisions."

"Yes. But you haven't heard the worst of it yet. I got there on Thursday night pretty late and I went over to the stalls to see who was around, and her stall area was deserted."

"How late was it?"

"Around 10, but the show didn't end until after 9. I figured she would still be around. The tack room was locked up but the aisle hadn't been swept and Sneaky's stall was filthy. I cleaned it myself."

"Did you call her?"

"I was too upset. I didn't see her until the next morning. I went over pretty early and she was there, but she looked like hell. When I told her that I'd been there the night before and that I'd had to clean Sneaky's stall, she told me that the groom had tried to extort her and that she thought she had the flu. She certainly didn't look healthy."

"That could explain why everything was in disarray," Karen's tone indicates that she knows more is coming.

"It could, except that I am certain that she had alcohol on her breath and her clothes looked slept in."

Karen straightens at this news and cocks her head. "In the morning? And you're sure it wasn't just cold medicine?"

"I know the stench of whiskey when I smell it." Eileen sighs deeply.

"Did you say anything about it?"

"Not then. But after Sneaky placed 7th out of 8 in her class, only 10 weeks after winning a world championship, I lost my cool. I followed her back to the stalls and I waited until no one could overhear us and I asked her what the hell was going on."

"And?"

"That's when I got all the excuses that I already recited. I told her that I didn't give a damn about anything other than a certainty that my horse was being given exceptional care. I don't care if the fences need to be painted and the sprinkler system leaks. But the moment I suspect that my horse is underfed and under-conditioned, we have a problem."

"What did she say?"

"She cried and then she asked me for a loan. A big loan." Eileen pauses to sip wine.

"Wow. What are you going to do?"

"I told her I had to think about it. And I can't decide, so I need your advice."

"Talk me through it."

"I think I have two choices. Either I give her the money and trust that she's spending it taking care of my horse and getting her own shit together…"

Karen interrupts, "Or you move your horses from that barn and find a different home for them."

"Yes. But that isn't as simple as it sounds."

"Why not? Any trainer out there would be thrilled to have you."

"I have four horses, and one of them is a stud."

"But you could move him back to the stud farm that he was standing at before Holly moved."

"I could. And I know that he gets good care there. But what about the other three? I don't know the Kentucky trainers and I don't know if anyone good would take them all and I hate to split them up."

"Why? It isn't like they're bonded to each other. You have Sneaky Suspicion, who just happens to be a World Champion Fine Harness horse. You have a three-year-old, and a two-year-old, right?"

"I also feel a personal obligation. Holly has always been so honest and trustworthy that I feel like I owe it to her to give her time to get her feet under her. She saved Spy Master from certain death more than once."

Karen nods. "I can see why you want to give her the benefit of the doubt."

"And I can afford to help her."

"But something is holding you back. What is it?"

Eileen sighs again. "I'm worried about her drinking. My dad was an alcoholic and I know what that disease does to people and the lives of those around them. Holly may not be able to fix whatever is wrong with just money."

"Maybe she's just reacting poorly to stress and had too much to drink that one night."

"Maybe. But she just seemed off and I recognize the look and behaviors from my dad. She couldn't wait to get away from me to be by herself and she just didn't look bright, if you know what I mean. She looked rumpled and bleary. I don't even know how to describe it. I could only say that it sparked this recognition in me. All these old memories of my dad came rushing back."

Karen gives her friend time to dab tears from her eyes. "I haven't ever been around alcoholism and don't understand it. But you might be jumping to conclusions. I've never seen any signs of that as long as I've known Holly, and I had horses with her for seven years. We saw each other in all kinds of social situations. Sure, she might have too much to drink once in a while, but I don't think she was any worse than the rest of us."

"You might be right, but I suspect that she lacks the ability to control her drinking."

"Did you tell her that?"

"I did and she denied it. Vehemently. But that's a very common response. She got so belligerent about it that it actually made me more certain that something is amiss."

"What are you going to do?"

"I think I'm going to give her the loan and a deadline. I haven't thought through the details yet."

"My recommendation would be that you tell her that you'll pay some of her suppliers directly. That way you'll know that the money is getting spent on things that benefit your horses."

"That's a good idea. I knew that if I told you this story, you'd have some good advice."

"I'd ask her who she owes and how much, and I'd decide which of those bills I was willing to pay and which suppliers I would want to set up with direct billing."

"Like feed and maybe the footing?"

"Yes. And I'd make sure she signed an agreement to pay you back with specific terms in it so that you have a legal document to point at if things go south. If you're paying the mortgage, make sure that the agreement has a provision for you to share in any equity. And you'll have had to think through how long you're willing to do this."

"Do you think I'm being stupid?"

"Stupid? No. You're incapable of being stupid. You're being generous and you're trying to do right by someone you care about. I do think the hard part will be monitoring how your horses are. Have you thought about that?"

"I have, but I don't have any solutions."

"Who was the guy that was Holly's friend that kept Spy Master for you the year he won second at Louisville?"

"His name is Kenny Rivers, but he isn't in Kentucky any more. He moved to Wyoming."

"Wyoming?"

"Yes, his family has a ranch up there, I think. But you're right. I need someone to keep an eye on things."

"Either that or you're going to need to make a lot of trips to Kentucky yourself. Have you thought about buying a condo there? I bet you wouldn't have to spend very much money compared to what it would cost here."

"It's probably worth thinking about. Thanks for listening, sweetie. I needed someone to help me think this through."

CHAPTER 16

"My goodness! I believe you're getting the hang of this driving thing!" Roger enters the practice ring as Melody coaches Helen through her last pass with Buddy.

After Helen practices lining up and then backing, Melody and Roger both help her from the cart while Matthew hands her a cane. Despite wincing briefly at the pain in her feet, she is smiling broadly. "Thanks Roger! It's just Buddy, though. He's such a sweet boy and he tolerates my mistakes. In fact, he even pretends I'm not making them." She pats the horse's neck as Melody and Roger release him from the jog cart and a groom steps up to lead him back to his stall.

"Is it fun?" Matthew asks.

"I'm ashamed to admit that I didn't think it would be fun. It's surprising that you feel as much connection with the horse as if you're riding. It's just different."

Melody laughs, "I noticed you were giving him leg aids on the corner."

"I caught myself doing that! Isn't it weird that it didn't help?" Helen giggles at her joke. "There's a level of finesse to driving that I never appreciated as a spectator."

"Just wait until you sit behind a nice horse in a fine harness buggy," Roger says. "It's an adrenaline rush of a different kind. I went through some old videos last night and pulled out some snippets of really wonderful drives so that you could see how exciting it can be. I'll email them to you."

"Does this mean that we're officially shopping for a harness horse?" Matthew asks, his arm around his wife.

"We need to sell Glitter Girl first, but yes, I think I could really enjoy this."

As the four of them walk out of the ring together, Melody says, "Send me all your videos and photos of Glitter Girl and I'll have a sale video made so that we're prepared to deal with the inquiries when we advertise her. Getting her sold will give you time to think about what kind of harness horse you want."

"It will also determine how much we can spend," Helen says soberly.

"Glitter Girl must be worth a lot," Matthew offers. "She's only nine years old and she was third last year in the Amateur Gaited Championship in Louisville."

"Yes, she is worth good money," Roger agrees. "The only disadvantage is that she's out here in Denver, so it's harder for the Kentucky crowd to come try her. And we'll want to balance the price you ask with how patient you can be."

After making eye contact with Matthew, Helen says, "I'm the practical one in our house, so we want enough money to be able to afford a nice harness horse."

"Do you think you want a pleasure driving horse or a fine harness horse?"

"Let's talk about the differences," Helen suggests. "Since I'm doing this because I have balance issues, I'd especially like to talk through whether that will impact my ability to be successful in a cart."

The two couples settle themselves in the barn office, and Roger begins. "In fine harness, you're driving a small buggy with four wire wheels. The gaits in an Amateur Fine Harness class are the animated walk and the park trot. Your horse is required to stand quietly but is not required to back."

Melody continues, "In pleasure driving, your horse must back, and you're driving a two-wheeled cart, much like the cart you were in today. The gaits include a flat walk, trot, and extended trot. Theoretically, just like in under saddle classes, speed is supposed to be penalized and a pleasure driving horse has to behave. They are penalized for pulling, tossing their head, switching their tail, and any bad behavior in the ring. But pleasure driving horses can look pretty darn fancy these days."

"I think we want a fine harness horse," Matthew says.

"You're just biased against pleasure classes," Helen teases him. "He says the classes are too slow. I don't like that the classes are so big. The traffic is hard to handle."

"They are larger," Roger agrees. "In thinking about your balance issues, there might be other important differences between the two divisions. In a pleasure cart, the audience doesn't see your feet and you have more cushion and a higher back rim. In a fine harness buggy, your feet are visible, the bench is narrower, and you sit up higher. I think balance might be harder to achieve."

"Can the carts be modified to accommodate someone with a physical disability?" Helen asks. "I certainly don't need it now, but if my neuropathy keeps progressing, I might need some sort of way to safely anchor my feet in the cart."

"It's an interesting question. I'll need to do some research into that." Melody answers. "But there is also a lot that riding and driving have in common. Regardless of the tools available, you still need to keep a horse balanced. In both cases, you're trying to achieve a lofty step and keep your horse straight. From a physical perspective, you need to use your core for stability and to stay still in the cart. You lengthen and straighten your upper body in both cases. Also, light hands are important in both cases. And while it isn't the same, sometimes driving a strong horse requires back and leg strength." She pours herself a fresh cup of coffee. "In harness, you really have less information about your horse's intent so you have to watch for clues, whereas when you're riding, you can feel the clues more readily. And we already learned about having to think ahead."

"Poor Buddy," Helen tells Matthew. "I asked him to go straight into the wall. Fortunately, he knew that I didn't really mean it, even though he had blinkers on and I was the one with a full range of vision."

"Driving does require a greater sense of space and the driver is fully responsible for paying attention to what's happening around them." Melody smiles. "Maybe most importantly, though, is that we're going to need to find a horse that you really love. I think that a strong bond between you and your horse will allow you to be more successful if your neuropathy progresses to your hands. You'll need to use your voice more and perhaps shift your weight in the cart. You'll need a horse that accommodates any inconsistency in your hands or how you use the whip."

Roger notices Helen's face begin to crumple at this and interjects, "Don't be discouraged. Just be comfortable that we will all think through this together and help you be successful and have fun. Heck! A guy named Amos Rockwell was famous for driving his Morgan horses without a bridle at all." He laughs, "I'm not saying that we're the trainers that he was, but I am saying that you shouldn't be discouraged. We can definitely make this work for you."

"While you're finding the right horse, I'm going to hit the gym," Helen admits. "I'm going to have to build some muscle in my upper arms to hold the reins up and to keep them from getting under his tail."

CHAPTER 17

"I'll warm her up for you," Bobby says, leading Texas Debutaunt from her stall towards the ring.

"How have you been getting along with her?" Missy follows them down the barn aisle, raising her voice to be heard above the mare's shoes ringing against the concrete.

"Good. We've had her about 10 days now. It took her a while to settle in, but I think she's finally starting to relax a bit."

"Have you found any holes?"

"Nothing that worries me." The mare stands quietly as he mounts and waits for him to cluck gently before walking off. He walks her around the entire ring once, coaxing her forward when she shies at a sunspot on the ground, and then asks for a trot. Texas Debutaunt pricks her ears forward and gains speed as she works her way around the ring, now ignoring the sunspot. Her head is high and she appears to gain confidence as she trots. When Bobby reverses her through the center of the ring, she notices the original sunspot again, stutter-stepping as she approaches it, and accelerating after Bobby uses his legs and voice to coax her past it.

After slow gaiting her both directions, Bobby halts her in front of Missy. "Ready?"

"I am. What do I need to know?"

"I'm sure you noticed that she's aware of every little change. She'll probably act like she's never seen that sunspot before, so just drive her forward with your legs. She won't do anything bad, but she's pretty cautious about anything she thinks is new. Just be patient and let her get used to you."

"What about the bits?" Missy asks, gesturing toward the double-bitted show bridle on the mare.

"She's very light, like we noticed when you rode her in front of Amber. She just likes a very light touch on the snaffle and the curb. I tried to switch her bits up a little to see if we could find something that would allow her to take a little better hold of her bit, but I haven't found anything yet, so this is the same bit Amber uses on her."

63

Missy mounts and gathers up her reins while Texas Debutaunt stands quietly. When Missy clucks, the mare obediently flat walks to the side of the ring.

"Go ahead and ask her to trot, Missy." Bobby says. "Don't forget to keep your legs on her to give her some security. She likes to feel your leg against her side." He watches quietly while the mare shies again at the same sunspot the first time they pass it, ignoring it the next time. "Push her forward, now. She's got at least one more gear," he encourages. "That's better," he yells when the mare becomes more animated. "Keep her collected, dig in with your seat in the corners."

Jennifer joins Bobby in the barn, watching carefully as Missy guides the mare around the ring.

"Let her walk and then slow gait," he tells Missy. "Be as quiet as you can with your hands in the transition. Keep your hands low, just separate them and give her a gentle signal. Keep your legs on her."

"How's it going?" Jennifer asks quietly, watching as Missy and the mare transition to the slow gait.

"Okay," Bobby responds without taking his eyes off his rider. "Missy, she's getting a little strung out. Sit really deep and squeeze your legs to get her to come back to you." After a few strides, "There it is! That's it!" He glances at his wife, who is smiling and nodding.

"Go the other direction and this time I'll just be quiet and let you figure it out," he tells Missy.

Missy reverses through the middle of the ring, clucking when the mare shies at the same sunspot she has now passed several times. Bobby and Jennifer watch the remainder of the work out, stepping forward to help Missy dismount at the end of the ride.

"What do you think?" Bobby asks.

"Amber must have legs of steel. It's a lot of work to ride her."

"I think she's just a little insecure. I've noticed that she requires less leg the more she works."

"She seems to notice everything. Like that sunspot. You'd think that she'd realize she's been past it before and it didn't bite her, but every change of gait and direction made her notice it all over again."

64

"Yes. She's very sensitive to change. It could be because she's had a very predictable environment in her training. She's actually calmed down a lot in just 10 days, so I think she'll become more tolerant as time goes on. I've experimented a bit with moving her stall around and simple changes like that, and each one causes her to quit eating for about a day. But I don't think that's a big deal. It will just take a little time to help her learn how to be more adaptable."

"She's wonderful to ride. Her slow gait and rack are very steady. She never tries to cheat on the corners." Missy says. "And I really like how she waits for signals. She doesn't hop around, anticipating the transitions."

"I like that, too. For a mare that is so watchful about her environment, she's really patient in her gaits and she's got wonderful ground manners."

"That's an interesting combination of behaviors," Jennifer comments.

"I've decided that Amber must switch up her training a lot, so she can't anticipate what's coming next. Maybe some days she only trots and other days she canters patterns."

"More like a dressage trainer might work a horse?" Missy asks.

"That would explain why this mare likes so much leg," Jennifer adds. "And if you're working alone like Amber is, the ground manners would be a necessity. You'd have to make sure your horse waited quietly for mounting just for safety's sake if for no other reason."

Bobby motions for a groom to take the mare back to her stall and asks Missy, "Do you like her enough to buy her?"

"I like her a lot, but I'm not yet convinced she's the one for me," she says uncertainly.

"What do you think she's lacking?" Jennifer asks.

"I'm not sure I can put my finger on it. I own her mother and I saw her show at Fall Classic, so I'm not concerned about her quality." Missy hesitates, "This is going to sound weird, but maybe it's her personality. She's so stand-offish."

Bobby cocks his head at her, thinking about her statement for a few moments. "I kind of see what you mean. When you think about it, she seems a little introverted."

"But kind of haughty at the same time," Missy agrees., "And it seems like such a weird thing to even care about. How much time do I have to think about it?"

"I told Amber we'd need a couple of weeks, so the mare needs to go back in another two or three days."

"I just don't feel like I'm ready to be done looking. Holly McNair told me that she has a three-year-old Spy Master filly that I need to come look at."

Bobby and Jennifer make eye contact, but before either can remark, "I think I'd like to make Amber an offer, but I want to low-ball it," Missy says suddenly, naming a figure that is slightly more than half of what Amber is asking.

Bobby hesitates, "That's pretty low for a horse with this quality. She's a very nice mare."

"Yes, but Amber might take it. That's still a lot of money for someone like her. What's the worst thing that can happen? If she doesn't take it and I don't find something else in a couple months, I can always go back and improve the offer," Missy shrugs.

Jennifer asks Bobby, "Did you get a sense for how motivated Amber is to sell her?"

"I don't really know. She's such a quiet person that I can't really read her."

"I have to get going, but let me know what she says about the offer," Missy says her goodbyes and leaves the barn.

"What the heck just happened?" Jennifer asks. "Did Missy just tell us that she was going to go try out a three-year-old by herself?"

"I think she did. She certainly didn't invite us to go with her. And she also instructed us to give an embarrassingly bad offer for a really good horse, just because she thinks she can take advantage of a seller?"

"Wow. This isn't the Missy that I'm used to dealing with. I wonder what's going on with her. Do you think there's any chance that Holly McNair is trying to poach our client?"

Bobby takes his time to answer. "I don't know, but I also don't know what we can do about it even if it's true."

"I could kick Holly's ass," Jennifer jokes, then more seriously. "I just think it's weird that a client we've had for such a long time casually announces that she's going to another barn to look at a young horse and doesn't invite one of us. She clearly doesn't intend to bring the horse back here if she buys it."

"Well, she's free to take her business anywhere she wants. If she isn't pleased, I'm certainly not going to beg her to stay."

"True, but it just feels a little fishy to me. What are you going to tell Amber?"

"Well, I can tell you what I'm not going to do. I'm not going to give her that lame offer of Missy's. That's a slap in the face for a horse like Texas Debutaunt. And it is offensive to suggest that Amber's effort shouldn't be rewarded fairly. I think we should show the mare to Marianne."

"Would she make a nice horse for Blair? It seems like the idiosyncrasies she has wouldn't match well with a rider with some of the same insecurities."

"I've been thinking that it might work the other way around. They're very much alike, personality-wise. It might be a match made in heaven."

"We certainly can't let Marianne know that Missy rejected the mare."

"Missy didn't reject her. From my perspective, Missy didn't spend the money it would take to buy a horse this nice."

Jennifer looks at her husband in surprise. "Well, listen to you! Getting so creative with the spin!"

"Well, it's the truth. I'm going to call Amber and see if we can keep the mare for another week so that we can get Marianne in here to look at her. And I'd like you to ride her for Marianne because you're about Blair's size and I want her to be able to visualize how nicely Blair would fit on her."

CHAPTER 18

"Can I be excused?" Jeremy asks his mom. "I really need to finish my Biology paper. It's due tomorrow."

"Of course. Is that the paper on genetics?"

"Yeah."

"How did it turn out?"

"I think it's okay," Jeremy answers cautiously, turning to his dad. "I'm not sure if you'll like it, though. Do you have time to read it tonight and tell me what you think?"

"Of course. Print a draft off and I'll start on it as soon as we get the kitchen cleaned up."

It only takes a few moments for Jeremy to reappear in the kitchen with a sheaf of papers. "It has four parts. We have to start with a hypothesis that's stated as an if-then sentence and then write an impact statement. The impact statement is supposed to describe what would happen if the hypothesis is true. In the third part, we have to describe the evidence we already have that leads us to believe the hypothesis might be true. Finally, we have to lay out the experiment we need to run to prove our hypothesis."

"Sounds cool," Kenny accepts the papers. "How long does it have to be?"

"My teacher said we should try to be concise, so I don't think she's expecting it to be too long."

"She probably doesn't want to read novels," Angela laughs. "She's a smart gal."

A few minutes later, Kenny and Angela settle into their favorite chairs in the family room, and Kenny begins reading. Within thirty seconds, Angela hears him say, "Holy shit."

"What?"

"Listen to this hypothesis." Reading from the paper, "If the famous Saddlebred stallion Spy Master carries the Polysaccharide Storage Myopathy (PSSM) gene, then his foals will have a predisposition to colic."

Angela looks up from her book. "So?"

"His hypothesis is that the most valuable stallion in our industry carries a gene that causes colic."

68

"It's only a hypothesis, Kenny. I could easily hypothesize that the world is flat. It doesn't make it true."

Kenny continues reading, getting more tense as he proceeds. Finally, he slams his recliner to an upright position and yells, "Jeremy!"

His son must have been waiting close by, as he appears in the room in just seconds. "I guess you've read it?"

"Not all of it," Kenny is clearly agitated. "You're suggesting that the most prolific stallion in our industry carries a gene that could cause his foals to colic. Where in the world did you get such an idea? It's a libelous statement. You can't make stuff like this up. You need to understand how damaging it could be to even suggest such a thing."

"I don't think so," Jeremy says calmly. "We talked about it in class. For it to be libel, it would have to be false and malicious. I know it isn't malicious. And I don't believe it's false. Have you read the evidence section?"

"I'm still on the impact statement. Where did you get these numbers?"

"I did some research in the registry. Everything is on-line. Spy Master has been an active sire for six years. He has almost 300 foals in the registry already."

"But you're not counting all the foals that weren't registered and all the second- or third-generation foals."

"Right. I didn't want to get bogged down and decided to estimate on the low side."

"So, are you saying that those 300 foals, a few of whom are on this very ranch, are susceptible to colic?"

"Kind of. I found it by looking up Monday Morning Disease. That's what I've heard you call it. On the web, they describe it as colic-like symptoms. So, then I found a bunch of stuff on the internet about certain breeds being more likely to colic than others." He continues uncertainly, "One link said there are they've found mutated genes in some of these horses and they have linked it to something called Exertional Rhabdomyolysis." Jeremy stumbles over the pronunciation.

"Jeremy, I've never even heard of that. That sounds really far-fetched."

69

"You can read about it yourself," Jeremy says defensively. But the symptoms they describe are a lot like what we're seeing in some of our horses. Why couldn't it be true?"

"It's a big leap to take a few horses that are stiff and sore if they have some time off and draw the wild conclusion in your hypothesis," Kenny says.

"But it isn't a conclusion," Jeremy's voice is more defensive. "It's a hypothesis."

"Son, what you're suggesting could damage a lot of people, including us. What in the world drove you to such an idea?"

"If you had kept reading, you would understand. I found a lot of information about it on the web. This genetic disease is called PSSM. When I read about it, I realized that it explains some of the things I've noticed in a few of our horses."

Angela interjects, "But honey, it's like what they say about WebMD. That you read about some disease on the web and think you have the symptoms, only to find out that it only occurs if you live on a tropical island."

"But PSSM is plausible," Jeremy insists stubbornly, his voice rising. "The researchers describe it as exercise intolerance due to muscle wasting, stiffness, and pain." He turns back to his dad, "You've noticed yourself that some of our horses have weird stiffness and lameness issues that improve when they work. We always blame how cold it is up here, but it even happens in the summer."

"We have more horses that don't have that trait than those that do," Kenny interrupts.

"True, which actually is even more evidence that it might be PSSM. If all our horses had the issue, then it might be training or feed or something." Jeremy triumphantly takes the papers from Kenny, "Listen to these symptoms." He reads from his paper, "Changes in temperament/behavior because of pain; gait and coordination problems; shifting lameness; local muscle wasting." He looks up, "I looked that one up, and there are pictures of what it means. It totally explains those small divots in a couple of our horse's muscles that look like kick marks. I've always wondered what they were." He goes back to reading from the paper. "Symptoms also include frequent tying up; stiff hindquarters;

70

muscle tremors; gait changes like cross-firing or disunited canter." He pauses, glancing up to gauge his dad's reaction. "This is a list I got right from the Michigan State University Veterinary School website. It sounds familiar, right?"

Kenny shrugs and Jeremy interprets this as encouragement to continue. "You need to read about it yourself, Dad."

"But what breeds have been shown to have PSSM? Has it ever shown up in Saddlebreds?"

"It isn't rare. They've found PSSM in more than 20 breeds. I've read about Quarter Horses, Morgans, Paints, Appaloosas, Arabians, Quarter Horse/Thoroughbred crosses, draft horses, Standardbreds, and warmbloods all having PSSM. I'm not sure about Saddlebreds. But that's why this is a hypothesis," he points out.

Kenny's face shows his concern. "Go on."

"It just sounded familiar to me. We have at least four horses in the barn now that have these symptoms."

"What's the cure?" Angela asks.

"There is no cure," Jeremy answers. "At least not yet. But the articles I read say that diet and exercise help." Turning to his dad again, "You've said yourself that you thought diet helped some of our horses move better."

"It certainly sounds like you've done your homework," Angela says, watching Kenny's reaction.

Kenny reaches for the sheaf of papers Jeremy is still holding. "Let me read the whole thing. And I'll look at your references on the internet. But I'm concerned that you don't really understand the implications here. If you're right, then it will ruin Spy Master's value and the value of his off-spring. The young fillies we have that are Spy Master's will have no value as breeding stock."

"There's a genetic test that they use to diagnose it," Jeremy counters. "Next semester we actually do the experiment to try to prove our hypothesis. I'm hoping that we could get a few of our horses tested. Or maybe even get a genetic test for Spy Master. Then we'll know whether I'm right."

"Regardless, I'm worried about you turning this paper in tomorrow. If word were to get out that Spy Master could have a genetic defect, all hell would break loose in the Saddlebred community."

"Kenny, it's just a high school biology paper in a small town in Wyoming," Angela's voice is calm. "I think you might be over-reacting."

"Maybe, but if we blindside people with this, even if it doesn't turn out to be true, it will hurt a lot of people I care about."

"Like Holly McNair?" Angela asks. "Frankly, I think it's more important that it would devalue the horses in our program. Perhaps we need to breed our mares to something other than Spy Master this year."

CHAPTER 19

"I don't have much time, so why don't you tell me what I'm here to look at." Marianne demands, removing her soft leather gloves and placing them in her Louis Vuitton bag.

"Jennifer is bringing out Texas Debutaunt. This mare is six years old. She hasn't been shown much. She was bred by Louise Clancy-Mellon and was trained by an Amateur Owner Trainer. She needs a little finishing, but I've had her in the barn for a couple of weeks to try her out and I want you to see her."

"What's her breeding?"

Bobby knew this would be Marianne's first question, and he has thought carefully about how to present the information that Texas Debutaunt is a foal of one of Vendome Copper's in-barn rivals. "She's the result of an embryo transfer from Texas Beauty Queen, believe it or not. But Louise was a really thoughtful breeder. She used that young stud out of Alabama that was killed in the barn fire a couple of years ago. Consequently, there aren't many of his foals around to compare this one to, but I think he's given her a much more elegant and refined look than Texas Beauty Queen has. This mare also has a very precise gait and a willingness to listen to her rider that Texas Beauty Queen lacks."

"I've never really understood why everyone likes that Texas Beauty Queen so much. I've always thought she was a little coarse. I think Missy Phillips does so well on her because Missy's father is a Senator." Marianne accompanies her unsupported opinion with a satisfied smile, validating Bobby's strategy to downplay the relationship between the two mares, and they both watch Jennifer trot the bay mare into the ring.

Bobby waits until the mare turns the corner towards him and then whistles sharply. Texas Debutaunt's head raises another full inch as she trots toward him, her four white feet flashing. Bobby watches Marianne in his peripheral vision, relaxing slightly when he sees a small nod.

After two more passes, he says "Go ahead and slow gait her, Jenn."

Jennifer stops the mare and then cues her to slow gait. Bobby waits for the pair to begin the straight-away towards Marianne, and then rattles a can full of marbles. Texas Debutaunt squats low, making him worry that he's overdone it, but Jennifer's strong legs drive her forward down the rail.

"Isn't she a sight?" Bobby had planned to keep quiet to let Marianne evaluate the mare, but he can't stop himself from marveling at the momentary suspension the mare achieves before taking each elevated stride. "You don't see a real slow gait anymore, but ridden correctly, this mare can do it as well as any I've ever seen."

Marianne is quiet, so Bobby decides to push it a bit more. "There aren't many riders that will be able to get the best out of her."

"Well, Blair is a beautiful rider. I'm sure she won't have a problem." Marianne is brusque, "Have her go the second direction."

Bobby tells Jennifer to reverse direction and he and Marianne watch quietly while the mare trots, slow gaits, and racks. Finally, Jennifer halts the mare in the middle of the ring and she and Bobby wait for Marianne's reaction.

"Is anyone else interested in her?"

Bobby carefully dodges the question, "Amber Gianelli owns her and trained her. She hasn't been shown much. Amber wants a lot of money for her and I think she's worth it, but there aren't many amateur riders out there that will be able to get the best out of this mare. And she needs a little finishing to make her more confident."

"Be more specific. What kind of finishing?"

"I just think she needs to be exposed to more. She needs to go to a lot of shows, and she needs some muscle. I don't think Amber jogs her, so I'd muscle up her back end by using the jog cart.

"I think she looks a little underfed," Marianne comments.

"I'm impressed you noticed that," he flatters. "If she were mine, I'd amp up her feed with some high-quality vitamin packs. She just needs a little plumping up and a little shine."

"How long has she been for sale?"

"That's a hard question. I'm still not all that sure that Amber wants to sell her. It will take some money to pry this horse out of her hands." Bobby begins. "I'm not completely sure that we can get it done. I think that Amber will care that a rider like Blair will have her and will be able to show her to her full potential. Horses like this are rare."

"I'll authorize up to twice what we spent on Vendome Copper," Marianne says, putting her gloves back on. "I'll expect an answer by the end of the day. Then it will be up to you to have her in perfect condition for presentation to Blair at Christmas."

Bobby manages to suppress his grin until she leaves the barn, and then he jubilantly follows Jennifer and the mare back to the stalls.

"I know you're excited," Jennifer says, "but I'm still worried she's going to find out that she just bought Missy's reject."

"I'm not worried about it at all. I've set it up so that all we have to say is that the mare didn't perform as well when Missy was riding her. It's a completely true statement. She was perfect for you."

"I hope she'll be perfect for Blair," Jennifer worries. "I wouldn't be surprised if Blair just rejects her. She adores Vendome Copper."

"Yes, my next trick will be convincing Marianne to keep them both. Vendome Copper will be a perfect gaited pleasure horse. He flat walks perfectly. I need to help Marianne understand that the true and only path to Blair's pure happiness and Marianne's total domination of the amateur gaited classes is to show both horses."

Jennifer shakes her head in amusement. "Who are you and what have you done with my husband?"

CHAPTER 20

Annie carefully removes a heating pad from underneath her bathroom sink, wincing as she straightens, and then slowly walks to her couch. She groans when she leans over to plug it into the nearby wall socket and then slowly lowers herself onto the leather cushions, removing her stocking cap from her short, straight, graying hair. "It's true what they say," she tells the orange cat that leaps up onto her lap. "Getting old is not for sissies."

She pulls her cell phone from her pocket, pokes experimentally at the cracked screen, and mutters, "At least the damn thing still works." As she waits for the connection to go through, she composes the message she wants to leave in her mind, and is surprised when she hears a soft, tentative "Hello?"

It takes Annie a second to react, "Amber? Is this Amber Gianelli?"

"It is," Amber admits uncertainly.

"This is Annie Jessup."

"Oh! Hi Annie," Amber's reply is much warmer now. "How are you?"

"Well, not very well at the moment, but that's neither here nor there."

"What happened?"

"One of these two-year-olds I have in the barn dumped me into the wall and I'm feeling my age just now."

"Oh no! Are you all right?"

"No serious damage, except to my pride, that is." Annie admits in her hoarse voice, earned from years of smoking. "But that's not really why I'm calling you. Or maybe it is." Annie hears herself starting to ramble. "I wanted to congratulate you. I saw on-line that you sold your mare."

"I did. But I'm not sure I should be congratulated. I'm a little sad. She's a nice horse."

"Yes. She was. But you're young. You have a lot of nice horses to look forward to. That's actually why I called."

76

"I bet you have a nice horse or two that I could buy," Amber says, laughing lightly.

"Well, I certainly do. But again, that's not why I called."

"Okay. I give up. Why did you call?"

"I want to know if you are interested in moving out here to North Carolina and becoming my assistant trainer."

When Amber makes no sound for several seconds, Annie says, "Damn phone! It's probably busted. Amber? Are you there?"

"I'm here. I'm just surprised. Why me?"

"I've seen you work your mare. You're quiet and calm, and you can certainly ride a horse."

"But I don't really know anything at all about horse training."

"I will teach you everything I know. Of course, I don't know what we'll do in the afternoon," Annie jokes, and is rewarded by Amber's laughter on the line. "You're an accountant, aren't you?"

"I am."

"Do you like what you do? Do you wake up each morning excited about your job? So much so that you can't wait to get dressed? Do you eat breakfast on the way to your office because you can't get there soon enough?"

"No. I eat breakfast on the way to my job because I didn't leave soon enough to get there on time."

"See? If you come out here to Big View, you'll just have to walk across the driveway to get to your job. I supply housing, a lousy salary, fresh eggs from the chickens, and the best young horses on the planet to ride every day."

"Oh my gosh. That sounds so tempting."

"What's holding you back?

"This will sound dumb, but I've dreamed my whole life of winning the Amateur Gaited Stake at Louisville. I used to fall asleep as a kid thinking about what that victory pass would be like. And I know a few people that gave up their amateur status and regretted it. It isn't easy to get it back."

Annie hesitates. "It doesn't sound dumb. I understand your desire to win that class. We all have dreams like that. I'd like to win the Gaited Stake someday, but I will tell you that my real joy as a breeder and trainer is in watching a horse I started do well, and in pairing one of my riders with a horse and watching them fall in love and be successful. I'm not exaggerating when I say that I get true satisfaction from every ribbon that I helped someone else win. In some ways, I think watching a horse you bred and trained make a victory pass and seeing the smile on that rider's face is even more satisfying than doing the ride yourself."

Amber is quiet for several seconds. "You're a really good saleswoman. Maybe there is middle ground here. Selling my mare has given me a little breathing room, financially. Would you be open to having me come over and spend a few months with you without pay? Maybe I could see what it's like to be a trainer but hang on to my amateur status for this next season? Maybe I could help you, but also pick up some catch rides?"

"How could I ever say no to that? You want to come here and help me for free? No one gets rich being a horse trainer, but you're taking that to extremes," Annie jokes. "I'll check the rules, but I imagine I can give you a pretty good deal on rent." Annie takes a deep breath, "In case you need extra incentive, I do want to be really clear about what I'm offering. I'm 60 years old. I never married or had any kids. I own this place free and clear. I'm offering you the best job in the world, housing, and mentorship. Ultimately, I'd like to turn this place over to a protege so that my life's work doesn't just go to some sad dispersal sale when I leave this world. I'm hopeful that you could be that protégé. I won't lie. It's hard work and I can be a real bitch some days, but I promise you that you will have fun and you'll never be sorry."

"How soon do you want me?"

"How soon can you get here?"

CHAPTER 21

"I wish you would stop pacing around and just call her," Angela is clearly exasperated. "You're driving me insane!"

"But what am I going to say? Hey Holly, my 16-year-old son thinks the stud that is the focal point of your business might have a genetic defect? How's the weather out there?" Kenny scoffs. "That'll go well, I'm sure."

"I just think you need to get this off your chest so that you'll quit obsessing about it."

Kenny sighs, dialing Holly's number. She answers on the first ring and after some small talk, Holly asks about his family. "Everyone's fine. But that's actually why I called. Jeremy has been doing this research project in his Biology class and he happened to get interested in this inherited condition in horses called PSSM. Have you ever heard of it before?"

"No. What is it?"

"It's something they see in Quarter Horses and some other breeds. I think it's the same thing that my Dad used to call Monday Morning Disease."

"Oh. I think I have heard of that. Isn't that when a horse gets muscle stiffness after having time off work?"

"Right. And it can even look like a lameness that the horse works out of with exercise." He pauses and then dives in. "Jeremy got interested in it because he thinks it might explain some of the behaviors we've been seeing in a few of our young horses. They're slow to warm up, short-strided, and stiff."

"Really? But I didn't know you had any Quarter Horses."

"I don't, Holly. We've only got Saddlebreds."

"What are you trying to say, Kenny?"

"I'm trying to say that the research Jeremy is doing has made me wonder if there might be a genetic defect in a few of my young horses and the only bloodline they all have in common is Spy Master."

Holly remains silent for a long moment. "Let me get this straight. You called to tell me that you think Spy Master has a

79

genetic defect because of some school work your teenage son is doing?"

Kenny can't tell if she is amused or angry and decides it might be a mixture of both. "I've read his research, Holly, and I've done a bit of my own. I think there's a chance he could be right."

"Let me make sure I understand." Now there is no mistaking the fury in her clipped voice. "You called me to tell me that you and your son think that the stallion whose foals dominated the top 10 in every division this year has a genetic defect?" He hears her take a deep breath. "Until this very moment, I would have told anybody that you were one of my best friends in the world. But I guess I was wrong. It is now clear to me that you are jealous of my ability to win a World Championship, which is something you will never do. You don't even have the guts to compete much less the skill to win. So now you're trying to bring me down to your level. That's what this is about."

Kenny expected a poor reaction, but he is ill-equipped to handle her vitriol, "There might not be anything to this, Holly, and we could resolve it quickly with a simple DNA test. And even if it comes back positive…"

She interrupts him, "If you think for one moment that I'm going to submit Spy Master to a genetic test, then you must be smoking dope."

"Holly. Calm down. We're friends and we have the same interest here. I thought you would want to know about this as soon as I suspected he might have something. You have to admit that it resonates with Spy Master's history of colic."

"Who else have you told about this?"

"No one. Like I said, it's a high school Biology project."

"I'd better not find out that you're spreading lies about me, Kenny Rivers, or I will ruin you." She immediately disconnects the call.

Kenny slowly takes the phone from his ear and looks up to see Angela watching him from the doorway. "That didn't sound good."

"No. She completely lost it."

"Yeah, I could tell. I could hear her screaming from over here."

"I knew it wasn't something she'd want to hear, but I didn't expect her to go nuts. She accused me of making this up because I'm jealous of her."

Angela shakes her head in sympathy. "I'm sorry. I know her friendship means a lot to you."

"It just seems so out of character. I've never known her to get so mad so fast."

"Maybe she's just feeling the stress of the move to Kentucky. We know what the business is like out there. We certainly know how hard it is to succeed."

"Yeah, but she's got Eileen Miller as a client, a World Champion harness horse in the barn, and the leading Saddlebred stud. It seems to me that she has already succeeded."

"And you just suggested to her that it could all come crashing down in a second. It's no wonder that she flipped out." Angela takes a deep breath, "So what are we going to do?"

"What do you mean?"

"If part of our herd has a genetic defect, then we are in big trouble. Holly isn't the only one that is going to get hurt if this turns out to be true."

"I'm not sure what we can do."

"Maybe it's time to go see someone at the veterinary school in Fort Collins. It's not that far away. I'm sure there's someone there that can educate us. I think we're going to be better off armed with facts. Right now, I feel like we're just armed with fears."

"That's a good idea. I'll make some calls."

CHAPTER 22

3 PM December 8, Spy Hill Barn, KY

Missy walks by several empty stalls as she makes her way down the aisle at Spy Hill Barn. She notices a grooming box on the aisle floor next to an open stall door and heads toward it. Just as she gets close, Holly emerges.

"I thought I heard someone drive up! Welcome to Spy Hill! You've been here before, right?"

"Thanks! Yes, I had Toreador in training with Johnnie Stuart for a while," Missy answers, avoiding the memory of the conflicts that resulted from that association. "I think he built this place from scratch."

"Yes, he did. But it fell into disrepair after he moved out. This poor barn needs more repairs than I expected when I bought it," Holly explains.

"It looks like you've got plenty of room here," Missy gestures at the unoccupied stalls.

"I've got some construction workers coming tomorrow to rework some of the stalls. It feels so empty because I've moved a bunch of horses into the breeding barn so they won't be disturbed by all the noise and activity."

Missy makes sympathetic noises, but notices that the stalls in question show no signs of recent habitation, with stale wisps of bedding in the corners and a vacant air. "I can only imagine. Johnnie has been gone almost five years, I think. I always wondered why it stood empty for so long."

"I suspect he thought that his appeal of his expulsion from the Saddlebred Association would be successful. It just got resolved and upheld about six months ago, and that's when he got serious about selling. It will take me a while to get it into shape," Holly leads Missy down the aisle, stopping at an open stall door. "Here's the filly that you came to see."

"Tell me more about her," Missy stands back from the door of the stall to let Holly enter it.

"She's a coming four-year-old. Her name is Secret Agent. Her sire is Spy Master and her dam is a mare that one of my California clients owns. She's very well bred." Holly releases the filly from the cross ties and leads her into the aisle, posing her for Missy's benefit. "I bought her as a yearling, started her as a two-year-old, and gaited her last Spring."

"Oh!" Missy is clearly surprised. "I didn't realize that you own her yourself."

"Yeah, owning horses yourself is the big no-no for a horse trainer, isn't it? When a barn gets busy, they're the ones that get overlooked, just like in the old saying where the shoemaker's kids are the ones that are barefoot." She admires the filly, "I just couldn't resist this one, though."

"Have you shown her?"

"No, I haven't yet. I've been waiting for her to get more solid so that I give her a good experience and avoid the setbacks that come from rushing them. I'm very careful about letting the horse tell me when they're ready for the next step. And the move from California put her training a little behind."

Missy stands back, noticing that the leggy chestnut filly has no white markings. "She has a beautiful neck. She actually looks like she could be a walk-trot."

"Yes. I think you're right that she could be successful as a three-gaited horse, but just wait until you see her rack. But it could always be a fallback for an owner if she ever stops racking or needs a change of pace." Holly leads the horse towards the practice ring, "I'll ride her first and then give you a chance to try her."

Missy follows her down the aisle, continuing to notice that few stalls are currently occupied and that no other people seem to be around. "Are you here all by yourself?"

"I've got some grooms, but they're out getting a load of feed right now," Holly explains. "Although I admit that I've had trouble getting good help. Labor here is cheaper than it was in California, so I thought that I'd be able to lure help away from other barns, but other trainers are finding ways to keep their people. The living quarters I have to offer the grooms are a little rundown, so that doesn't help."

"Everyone in the industry is talking about how hard it is to find good grooms and assistants," Missy agrees. "But it doesn't seem safe for you to be working young horses by yourself. Doesn't it worry you?"

"My motto is that everything worthwhile in life comes with some risk," Holly carefully mounts the filly, barely getting her reins gathered before the young horse jogs off, tossing her head.

Missy stands in the center of the ring, watching as the filly trots and slow gaits both directions, noticing that Holly rides with careful concentration. Secret Agent spooks and darts sideways several times as she makes her away around the arena, laying her ears back when Holly gently corrects her. Despite her obvious inexperience, the filly is athletic and energetic, trotting well above level in the front.

When Holly halts her in the center, "Do you want to give her a try?"

"I don't think so. She's still a little too green for me," Missy laughs lightly. "I'm pretty sure she'd dump me in a heap just for the fun of it. She's a very nice filly, though. I absolutely love her hocks. At the trot, her hind feet nearly touch her belly."

"She's only got plates on," Holly proudly points to the very light shoes that the horse wears. "Imagine what she'll look like with a little more shoe. Her great hocks have been my biggest training challenge with her. The exceptional bend in her hind legs suit the rack perfectly, but I have to keep encouraging her to take a longer step. One of the benefits of my move to Kentucky is that I now have access to some of the best Saddlebred farriers in the world, and I think that is going to make all the difference with this horse. Last week, my farrier suggested that we put rocker toe shoes on her hind feet to help her stretch and reach, which will allow her to rack faster. But I knew you were coming to look at her today and I didn't want to change her shoes right before showing her to you."

"I'm not familiar with a rocker toe. What is that?"

"It's a shoe that is turned slightly upward in the toe, kind of like a ski. My farrier thinks it will really teach her to lengthen her step. I just want to make sure we don't take away her fantastic trot. As you know, it's a difficult balancing act that changes constantly as they grow and develop."

"She's breathtaking, especially when she comes around the corner and focuses on getting to the end of the straightaway. Does she wear a curb bit?" Missy motions toward the snaffle bit in Secret Agent's bridle.

"I'm long-lining her with the curb, and will probably ride her with it in the next few days. She hasn't given me any problems, but I'm taking it slow. As you probably noticed with her spooking, she's very aware and reactive. I've learned the hard way that going slow and being patient is the best way to work her." Holly pats the filly proudly, "Gaiting her has been one of my greatest achievements. She pops her knees so high and is so game that for the first couple of weeks, I could only get a couple of steps before she'd crow-hop across the ring with me. It took me forever to get her to do an entire straightaway, and only then did I even attempt a corner."

"Well she certainly has the rack down flat."

"Yes, she does. I'm convinced she's the real deal."

"She's gorgeous. Even though I'm actually looking for something that is closer to being ready for me to take to the ring, I'll admit that she's tempting."

"Since we're getting to be friends, I wouldn't lead you astray, Missy. Her price is only going to go up as she gets more consistent. This filly is special. You really should snap her up."

"Let me think about it a bit," Missy muses as they lead the filly back to her stall.

"Don't think too long. Once word gets out, she could go fast."

CHAPTER 23

Bobby and Jennifer are working quickly to make sure that Texas Debutaunt is ready for presentation to Blair. As they fasten a big red bow around her neck, Bobby asks, "Did Missy ever say anything to you about how her visit to Spy Hill went? Did she look at a horse over there?"

"I had to drag some information out of her," his wife answers, wetting a soft brush and using it to smooth the mare's mane. "She finally told me that she looked at a three-year-old that hasn't been shown yet."

"Did she like it?"

"I'm not really sure. She would only say that it still needed some work. It sounded to me like she was considering buying it."

"That's interesting. Did she tell you whether she would bring it over here?"

"I was afraid to ask and she didn't make it easy. She was really evasive."

Their conversation is interrupted by Marianne's voice in the barn aisle. "Bobby? Jennifer? Where are you? I told you we would be here at precisely 11 AM."

Jennifer rolls her eyes at Bobby and steps out into the aisle. "Right here, Marianne."

Bobby hears the footsteps quicken and he also steps out to greet their client just in time to hear her say, "I told Blair she had food in her teeth and sent her to the restroom. Is everything ready?"

"It is," Bobby steps away from the door so that Marianne can see the big bay mare, her four white feet and broad white blaze sparkling.

"Did you get the right halter on?" Marianne asks, her voice hushed as they hear Blair's steps at the end of the hall.

"Of course," Bobby answers, detaching the mare from the cross ties in the stall and attaching a leather lead with a brass tag engraved with Blair's name. He turns the mare's face so Marianne can see the name tag on the halter has Texas Debutaunt in large script.

86

Marianne obviously checks to be sure the spelling is accurate and then nods curtly. "Straighten that bow and then you'd better bring her out in the aisle. Otherwise it will take Blair all day to get here. She brought peppermints for every horse in the barn and she'll stop at every stall if we don't do something to hurry her along."

Bobby pats the mare on the neck as Jennifer slides the stall door wide open, checking to be sure the latch is fully retracted and then takes out her camera phone and stands back, ready to record Blair's surprise.

As Bobby leads the horse into the hall, Marianne summons her daughter, "Blair, dear? Come meet your new partner."

Later, after Marianne and Blair have departed and Texas Debutaunt is back in her comfortable stall, Bobby asks Jennifer, "Am I wrong, or was Blair underwhelmed?"

"That's an understatement. I followed her into the bathroom just before they left and found her sobbing."

"Sobbing? Why?" Bobby is incredulous.

"She thinks her mother is going to make her sell Vendome Copper. She adores that horse. She told me that she'd rather sell her own arm."

"That's a bit dramatic."

"Yes, but she's got a soft heart. I told her that we think she could move Vendome to the Ladies division and be successful, and that if she wanted to do that, we could help her figure out how to convince her mother to keep both horses."

"So that's what was behind all of that conversation about needing to keep Vendome until Spring so that Blair would be able to stay in shape while she slowly transitioned to the new horse?"

"Yeah. It buys us some time. Thanks for going along with that."

"I know when to keep my mouth shut." Bobby smiles. "And I truly believe what I told her about the market being better in the Spring and that it is better for older gaited horses to stay in light training all winter, rather than getting turned out."

"As tiresome as Marianne can be, we're very lucky to have a customer who can afford to keep two horses in training year-around."

"True. But it was pretty funny that she had to double check that we had the right halter on her horse." Bobby laughs. "But if we can figure out how to keep Vendome in the barn, she can come out and double check my work all day every day."

CHAPTER 24

After negotiating the automatic telephone directory for the Colorado State University Veterinary School, Kenny is finally connected to the faculty member that leads the genetic research laboratory, Dr. Michael Adams. Kenny introduces himself as a Saddlebred breeder and explains that he is seeing some symptoms that several of his horses share and he's concerned there might be a genetic link. Kenny mentions that he's been doing some reading and suspects something like PSSM.

After asking some basic questions, Dr. Adams says, "Let's start at the beginning. What symptoms are you seeing?"

"I'm seeing muscle stiffness, particularly if the horse has had a day of rest. In a couple of my young horses, it is pronounced enough that I think they're lame, but the symptoms go away after they work for a little while. It doesn't seem to be weather-related."

"Do you see excess sweat? Does the horse act like it has cramps?"

Kenny affirms this and adds, "Sometimes it is even bad enough that I actually think the horse is colicking. But that's pretty rare. It usually just seems like they're a little achy."

After asking several other questions about whether the horses have temperatures and increased respiration rates, Dr. Adams says, "The symptoms you're describing sound like a fairly minor case of tying up. When this happens on a regular basis, we call it Recurrent Exertional Rhabdomyolysis, or RER for short. Some horses sporadically develop exertional muscle damage as a result of nutritional, training, or environmental factors. Others develop RER in spite of a sound diet and environment. In fact, RER can be caused by several problems, including PSSM Types 1 and 2 and something called Malignant Hyperthermia. But there are other potential causes as well."

"I'd appreciate an education on what they might be, Dr. Adams. I've done some reading, but I admit that I can't even begin to understand some of it."

89

The vet's voice changes from his previous conversational tone to a cadence that reminds Kenny of the hours he spent attending lectures at William Woods University. "Let's start with the basics. As you know already, there are two types of PSSM. PSSM Type 1 is a point mutation in a gene that causes the glycogen synthase enzyme to be overactive. Simply, it is the inability to store and use sugars in skeletal muscles. The genetic malfunction overstimulates the production of glycogen and impairs its breakdown. This impairment results in the muscle not getting enough energy. That's why a PSSM 1 horse is actually made worse if it is fed carbohydrates that are high in starch, such as sweet feed, corn, wheat, oats, barley, and molasses. Rather, you should feed a PSSM 1 horse a high fat diet to give them the calories they need. The inability of a PSSM 1 horse to break down sugars for energy is also the reason that you need to give that horse daily exercise to enhance glucose utilization and improve energy metabolism in skeletal muscle. The success of a high fat, low sugar diet and a disciplined exercise program is well-documented and 90% of horses have improved. We can determine whether your horses have PSSM Type 1 with a fairly simple muscle biopsy. We'll process the tissue in our laboratory and you should have results in about 10 days."

Dr. Adams pauses, giving Kenny time to react to the information. "I'm surprised. I thought it would take a genetic test."

"For a definitive diagnosis, we would do genetic testing, but your local vet could do the biopsy from the rear leg hamstring muscle and send us the sample, so you wouldn't have to bring your horses all the way down here to Fort Collins for that."

"I see," Kenny says thoughtfully.

"Without testing, I kind of doubt you have PSSM 1, for several reasons. First, you told me that you have American Saddlebreds. That isn't a breed we see too much of in Colorado, so I don't know a lot about them. But I do know that PSSM 1 has been identified in several breeds, most commonly in draft horses in Europe. Here in Colorado, we see it in halter-type Quarter Horses. I don't believe it has ever been identified in Saddlebreds, although it might just be because it is relatively rare in that breed.

I'd need to do a thorough check of the literature to be sure. The second reason that I doubt you're seeing PSSM 1 is that the symptoms don't typically show up in young horses. Although it isn't unheard of to see symptoms in a yearling or two-year-old, it is more typical to see symptoms appear at around age six. Finally, we more commonly see PSSM 1 symptoms in calm and sedate horses. Since Saddlebreds are known to be high-spirited show horses, I think PSSM 1 is probably unlikely."

"I guess that's good news. So what about PSSM Type 2?"

"PSSM Type 2 is what we've come to call the disease that has the same symptoms as PSSM 1 but the horse tests negative for the gene mutation."

"Just to be sure I'm understanding your point, I think you're saying that a muscle biopsy would show us whether we have a problem with the storage of sugars in the muscle. If that test is positive, but the genetic test for the mutation is negative, then the horse has PSSM Type 2?" Kenny asks.

"Right. They're currently doing research to see whether they can find a genetic link to PSSM Type 2, but they haven't succeeded yet." Dr. Adams is clearly pleased that Kenny has come to the correct conclusion. "We've seen Type 2 in Morgans, Standardbreds, and Thoroughbreds. You'll notice that these breeds don't have the same calm temperament that I described when I talked about PSSM 1. So it isn't too much of a stretch to presume that it might be present in Saddlebreds."

"Are there differences in symptoms between Type 1 and Type 2?"

"Yes, but they're subtle. A Type 2 horse sometimes has painful and firm hindquarter muscles and sometimes we'll see painful back muscles. A symptomatic horse doesn't want to engage his hindquarters, so he'll get strung out at the trot."

"So this would make the horse difficult to collect," Kenny muses. "For a Saddlebred, this means that he wouldn't want to rack or slow gait."

"Right," Dr. Adams agrees. "PSSM cannot be cured. But if your horses have PSSM, there is some good news. You can manage the symptoms with diet and exercise."

Kenny laughs without any humor. "If it is Type 1, it would be terrible news because it would put a big hole in my breeding program."

"That's true. If it's genetic, it would have wide-ranging implications, not just for your breeding program, but for anyone in your breed with the same bloodlines. PSSM Type 1 is dominant. So only one copy of the gene needs to be passed on for the disease to manifest."

"Don't I know it," Kenny mutters. "There is a minimum 50% chance of getting an affected foal, even if one parent is PSSM Type 1 negative."

"Right. But if you end up with a PSSM diagnosis, there are ways to manage the disease. For Type 2 horses, it might just require dietary changes to high fat and protein feeds. I'd also supplement with some amino acids. I would recommend some adjustments to their training, such as a longer warmup and the diligent use of some stretching techniques. We can talk about details if our tests for PSSM are positive. But I'd also look at other possibilities to explain the symptoms you're seeing."

"Such as?"

"It could be Malignant Hyperthermia."

"Just the word 'malignant' is pretty frightening."

Dr. Adams' voice is calm. "It's another genetic disorder that we see in Quarter Horses, so it is probably a long shot. I've learned in my business that when you hear hoof beats, you should expect to see horses, not zebras."

"So what should my next step be?"

"I'd like to do a full genetic workup on four of your horses. I'd like you to bring down three that display the symptoms you describe, and one horse that doesn't display the symptoms. I think it'll take us a full day to do the work up, so we'll have to wait until after the holidays when my graduate students are back. When we're done talking, I'll send you back to my scheduler to make the appointment."

"Thank you, but I need to ask what this will cost."

"You're describing a very interesting case with important implications for our research here," Dr. Adams replies. "We'll do

92

the initial workup and genetic testing free of charge as long as you'll sign an agreement that allows us to publish our results."

CHAPTER 25

When Holly's phone rings, she checks the caller ID so that she can avoid Eileen and any collection calls from one of the many vendors that Eileen isn't paying. Seeing the North Carolina area code, she answers hesitantly, "Spy Hill Barn."

"This is Annie Jessup. Can I speak to someone about your stallion services?" The gravelly voice on the other end of the call asks.

"Hello Annie! This is Holly McNair. It's great to hear from you. How can I help you?"

After a minimum of small talk, Annie states, "I've been considering breeding Josephine's Dream to Spy Master. I think I saw in the Stallion Catalog that the stud fee is $6,000."

"Uh... oh..." Holly stammers, suddenly sensing an opportunity. "That advertisement is out of date. I'm so very sorry. His stud fee is now $9,500. We've had to raise it. The great results at Louisville this last year brought incredibly high demand and we need to be selective."

"So you're going to let the high fee separate the wheat from the chaff? That seems like an odd strategy. It seems like you'd be better off just being more selective about the quality of the mares you accept."

"Trust me, I know. But the owner makes the rules." Holly lies smoothly. "I told her that there were better ways to manage his career, but she calls all the shots. And I can see her point that Spy Master is worth the investment. He's a Reserve World Champion gaited horse in his own right, and just look at the results of his foals. He was the number one American Saddlebred sire last year. Who are you considering breeding him to?"

"I was considering matching him with my gaited mare, Josephine's Dream."

Holly notices that Annie has used the past tense and works to save the sale. "She's phenomenal and just imagine the foal they would produce," she effuses. "There'd be virtually no risk that the foal wouldn't rack. Gosh, you'd have buyers standing ten-

94

deep at the rail to watch that one show. The extra $3,500 now will be well worth it."

Annie takes a long time to reply, obviously thinking it over. "I assume you have a standard breeding contract?"

"Yes, I'll email it to you. Will you want frozen semen or will you bring your mare to us to be bred?"

"I'll want frozen. But I'll let you know if and when I want to move forward with this."

"You have such a high-quality mare that I think the foal would be really special. Let's be honest, a great foal will benefit Spy Master's career too." Holly hesitates, running a quick mental calculation of the impact extra board income the mare would generate. She lowers her voice and offers, "I probably shouldn't do this, but if you bring your mare to me, I can reduce the stud fee by $1000. But you'll have to keep this reduced rate confidential. I certainly can't afford to offer it to everyone and I don't want people to accuse me of playing favorites."

"I heard you are at Johnnie Stuart's old place. Is that right? I'd want to be sure that Josie would be in a top-notch place, even if it is only for a short time."

"I understand. I have made some substantial upgrades to the facilities since moving in."

"I can imagine they were needed. You can't leave a place like that vacant for long."

Holly laughs, "Don't I know it! I don't really understand how fences and stalls can come apart when there aren't even any horses leaning on them. I've spent an incredible amount of time whipping this place back into shape."

"Why don't you send me the breeding and mare care contracts and I'll review them? I'll let you know when I make a decision about my mare."

"I don't want to pressure you, but I'm likely to be at capacity this winter and spring. I'd like to say that I'd be able to create a spot for your mare, especially given her quality. But I'm filling up fast, so the sooner I get a contract back, the better."

After they end the call, Holly opens her email account to send the paperwork to Annie, wondering why skimming from Spy Master's stud fee hadn't occurred to her sooner. She does some quick mental calculations. Last year, Spy Master collected 40 stud fees. By getting an extra $2,500 for each, she could generate $100,000 and Eileen wouldn't even know about it! And if she could increase the number of mares to 60 in the coming season, she could clear $150,000. She leans back in her chair to think about the likelihood that Eileen will discover her dishonesty and wonders if she can depend on the mares' owners to not disclose the fee they are paying if they think they are getting a special rate. She launches a Google search for Non-Disclosure Agreements and downloads one of the simple forms. She starts typing, customizing the form by inserting the Spy Hill Barn logo and changing the language to threaten legal action if the stud fee is disclosed to anyone for three years. In less than 30 minutes, the new form is ready and she adds it to the contracts attached to the email to Annie Jessup. Before she can change her mind, she hits send, and then takes a swig of bourbon from the bottle she keeps in her desk drawer.

She then notices a message from Kenny in her inbox. She clicks on it and whispers the last line of the text aloud. "So, I'm taking several of my young horses to CSU to have them genetically tested and get muscle biopsies. I'll let you know how it goes."

"Shit!" The word explodes from her mouth.

CHAPTER 26

When Amber enters Annie's barn, she is greeted by the sounds and smells of horses enjoying their morning hay and grain. She squeezes past the tractor and feed trailer that block the aisle, nodding to the caretakers that are measuring rations into each horse's feed bin. Halfway down the aisle, she finds the side entrance to the indoor practice ring. She can hear a horse trotting in the ring and waits for it to pass the door before entering.

"Gosh, you're early," Annie calls as she trots by. "I didn't expect to see you until this afternoon."

Amber makes her way to the center of the ring, watching Annie work the young horse. "I couldn't sleep last night, so I just got up and took off," Amber explains.

"Let me finish working this one and then I'll give you a tour." After several more rounds of the ring, Annie dismounts and hands her sweaty horse off to a groom. "Welcome to Big View. I admit that I feel a bit guilty about having you here without being able to pay you. I went through the rule book pretty carefully to see if there was a loophole somewhere, but I didn't find one. At least if you were an intern, I could pay you minimum wage and reimburse expenses. But I can give you living quarters for the hours you work as a groom."

Amber acknowledges Annie's point, "Yes, the rules are really tight and I'll probably regret my decision to maintain my status, but I have some savings and I guess that's what they're for. It's so hard to get amateur status back once you give it up, that I'd rather keep it until I'm certain that this is for me."

"Yes, and the penalties for sneaking you any payment are huge for me, as well. So we'll have to keep our noses clean on this. Make sure you keep records of the hours that you're working as a groom. You can be sure that people will be watching."

Annie leads Amber into the barn aisle. "Let's start at one end and work our way up. My initial thought is that I'd give you one yearling, two two-year-olds, and two three-year-olds to work. You'll be responsible for all of their care and training, including

97

grooming and stall cleaning. I've already picked out candidates because I wanted to give you a variety of personality types and maturity levels." She moves to the first stall on the left side of the aisle, gently sliding the door open. "This is your yearling and he's as green as they get. We just brought him in from the field yesterday."

Amber looks at the young stud colt, a chestnut with a flaxen mane and a tail filled with cockle burrs. The young horse is standing as far back in the stall as possible, clearly frightened of his new surroundings. His morning rations are untouched. "He looks scared," she comments.

"He is, but he'll settle down in a day or so. We had a halter on him as a weanling and he learned really quickly. Since then, he's been out in the pasture for four months. He was born here on the farm and his dam was a really good amateur pleasure horse. She is smart as a whip and has an honest and forgiving attitude. From what I've seen so far, I think this colt has inherited those traits."

"What are your near-term goals for him?"

Annie nods approvingly, "I like the way you think, Amber. Always begin with the end in mind. In two weeks, I'd like to see him stand quietly in cross ties for grooming. He should allow you to pick up his feet and be calm and quiet for the farrier. He should be easy to catch and lead, and he should be working well on a lunge line, including halting and reversing."

"I haven't worked a yearling before," Amber admits nervously.

"That's what this is about," Annie smiles. "We're going to give you an education in horse training. And don't worry, I'll be here to help. I'm going to do my best to keep my mouth shut and not give you too much unsolicited advice because I believe that figuring it out and making a few mistakes along the way is how you learn. But I won't let things get out of hand if they're going the wrong direction. You can depend on me to step in if I see something going haywire. The one thing I will insist on is that you not turn a young horse into a gentle pet. I think that it's important to keep them a bit wary. When a young horse is too gentle, they tend to forget who the boss is and that makes them difficult and dangerous to work." Annie slides the stall door closed and continues down the aisle, introducing each horse as she goes.

It takes nearly an hour to walk through the 24-stall barn, when Annie finally arrives at the last stall. "They say a mother should never have a favorite child, but I do. And this is my favorite child, Dream Weaver." She slides the stall open and rewards the mare's nicker by offering a peppermint and stepping forward to pat her neck. The chestnut crunches the candy and then immediately turns back to her hay. "I swear I haven't turned her into a pet," Annie jokes. "She is my gaited mare's first foal."

"That's Josephine's Dream, right?"

"It is. She's currently the queen of the broodmare band."

"Didn't you sell her to Missy Phillips?"

"Yes, about eight years ago. Missy kept her about 2½ years and won the Amateur Stake at Louisville with her. Then she sold her to one of my juvenile riders. Abby won the 14-17 juvenile championship at Louisville, and eventually her family gifted her back to me. Josie is 14 now, and enjoying a well-deserved retirement."

"Wasn't she in a big trailer wreck?"

"She was. It happened on the way home from Louisville the very first year that Missy owned her. Even though she went on to win a World Championship, I think the wreck contributed to her early retirement. It was just hard to keep her joints comfortable, so I decided to stop asking so much from her. She certainly doesn't owe me anything."

"She must think she owes you something," Amber says. "Look at the beautiful filly she gave you."

"Yes, just look at her." Annie stands back to admire the horse. "I've already sold two of her siblings, so this is the only one of Josie's left in the barn. Although, I've got her little sister out in the yearling field."

"It's a nice place."

"Thank you. It's not huge and I've intentionally kept it that way. I usually have an assistant, but I don't want to have to rush through my work every day, so I've really tried to keep my own string down to about 15 horses. There are 20 in training now, counting the five I've allocated to you. There are four more show horses that are on their winter break, so they'll be coming back into the barn next month."

"Do you have a lot of amateur clients?"

"No, that's also something I've been deliberately reducing over the years. I have one amateur and three juveniles. I enjoy teaching them, but I don't really enjoy dragging a huge bunch of finished horses to a dozen shows in the summer." Annie turns to lead Amber back up the aisle. "If everything works out and you decide you like this life, we may want to reverse that trend. Having a barn filled with amateurs and juveniles is a blessing and a curse. I like the energy that it brings, but I don't like the drama. I'm really happiest just working a young horse quietly and helping it develop and grow."

"I'm so thankful to be here. Can I get started now?"

"Absolutely. Just hunt around for anything you need. Everyone here behaves as a team, so they'll all be willing to help you."

CHAPTER 27

Melody helps Helen out of the pleasure cart, "Well done, Helen."

"Well done?" Helen responds in disbelief, her eyes filling with tears. "Poor Buddy! I nearly ran him into the side of the ring three times! I mashed two of your cones into oblivion! I went right when you said left! When you told me to reverse in the bull pen, I didn't give myself enough room to turn and you had to lead Buddy out of the mess I got us into!" She accompanies her statements with dramatic expressions and hand gestures, and by the time she takes a breath, Melody is laughing out loud.

"But that's the point!" Melody gasps. "I wanted all those things to happen. I even tried to get you to hang a hub up on the doorway, but NO!" She widens her eyes and spreads her hands, "You had to find something to fail at."

Helen stares at her in disbelief and then starts to giggle. "Well then, let me back in that cart. I bet if I keep trying, I can accomplish that!"

"What's going on in here?" Roger has obviously been attracted by the gales of laughter coming from the ring.

Helen straightens her expression and says with mock seriousness, "Melody was just saying that she mistook me for the famous and elegant Donna Moore in my driving lesson today."

This unlikely comparison to one of the most skilled trainers and harness horse drivers in the history of American Saddlebreds causes Melody to erupt in more laughter. Between gasps, she wipes her eyes, "Helen fell into most of my traps in her driving lesson," she points at the mangled orange cones littering the ring. "But I told her that she had failed to hang the hub of the cart up on the doorway and she offered to try again."

Roger smiles, "I wanted to warn you, Helen. Melody's driving lessons are legendary. I think Buddy has learned to aim for the cones."

"Hey! I told you that I thought he went out of his way to kick that last one with his hind foot," Helen looks at Melody accusingly.

"I think Buddy has learned that he gets a treat for every cone that has to be pummeled back into shape at the end of one of these lessons," Roger unhooks Buddy from the cart. "Did she tell you to reverse in the bull ring, but she waited until you were far enough around the corner for it to be impossible? That's another one of her tricks."

Melody is serious now, "That's what these lessons are about, Helen. I'm trying to help you to experience everything that can go wrong when you're in a safe place with a bomb-proof horse. That will help you know how to react when you're in a show ring with a fancy horse."

"The biggest thing I learned was to keep going forward and to learn how to plan my route."

"Perfect. That's what I hoped you would learn. Did you have fun?"

"I had a blast. I had underestimated how much fun this could be. And I can see how much difference skill will make in being able to catch a judge's eye."

"And in staying safe." Melody adds.

"Yes. I was looking at some old videos on-line and there have been some terrible wrecks. I saw one where a horse got loose in a big class and was racing around at full speed, dragging the broken cart behind him. He collided with other horses and was completely out of control. I don't think anyone was killed, but it looked incredibly scary and dangerous."

"I think I might know the video you're talking about. It is infamous." Melody and Helen start walking back to the barn area together and Melody's tone is deadly serious. "There are a few things that you must always remember, no matter what else happens. First and foremost, don't allow your horse to balk. In that way, it's like riding. A balky horse that tries to rear is very dangerous. It is often caused by an inexperienced driver that is pulling too hard on the bit and not allowing the horse to go forward. It can lead to a very scary situation and the horse and driver can get badly hurt."

"Got it."

"Next, pay attention to your reins. Never allow a rein to get under your horse's tail. Even a saint like Buddy will kick when that happens, and that is only slightly less dangerous than a horse that rears."

"Got it," Helen repeats.

"And finally, the point you mentioned. You must stay calm and think ahead. Use all of your senses to anticipate what the horses ahead of you are likely to do and maneuver your horse to accommodate it."

"Practice defensive driving," Helen suggests.

"Exactly. It's critical in a big class."

"How many driving horses do they put in a ring?"

"Here in Denver, we never fill the ring. But I've seen as many as 18 in the same ring in Louisville."

"Wow. I've seen that ring with 23 riders in it and it is so full it's scary. Especially when everyone is reversing. A horse and driver are at least as big as two riders. Eighteen trying to reverse has to be frightening."

"It's nerve wracking enough when they're professionals, especially if the horses are young. But I know more than a few trainers who claim they've lost years off their lives watching their amateurs or juveniles in a ring that busy. In truth, though, there are really very few wrecks. And I'll do my job to make sure you're prepared before we ever get that far."

"Matthew and I talked, and I think that we're ready to start shopping for a harness horse as soon as we find a great new home for Glitter Girl."

Melody smiles, "Roger and I anticipated that. We have a buyer for Glitter Girl, if you're ready to sell. And Roger talked to Kenny Rivers. He's got a harness horse that might work for you."

"That's the trainer we got Glitter Girl from. Matthew and I watched him show a harness horse at the Fall show in Denver."

"It's probably the same horse. It's a gelding named Nile Ninja. He's five years old this year. Kenny does such a great job with his horses. They're all calm and sensible. Do you think you're ready for a road trip to Wyoming?"

"Let's do it!"

CHAPTER 28

"Today's the big day," Amber greets Annie as soon as the trainer enters the barn and hands her a steaming cup of coffee.

Annie pretends confusion, "Oh? I don't think anything special is on my calendar." Then, reading the disappointment in Amber's face, "Oh, that's right. You've been here two weeks and it's time for me to see whether you've worked any magic on your horses." It is clear from Annie's grin that she's been teasing.

Amber smiles, "You're so funny. I couldn't sleep last night for the pure excitement of showing you where I am with each of them. I know you said you wouldn't interfere but I didn't expect to be left completely alone for two weeks."

"Honey, that's how you figure stuff out. It is far more productive to learn by experimenting than it is for an old bag like me to just tell you how I'd do something. This is a two-way street you know. I'm hoping that I'll get a few new ideas from watching you."

"You don't fool me, Annie. I know you've been watching me out of the corner of your eye, so nothing I show you today will surprise you. But I do have a few questions I've been saving up."

"Well then, let's see what you've done with that yearling."

It takes nearly two hours for the two women to work all of Amber's string and discuss them, with Annie demonstrating techniques to help Amber iron out small issues with her young horses. After they finish, Annie gives Amber a small hug. "I'm so pleased with how they're coming along. They look beautiful, although I think we should try some different conditioner on that two-year-old's tail. Ask Maria about that. I'm sure she'll help you. She's a magician with tails. And I think your three-year-old filly is about ready to gait. Let's work with the farrier when he comes on Tuesday and then I'll show you how to start that process. I like to start them without any shoes in the front. I think it's easier for them to get the idea."

"What would you like me to do next with the yearling?"

"You've done everything we need with that one at this point. I'd like to kick him back out into the yearling pasture and let him

104

grow up. We'll see him again in the Fall when we're ready to put tack on him."

Amber looks a little disappointed at this news. "Oh. I really like working with him."

"Don't worry, there are a lot of youngsters to go around. Let's walk out to the yearling pasture and pick out your next victim," Annie grabs her heavy coat off the coat rack.

Amber grins and quickly follows suit. "Seriously? That's great! What do I look for?"

"If you think I'm going to give away all my secrets in the first two weeks of you being here, you're crazy. If I did that, you'd get all the nice ones to work and I'd get the duds." Annie buttons her coat and starts walking towards the barn door, with Amber hurrying to follow.

"I don't believe you have many duds."

"Not many, but it happens."

"What do you do then?"

"It's a hard problem and a real challenge for our industry. I do everything I can to make sure that I've trained a useful horse, even if they aren't show ring quality. I make sure they are safe for people to be around. If they aren't safe or sound, either because there is a congenital defect of some sort or they're just not right mentally, then I consider euthanizing. That doesn't happen often, but I won't dump a horse on the market that isn't healthy or that might hurt someone. And I certainly don't want their defect polluting my gene pool. I've worked far too long and too hard to let my heart get ahead of my head."

"I bet that's a tough decision. I'm not sure I could do it."

"You could," Annie states with certainty. "You really have no other choice. It's the most ethical decision in some cases."

"What do you do with horses that aren't show quality but are safe and healthy?"

"We do get a few horses that don't have the desire and ambition needed to be show horses. I work hard to make them useful as pleasure horses, trail horses, or even lesson horses. It is one reason that I donate time and money to academy programs. Those kids need something good to ride and I'd rather donate a horse to one of their programs than send it to an auction where I wouldn't know what happened to it."

"The auctions are controversial."

"Some of them are. The Saddlebred auctions every year are wonderful. They're a very good way for someone to get a decent horse for not too much money, and they serve an important role. But I think you're talking about the auctions that the kill buyers show up at."

"Yes. I see a lot of stuff about it on social media."

"I understand why they exist, but it is heart-wrenching to see what goes on there. And it isn't just a Saddlebred problem. Horses of all breeds end up in those auctions. I believe it is far kinder to gently euthanize a horse that isn't suitable for anyone to use than it is to send the poor creature through the fright and pain of an auction. But that's my personal view. All I can really do is be a careful shepherd of my own flock and do right by them."

"But once a horse leaves your ownership, do you worry about it?"

"Oh yes! I certainly do. I'm not a huge breeder, so I'm better able to keep my eyes on them and pay attention to where they are and what's happening to them than some breeders. And rarely, I've had to step in to recover a horse that is headed down a sad path." She pauses at the fence and looks at the yearling herd. "I think the most upsetting thing that ever happened was when I got a call from one of the rescue organizations telling me that they had saved an old gelding from slaughter. They had done a DNA test and learned he was one of mine."

"Oh no."

"Yes. I had sold him to some people and they'd sold him when their daughter went to college. After that, he'd changed hands several times. I hadn't even noticed that he'd kind of disappeared from sight. I'm not even sure when or how he got separated from his papers."

"So what did you do?"

"Oh! I went and got him right away. I think it is a tragic thing for a horse to get separated from their name. But that's him standing under the tree over there. He's the old soul that keeps the yearlings from getting too crazy."

"That's a sweet story."

"It could have ended very differently for him. I'm lucky in that I have the room and the resources to give him a soft landing. Not everyone can do that." Annie abruptly changes the subject. "But enough with the sad stories. Let's find you another project."

"What am I looking for?"

"What did you like best about the last one you had?"

"His curiosity."

"That's a very good answer. A horse that is curious is one that is intelligent and will learn quickly." Annie whistles sharply. "You'll see that all of them in this crowd pick up their ears and turn towards us, but wait and see who turns back to the hay and who approaches. I'd pick from the ones that approach. What else would you look for?"

"Talent and conformation."

"That would be true if you were buying a horse, but I need you to think like a trainer. Every yearling in this pasture is going to make their way into the barn this winter. You want to find a youngster that is ready to start learning and pick them first."

"That makes sense. I want one that isn't a scaredy cat."

"Yes! And maybe one that wants to show off a bit." Annie shakes a plastic bag she has stuffed into her coat pocket and several of the yearlings startle and race to the far corner of the pasture. Three of the youngsters prance several steps and then turn to watch the women.

"I want the middle one," Amber says with certainty, motioning to the group of three.

"Good choice. That's a very nice yearling. She's out of Josie."

"What's her name?"

"Josephine's Joy."

"Joy," Amber says softly. "I like that."

CHAPTER 29

"The vet from CSU called back today." Kenny tells Angela softly, although there is little chance the kids will overhear as they are up in their rooms, presumably doing homework.

His wife pales and sets down the wooden spoon she is using to stir the beef browning in the pot on the stove. "What did he say?"

"There is good news and bad, so I'll tell you the good news first. None of the fillies I took down tested positive for PSSM Type 1."

"From what you told me, that isn't a surprise. They already told you that they'd never seen that disease in Saddlebreds. So what's the bad news?"

"Two of the four's muscle biopsies showed muscle fibers that have an overactive glycogen synthase enzyme."

"What does that mean in plain English?"

"He stopped short of diagnosing PSSM Type 2, although he says that the muscle biopsies indicate it."

"So why didn't he diagnose it?"

"He said that it is easy to get a false positive in a young horse because the muscle fibers are regenerating naturally."

Angela runs her fingers through her blond hair. "Wait. I'm confused. What does this mean for us?"

"It means that they didn't find a genetic issue to explain the symptoms I've noticed. And of the three fillies that I thought had symptoms, only two showed the muscular changes that explain them. Dr. Adams cautioned me that the veterinary medicine research community is still looking for a genetic link to PSSM Type 2, but they haven't yet found one."

"Does this mean that Spy Master is in the clear? And if so, what's causing the symptoms?"

"It's still a puzzle. As I understand it, it could be nothing. In other words, it's a false positive like he told me."

"That's the best possible case. What else could it be?"

108

"He said it could be environmental. Something to do with the feed or water, maybe." He shakes his head, "I suppose it's possible, but I kind of doubt that."

"Okay. But what's the worst thing that it could be?"

"The two fillies that tested positive are from dams that are sisters."

"What are you saying?"

"I'm saying that if PSSM Type 2 actually is genetic, it could be coming from our mares, not from Spy Master."

Angela turns back to the sizzling pot on the stove. "I'm still confused. But most importantly, I don't know what we do next."

"We have several choices. The first is that we change the horses' diets. Dr. Adams is sending me a recommended diet that will increase turnover of the muscle fibers. It has low starch and sugar content and includes a whey-based protein supplement. We'd also make sure that we warm them up slowly and work them thoroughly every day. We need to work them long and low for about 15 minutes a day to engage their topline and core."

"That sounds like expensive and time-consuming changes for you, but easy enough. What's the second choice?"

"We can continue to pursue the cause of this. I think that would mean doing a muscle biopsy of the two mares. If they show positive, then we probably have a genetic problem and it's in our mares."

"I think we have to be careful asking a question that we don't want to know the answer to. But let's just say that they test negative. Then what?"

"We'd want to get a biopsy from the sire."

"There's no way that they're going to agree to that, are they? Why would Holly submit Spy Master to a test that could destroy his value?"

"It isn't Holly's decision. It's the owner's decision."

Angela turns back to him. "Okay. That's true. But my point is still the same. Why would the owner do that? Isn't her name Eileen? What does she have to gain from it?"

"If he tests negative, it could remove any doubt that this problem is linked to him."

"But the vets don't even know that it's genetic, anyway. If I were her, I'd laugh you out of the room." She adopts an older woman's voice, playing the role of Eileen. "Excuse me? You want me to do a muscle biopsy on my world-famous stallion to satisfy your curiosity as to whether your fillies could have inherited a disease from him that the veterinarians don't even know is genetic?" She widens her eyes in mock disbelief. "You must be kidding me."

"Okay. I see your point. No need to be catty." Kenny starts setting the table. "What do you think we should do?"

"Make the diet and exercise changes and do nothing else."

"Not even test the mares?" Now Kenny is the one that is in disbelief. "I was planning on breeding them in March. What if we're just perpetuating our problem?"

"What would you do if they tested positive?"

"I'd quit breeding them."

"And if they test negative?"

"I'd probably continue breeding them."

"Are you going to stop breeding to Spy Master, even if they don't test him?"

"That's why I want them to test Spy Master," Kenny replies, his voice rising in frustration. "His foals are easy to sell and he matches well with my mares, but I don't think I can risk getting more foals that might have this enzyme. Even though they haven't found a genetic link, it doesn't mean that it isn't there."

Angela nods in agreement. "I agree. It sounds like we have several decisions to make. First, do we test our mares? Second, do you tell Eileen what you know and ask her to test Spy Master? Third, do we test our entire herd?"

"Our entire herd?" Kenny echoes, his voice rising.

"I'm just following your reasoning to its logical conclusion," she says defensively. "You said that if the mares tested positive, you'd quit breeding them. What if it is a recessive gene? If it is, then the two fillies you took to CSU that tested negative might actually have dams that would test positive, right? Don't we have to do muscle biopsies of every horse to figure out who might be a carrier?" She stresses the 'might' in her sentence.

110

Kenny's mouth tightens as he follows her reasoning. "Oh man. I think you're right."

"But let's think this through. Let's just say that the worst possible result happens and a good portion of our herd tests positive. What are the ethical implications? Would we have to disclose to all our previous buyers that the horses they bought over the many years we've been doing this might have PSSM Type 2? It would ruin our business." She turns back to him, "It isn't a fatal disease. There is no evidence it is genetic. Why are we asking questions when we don't want to know the answer?"

"But what are you saying? That we just forget the whole thing?"

"I'm suggesting we stop breeding to Spy Master and wait to see how next year's foal crop turns out. If you see foals that you think have the same symptoms that started this whole thing in the first place, then we test our mares."

"But that's kicking the can down the road. We won't know for a couple of years whether we have potential issues."

"But the alternative choice of testing everything and risking that we find a pervasive problem is not a reasonable solution. Our horse business would be finished."

The kitchen is suddenly silent as Kenny thinks through her logic. "So you're saying we just bury this whole issue?"

Angela softens her voice and says reasonably, "Those people from Denver are coming to look at Nile Ninja next week, right? Are you planning to tell them that he might have a problem with his muscle enzymes?"

"I don't know. I hadn't thought it through."

"Have you noticed these symptoms with him?"

"I'm not sure. He's definitely slow to warm up. I think I'd say that he's got some of the same symptoms, but they aren't as obvious as some of the herd."

"But he's a gelding, so even if it is a genetic problem, he can't pass it on."

"Angela, I see your point. But what if Roger wants to buy one of the fillies that tested positive? Are you saying that I shouldn't disclose it?"

"I admit that's a more difficult point. But it is possible she got a false positive. And don't most buyers do their own vet checks?"

"They never check for this. I think it would be unethical to not tell them of a medical problem that we're aware of."

"But is that even true if the diet and exercise changes work? Couldn't you just recommend a specific diet and training regimen and leave it at that?"

"I don't know. I need to think about it."

CHAPTER 30

"What a crazy day," Jennifer gives Bobby a hug as they leave the barn together. "I'm so glad it's over."

"Yeah. This week has been full of ups and downs. I can't believe that Missy sold Texas Beauty Queen. She gets along so well with that mare that I thought she'd have her for a few more years. I'm getting worried that she's slowly becoming more disconnected from our barn."

"I understand why she did it, though. Queen is 13 this year, and that's starting to get to the upper end for a gaited show horse. And the lady that bought her has a lot of property and a big broodmare band. It made Missy feel good to know that Queen would have a comfortable home when she can no longer show."

"I really liked that mare. I'm a little sad that my favorites are getting old. Between Queen and Vendome, I'm losing two of my favorite rides."

"Missy still has War Paint here, and he'll come back in from his winter break next week. So we'll get to see her more often and we can bring her back into the fold." Jennifer kicks off her muddy boots outside the door to their home. "Speaking of Vendome, we need to figure something different out with Blair. She just isn't gelling with Texas Debutaunt."

"I know. I've been giving that some thought." Bobby is already rummaging through the refrigerator, looking for something to make for dinner. "Blair is actually riding her pretty well, but this morning she was really frustrated and short-tempered when she kept missing that left lead. I think it's pretty weird that Blair doesn't act pleased when we praise her. It's almost like she just doesn't care that much. I'm starting to worry that this might not work out, not because Blair can't ride her but because she just doesn't like her."

"Personally, I think she's afraid that liking Texas Debutaunt will somehow be disloyal to Vendome."

"Really? Maybe you're right. I guess that I was just assuming that she might be trying to make a point with her mother." Bobby places a package of ground beef on the counter.

"Blair certainly knows by now that Marianne is domineering. She should be used to that by now." Jennifer reaches for vegetables to make a salad.

"True. I just think that maybe it has to do with Debutaunt being a completely different personality from Vendome. Vendome's a real love and he obviously likes people and loves Blair. He recognizes her footsteps and nickers as soon as he knows she is in the barn. Debutaunt is stand-offish. I think a lot of the difference is just natural. In my experience, mares are just not as easy going as geldings as a rule. And Blair hasn't actually spent much time getting to know the mare. We have her groomed and warmed up when Blair arrives and we cool her out."

Jennifer pauses, and leans back against the kitchen counter. "You might have given me an idea. Maybe we should figure out a way for Blair to spend more quality time with the mare."

"What do you mean?"

"Maybe when she comes to ride next week, we could let her free ride. Clearly, we need to have someone in the ring just to make sure that nothing awful happens, but maybe Blair would benefit from a little time to just get to know her mare. And I think it would help a lot if she cooled her out and brushed her."

By now, Bobby has the burgers sizzling in the pan. "It certainly won't hurt to try that. We might also find a way to lighten up when she comes to ride. I don't spend much time talking to her about how great this mare is and what I like about her. We're pretty much all business. Maybe we need to make it a little more fun."

"It certainly can't hurt to try."

CHAPTER 31

Eileen and Karen greet each other with hugs at the front door of their favorite restaurant in La Jolla.

"I can't believe I haven't seen you in three months!" Karen gushes. "Your hair is darker and it looks amazing!"

"I decided to try a different color for winter. The ash blond was looking kind of tired," Eileen runs her hands through her hair. "I've been looking forward to seeing you. I need some advice on what I'm now calling the 'Holly situation' and you're the most level-headed person I know. So I'm buying lunch today so I don't feel so guilty about it."

Karen laughs gaily. "Are you kidding? I'm dying to know what's happening with Spy Master and Sneaky Suspicion and the others. And what's up with Holly?"

By now they are seated at a table overlooking La Jolla Cove, watching a few tourists follow the path down to the beach. Eileen sips her water, "I'm kind of wondering where I should begin."

"Start with Spy Master. How is he?"

"As far as I know, he's good. We have tons of breeding contracts. Being named the Sire of the Year certainly increased his demand. Before breeding season started, I told Holly that I thought we should increase his stud fee a bit, but she convinced me that it was a bad idea."

"Really? Why?"

"We agreed that we wanted to be able to select the very best mares and that's not always consistent with owners having the most money to spend on stud fees."

"That makes sense." Karen peers over the top of her menu, "But I sense a 'but' coming."

"Right. I've left the selection of the mares in Holly's hands, but she doesn't appear to be very selective. When I asked her to send me a list of the mares, there were some on there that don't have any show history and their bloodlines aren't notable."

"What did she say when you asked her about it?"

"She said she'd looked at the mare and liked its conformation and that the lack of a good show record was not the mare's fault."

115

"Hm. I can see her point on that. You said that you're getting a lot of mares to come to him?"

"Yes. Nearly 50% higher than this time last year."

"I guess that's good if the mares are all as good as Holly says."

"Yes. I'm really not sure why it bothers me, except that I think it's odd that she came out so strongly against increasing his fee. She knows I'm paying most of the bills for the barn and the extra money would have come in handy."

"Eileen, Spy Master is your horse. It isn't clear to me why she has any say in what you charge for a stud fee."

"True. I've gotten in the habit of taking her advice when it comes to the horses."

"But this isn't really advice about horses, is it? Isn't it advice about finances?"

The waiter approaches the table to take their lunch orders, and Eileen uses the time to mull over Karen's point. Once they are alone again, she admits, "Of course you're right. And I'm not sure why I didn't see it that way. But it's a bit too late now to revisit his fee, since the contracts are already in place. I'll definitely readjust next year."

"Tell me what's happening with Sneaky Suspicion."

"I really need to get out there in the next month and drive her since I'll be showing her this next season. Holly says she enjoyed her time off and she started jogging her this week."

"That's good! You must be really excited about that."

Eileen leans back in her chair, smiling. "I'm experiencing that weird combination of excitement and nervousness in which you can't really tell the two emotions apart. It's her first year in the Amateur division and everyone has high expectations for her since she won the Open Harness World Championship last year. I'm a little worried about letting everyone down."

"Oh Eileen, you are one of the best amateur harness drivers in the industry! You're going to do great! Although I think we'll need to go shopping for a new gown or two or three." Karen laughs gaily, "In fact, I know a little boutique straight across the street that has some beautiful clothes."

Eileen shares the laugh, "Yes. We do need to make a date to do that."

"So how is Holly? The last time we talked, you seemed pretty concerned that she was having some financial trouble because of the move to Kentucky. From what you said just now, it sounds like you're still paying the bills for the barn."

"Yes. I took your advice and I'm paying the feed, shavings, and utility bills directly. And I've always paid the farrier and vet bills. She's still making the payments on the property. The previous owner holds the mortgage. I think she's really struggling to pay that much, but I didn't want to take all the pressure off."

"Oh lordy. That sounds expensive. I hope you put some sort of legal agreement in place so that you'll be reimbursed once things turn around."

"Yes. I took your advice on that, too. Although the last thing I want is to end up owning a horse barn in Kentucky." Eileen tucks her hair behind her ears. "The most worrisome thing, though, is Holly's state of mind."

"What do you mean?"

"Well, the last time I talked to her, she made a joke about how she now understands how valuable horses sometimes end up suddenly dead in their stalls."

"What?" Karen's eyes widen in disbelief. "What kind of joke is that?"

"She was making a point about how hard it has been to sell expensive horses this year. She has been trying to sell one for me and I think she really needs the commission. She knows my filly is insured for more than I'm likely to sell her for. I think she was referring to the horse being worth more dead than alive."

"Oh my gosh. That's not something I'd even joke about."

"Yes. She was in a dark mood. I simply asked her if she'd even shown the horse to anyone. She said that she hadn't and that I needed to advertise. But we'd need video and photos and she hasn't gotten around to doing them."

The waiter arrives at the table and sets down large salads in front of the women. They take a few bites before Karen asks delicately, "The last time we talked about Holly, I think you were afraid she was drinking too much. Are you still worried about that?"

"I'm not sure," Eileen admits. "I asked her how she was feeling and she said she was tired. She talked about how much work there is."

"I remember she was having trouble getting help."

"Yes. I send her money for two grooms though, so she did find help."

"You don't pay them directly?"

"It turned out to be so much simpler logistically for her to pay them, so I just put money in an account for her to use. They get paid every week and I didn't want the hassle of dealing with social security, etc. But more to your point, I can't tell from talking to her on the phone whether she's drinking like I suspected."

"It sounds to me like you need to get out there just to see what's up. Either that, or you need to find someone you trust to keep a close eye on things. Doesn't it make you nervous to be so far away from your horses?"

"I thought it was going to work out fine. A year ago, I wouldn't have thought twice about trusting Holly with them. Heck, I would have trusted Holly with my life."

"But now?" her friend coaxes.

"Now, I'm not so sure. You're certainly right that I need to be more present. I really wish that I knew more people in Kentucky so that I could get a read on what's happening from an outsider. I don't even know how she's perceived. If people don't like and trust her, they certainly won't bring clients by to buy a horse from her." She shakes her head in frustration and pastes a large smile on her face. "Enough about me and my horse problems. You're a brand-new Grandma! Tell me all about the baby!"

CHAPTER 32

"Welcome to Rivers Ranch!" Kenny greets Roger, Melody, Helen, and Matthew as they climb out of Roger's Ford 350 on a windy and cold Saturday morning. After exchanging brisk handshakes, he leads them all into the barn, where his daughter Emily is already pouring hot chocolate for the guests.

"Gosh, it's windy today," Helen remarks, using her fingers to untangle her curly red hair.

Kenny laughs. "Helen, it's windy every day up here. We like to say that if it weren't for the crappy weather, we'd have no weather at all. I guess we're trying to figure out a way to be thankful for it." After everyone has been served, he says, "I'm glad to see you brought a trailer because we have a lot to show you today and I'm hoping you'll find something that you want to take home with you. Angela has made a big pot of her famous chili, so we're going to have some fun and some great food."

"Thanks for the hospitality," Melody pipes up. "We've been looking forward to getting up here. You're the only Saddlebred trainer we know of in Wyoming and it must get a little lonely. How did you end up here?"

"It's a long and boring story," Kenny grins. "But the short version is that my great grandfather came to Wyoming from Missouri to work in the coal mines. He figured out pretty quickly that was a terrible idea, so he saved his money and bought a band of sheep, since he couldn't afford cows. Eventually, he upgraded from sheep to cows and built this ranch. He passed the ranch down to my grandfather, who passed it to his oldest son, my Uncle Jim. Uncle Jim and Aunt Marie didn't have any kids, so my parents in Missouri used to send me out here every summer to help Uncle Jim put up hay. I fell in love with the place and when Uncle Jim got ill, he asked me to move my family up here and take over the ranch."

"But how did you get into Saddlebreds?" Matthew asks curiously.

"I wanted to do something with horses, so I went to college at William Woods in Missouri. I didn't know anything about

119

Saddlebreds but during my very first class there I became friends with Holly McNair, who introduced me to them. It didn't take me long to know that I wanted to be a Saddlebred trainer."

"I didn't realize you'd been friends with Holly since college," Roger comments. "Is that how you formed the relationship with Spy Master? He's prominent in your breeding program."

"Yes. I helped Holly get Spy Master ready for the Louisville show the year he won the Reserve Championship in the Gaited Stake. It was a real pleasure to work with that horse. He's incredibly intelligent and surprisingly easy to work with for a stud."

"Why did they quit showing him?" Helen asks.

"He had a bout of colic at the Kansas City Royal that same year and I think the owner didn't want to stress him out with traveling to shows. Back then, Holly was training in California and every show required long trailer rides and overnight stays. It became a logistical struggle, so I think they just decided to send him to the breeding shed."

His guests all nod in understanding. "I wonder how Holly is doing in Kentucky," Melody comments. "It's got to be worlds different from her California experience."

"We don't talk that often," Kenny admits. "I know that her largest client moved with her, so that helped out. Having been a trainer there myself up until six or so years ago, I can attest to how hard it is to compete for clients and succeed there. There are dozens of good Saddlebred trainers in spitting distance, not to mention the great trainers down toward Versailles."

"So what's in store for us today?" Roger asks, looking around admiringly at the neat and clean barn.

"I thought we'd start out with something really different. I know your main purpose today is to see Nile Ninja, but I thought I'd show you some other stuff too, just in case I can pique your interest." He motions to Emily and then turns back to his visitors. "We've been seeing a lot of interest on the social web sites about the versatility of the Saddlebred. I thought we'd show you what versatility means in Wyoming."

Kenny leads the group down the barn aisle towards the indoor ring, but their progress is slow as they peer into each stall.

Melody comments, "I hadn't realized that each of your horses is named for a river. That's clever."

"My kids informed me that there are 165 major rivers in the world and several hundred lesser rivers in the United States, so we figured it would be a while before we ran out of names," Kenny laughs, leading the way into the ring. "My favorite river is the Gallatin because of the great fly fishing, so we named one of our best foals Gallatin Ghost." He motions to the large chestnut gelding that his daughter is mounted on. The horse is wearing western tack and protective skid boots on his hind legs. "Ghost is five years old. His sire is Spy Master and he was born and raised here at the ranch." He raises his voice, "Emily! Let it rip!"

The young girl nudges her horse into a relaxed lope and makes a small circle at the end of the ring. She then turns him up the center of the ring and accelerates to full speed, her blond ponytail sticking straight out behind her as she leans forward in the saddle. When she is nearly three quarters of the way down the ring, the visitors can see her sit deep in the saddle and say a soft "Whoa." Gallatin Ghost tucks his hind quarters under himself and digs his back legs into the footing, executing a perfectly straight sliding stop. As soon as he settles at a halt, she rides Ghost through three perfect clockwise spins, halting when he is facing the visitors. From there, she and Ghost lope a small figure eight, performing a flying lead change at the center of the pattern. She then increases their speed and completes a large figure eight, repeating the flying lead changes, and finally halting in the center.

All four visitors spontaneously applaud, bringing a broad smile to her face. "Well done!" Roger enthuses. "That's impressive."

Kenny smiles, appreciating the praise from a fellow trainer. "I had to show him off a bit. He's more up-headed than most reining horses, but he can get the job done. We're hoping to show him off this next summer at some of the local shows and see if we can convince people that the Saddlebred can compete in reining. It would open up a whole new market for us."

"That's impressive," Roger repeats. "I think you should video this and put it on You Tube. I think the Saddlebred Association would really appreciate the diversity that it shows."

"That's a good idea," Melody agrees, enthusiastically. "I've seen Saddlebreds as hunters, on trails, and even jumping fences. But I've never seen one compete in reining. Have you tried cutting?"

"I've thought about it," Kenny admits. "We have a neighbor that has some great cutting horses. But I'm not sure the Saddlebred is low enough to the ground to get face-to-face with a cow. It sure would be fun to try, though. They're definitely smart enough for it. But we've shown off enough. It's probably time to show you some horses that you might actually want to put in the trailer and take home." He whistles sharply and Jeremy leads Nile Ninja into the ring. "This is Nile Ninja. He's five years old and is also by Spy Master. Like Gallatin Ghost, he was born and raised here on the ranch. The only time he's been shown was at the Colorado Fall Classic. I think you saw him there," he says to Matthew and Helen.

"We did. He won that class," Helen says.

"He's a good boy. Very sensible, but with enough spunk and refinement that I believe he will make a top fine harness horse," Kenny says. "He learns fast and gets better the longer he works. Why don't I take a couple of rounds with him so you can see him work and then I'll hand the reins over?"

"That sounds great," Roger agrees, moving over to stand next to Helen. They watch while Kenny trots the horse both directions in the ring, quietly exchanging comments. When Kenny halts the horse in the center of the ring, Roger is the first to speak. "Thanks for showing him to us without any noisemakers. It's a lot easier to see the real horse inside. Will he flat walk?"

"It would take some work to get him to walk in a show ring," Kenny admits. "But I think he'd do it eventually. Why don't you take him for a spin?"

Roger and Kenny switch places while Jeremy holds Ninja's bit, and once seated, Roger clucks to get the horse to move off. After a couple of rounds and then several serpentines, he stops and asks Kenny, "How would he tolerate a little tighter overcheck?"

"Let's try it and see," Kenny gently tightens the chestnut's overcheck one notch.

When Roger trots him off, it takes two or three steps for Ninja to look comfortable with the higher head position, but he soon settles into it and strides powerfully down the ring, causing Melody to say admiringly, "He likes his job." When Roger rounds the end, she gives a sharp whistle, and Ninja crouches in his hind quarters, tips his ears sharply forward and brightens. "He's coming to the party," she says quietly and everyone in the ring murmurs their admiration.

Roger finally pulls the horse to a halt, "You're right that he gets better and better. He's very well-balanced, too. He doesn't seem to have a preference for direction."

"I think that's from all the work he gets outside of the ring. He's Jeremy's favorite horse to move cows on," Kenny says.

"Helen? Do you want to drive him?" Roger asks.

Matthew is already nodding when Helen says hesitantly, "Do you think he's ready for a beginner like me?"

"Of course," Kenny says. "He may look like a fire breathing dragon, but he's really a pussycat."

Roger and Melody help her into the cart and Roger gives advice. "A real soft cluck now," he says. "He's really responsive."

"Remember your lessons," Melody coaches. "Sit tall, with a straight back. Keep him straight and balanced, and use gentle fingers to keep his attention on you." She steps back and watches anxiously as Helen and Ninja move off at a jog.

"Use your voice," Kenny encourages, walking towards the far end of the ring to coach her in the corners. "If he gets going too fast, just say 'Easy' to get him to bring it down a notch.

Helen nods to confirm she's heard the trainer but her eyes are glued on Ninja's tail.

"Relax a little, drop your shoulders and lower your hands about an inch," Melody calls to her. "You're doing great."

"Yes! Perfect!" Kenny encourages when Helen makes the adjustments. "Let him trot on a bit faster and he'll straighten out.

That wiggle you're getting is because he's uncertain of what you want. Just be more deliberate and definite. Give him a cluck."

Helen obeys and Ninja lengthens his stride, focusing on the straightaway ahead of him.

"Take a little hold of him before you get to the corner to keep him balanced," Kenny says, watching intently. "That's it! Remember to use your voice."

"Easy," Helen commands, carefully steering Ninja around the corner.

"Now cluck just like you would have on Glitter Girl to get her to go down the straightaway boldly," Kenny calls, and whistles sharply as Ninja exits the corner.

Helen follows his instructions and is rewarded when Ninja increases his animation and speed, converting her tense expression to a happy smile.

"Same thing on the next corner. Slow and balance him several steps before you get there and then push him when he's coming out." Kenny glances at Roger and Melody, who are nervously watching Helen drive the powerful young gelding. He coaches Helen around the ring one more time and then tells her to halt in the middle.

Helen accomplishes the halt, laughing nervously and apologizing for the crooked parking job. Kenny steps forward to hold Ninja's bit, talking to him softly as Roger and Melody help Helen out of the cart. "Wow! That's a lot different than driving Buddy, the lesson horse," she says breathlessly. "I don't know why I'm so out of breath. He did all the work."

"Probably because you forgot to breathe," Melody jokes.

"Oh, yeah, that!" Helen laughs. "Holy smokes. That was fun! He's so powerful." She pats him on the neck, admiringly. "I felt like I was sitting in the back seat of a sports car."

"I'll go put him up and give you folks a chance to talk about him. And then I've got a couple of show pleasure prospects that I'd like to show you. I think you're really going to like them," Kenny says, leaving the ring with Ninja.

"You looked awesome, babe." Matthew puts his arm around his beaming wife. "I guess I don't need to ask you whether you've decided you like driving."

She laughs, "I finally understand why people like it so much. That was an adrenalin rush."

"He looks like a good fit," Roger says, and Melody nods. "He's square and balanced, and appears to have the perfect temperament. I'd still recommend that you do a full vet check, just to cover all the bases."

"Do you think Kenny would let us take him back to Colorado for a couple weeks just so we can work him at home, use our own vet, and make sure he's the right one?" Melody asks.

"I can always ask," Roger says. "Why don't you folks hang out here while I go talk to him?"

Three hours later, the foursome is back in the pickup and headed south to Colorado, towing a horse trailer loaded with three heavily blanketed horses.

CHAPTER 33

"Oh Blair! I meant to call you and see if we could postpone your ride on Texas Debutaunt, but I forgot! I'm so sorry. We just had a little emergency with a young horse up in the other barn and I need to help Bobby for a bit." Jennifer relies on Blair's normal timidity to keep her from questioning the unlikely story she is telling.

"Oh. No problem. I'll just feed some treats and come back another day."

"Oh no! Don't do that. Texas Debutaunt is ready to go. I'll warm her up and get you on. You can ride a bit while I run up and help Bobby, and then I'll come back and we'll finish."

An expression of horror crosses Blair's face and she says in disbelief, "You mean that I'll ride by myself?"

"Sure! I'll send one of the grooms in so that someone will be here just in case anything happens. But I should only be gone a few minutes. It will give you a chance to ride in peace."

Jennifer spends the next few moments warming up Texas Debutaunt as promised and helps Blair mount, brushing aside the woman's multiple offers to abbreviate or postpone the lesson.

"That's so sweet of you," Jennifer effuses as she summons one of the grooms to make sure Blair stays safe. "Just work on whatever you want. Do whatever makes you happy. Take advantage of this time to work on your transitions. I'll be back as soon as I can." She jogs out of the practice ring, quietly telling the groom to keep an eye on Blair and to call her cell phone immediately if anything goes sideways. When she reaches the upper barn, Bobby is waiting for her.

"Did she fall for it?"

"I'm pretty sure she believed me. She really didn't want to ride by herself, but I didn't give her much of a chance to get out of it. She's too polite to insist."

"I wish we had a camera in the practice ring. For all we know, she's already gotten off."

"I doubt it. She thinks I'm coming back in a few minutes to continue the lesson. I thought I'd wait ten minutes and then call

126

down and tell one of the grooms to make more excuses and have them tell Blair I'm delayed and to keep riding. Then I'll wait another ten and call down to suggest the groom help Blair put the mare back in her stall."

"It sounds like you have it all figured out."

"I don't want to annoy Blair, but I think we have to force the issue if we're ever going to get Blair to bond with Texas Debutaunt. I put a bucket with a bunch of treats next to the mare's stall. There's everything from apples and carrots to bananas and sweet potatoes in it. If Blair can resist giving them to her horse, I'll buy you dinner."

Bobby laughs, "I hope you're right."

"I just need to let her figure out that she can love two horses at once."

Thirty minutes later, when Bobby and Jennifer return to the large barn together, they can hear Blair's voice coming from Debutaunt's stall. Jennifer walks quickly to the open door, "I'm so sorry. That took so much longer than I dreamed. I apologize."

"Jennifer, you don't fool me a bit." Blair laughs, and then admits, "Well, maybe you fooled me for a moment. But it didn't take me long to realize that you staged this whole thing just so I would learn that this horse eats bananas."

Jennifer's face falls, "What? You knew all the time?"

"Come on. That whole scene was ridiculous. Who leaves a client out in the ring by herself and says something like 'do whatever makes you happy.'" She puts air quotes around the quote.

Bobby laughs loudly. "Jennifer, you didn't really say that, did you?"

"I guess I did. You're right. I overplayed my character."

"And I'd also like to know when you started putting bananas in a treat bucket next to a horse's stall. If I had any doubt at all that you were match-making, that cinched it."

Jennifer manages to look a little embarrassed. "I just couldn't figure out how to initiate a little bonding between you and your mare. I know how much you dote on Vendome, but you barely give this one a pat. I think you'll really like her once you get to know her."

"I appreciate that and you're right. I haven't invested any energy in getting to know this mare. I really don't want to sell Vendome Copper and I'm worried that if my mother sees me show any affection or loyalty to this mare, she'll push you to sell Vendome."

"I figured that was the problem," Jennifer admits. "But this mare is really special. She might not be as sweet as Vendome Copper, but she has a great personality. She's actually a little shy. I think the two of you will really thrive once you get to know each other. Vendome Copper will make a lovely horse for the Ladies division with his beauty and his perfect manners. I think we can help your mother realize that. I mean, what could be better than winning an Amateur Gaited class at a big show?"

Bobby interjects, "Let me guess, also winning the Ladies Gaited class?"

"I know it sounds silly," Blair says with tears in her eyes. "But I don't want to demote Vendome Copper. He's the current World Champion. It would seem ungrateful."

"Honey, I know he's smart, but he isn't that smart. As long as he can continue making victory passes, he's not getting demoted. But he is a much better fit for the Ladies division than Debutaunt is. She's a bit too feisty. And I truly believe that she's what you need to stretch yourself a bit. You know Vendome Copper so well and you're very comfortable together, but the competition is going to be coming for you this year and you need to step up your game and surprise them a bit. Debutaunt enables you to do that."

Blair nods, "I understand and I'm on board. But I need you to help me convince my mother to keep Vendome Copper. I owe him and I intend to keep him for the rest of his life."

CHAPTER 34

"Amber? Can you give me a hand with this one?" Amber hears Annie summoning her and quickly pauses her work cleaning one of her two-year-old's stalls.

"Sure! What do you need?"

"I was wondering if you'd like to ride Dreamy for me today."

"Are you kidding? That's like asking me if I'd like cheese on my hamburger! Yes, yes, and yes!" Amber smiles happily. "But she's your favorite one in the whole barn. Why do you want me to ride her? Are you looking for something specific?"

"I'm just curious about a few things and I'd like to get the same perspective that a judge has."

"Well you don't have to ask me twice," Amber quickly saddles the horse, checking the full bridle and other tack carefully before leading the mare out of her stall and towards the ring. "What would you like me to do with her?"

"Go ahead and warm her up and then we'll ride a class. I'll call the gaits but I'll let you figure her out as you go along. One thing that I'm checking is how tolerant she is of change."

Amber mounts and nudges Dreamy forward. The horse jogs off and it takes Amber more than half a ring length to get the mare to relax back into a walk. She walks an entire round and then begins trotting, with Dreamy picking up speed every step. Amber cuts across the middle, combining leg, seat, and hand cues to bend the four-year-old's body and distract her from the speed she obviously wants. After two rounds each direction, she stops at the end, separates her hands, and simultaneously uses her ring and small fingers to gently see-saw the reins while applying leg and clucking. Dreamy's front feet leave the ground as she leaps into the four-beat gait. It takes Amber half the ring length to steady the young horse's gait and even it out to a solid cadence. She completes a round, reverses by cutting diagonally across the middle, and completes a second round. She finally halts in the middle and laughs. "Holy smokes. You make it look so easy. I feel like I'm sitting on a stick of dynamite."

Annie smiles. "You're doing fine. You're starting to get her figured out. When you're ready, go ahead and start the class by trotting the first direction. Remember that I'm judging you, so try to get it right. If you have a problem, just ride through it."

Amber stays halted for several seconds, clearly gathering her thoughts for the ride. She then raises her hands, shortens all four reins slightly, walks her horse forward a couple of steps, and says "Whup trot."

Dreamy trots forward and Amber sits the gait until she feels the mare's lower back relax, enabling her shoulders and front legs to move more freely. After making sure the horse is square and even, she begins to post and concentrates on pushing with her seat every time she sits, using her legs to collect the horse and flexing her fingers and softening her wrists to contain the forward motion. She keeps trotting, using the ends of the ring to collect and square the horse, and tweaking the inside corner of Dreamy's snaffle bit to elevate her head as she completes the corner and begins the straightaway. After three complete revolutions of the ring, Amber hears Annie say, "Walk please."

She finishes the straightaway, slowing her post gradually so that by the time Dreamy reaches the corner, she's jogging. Amber allows her to continue the jog around the end of the ring and is nearly half way down the straight side of the ring when she hears Annie tell her to slow gait.

Amber takes a careful breath, gently separates her hands, sits deep in the saddle, and squeezes her legs. Dreamy's transition to the slow gait is rough. The young mare's front feet both leave the ground as she surges forward, taking two full canter steps before finally yielding to Amber's voice and body cues to slow gait.

Amber rides Dreamy through the other gaits as Annie calls them, continuing to improve her communication with the horse as they work. When she finally halts in the center of the ring, Amber's tanned face is shiny with sweat, despite the cool air in the ring.

"Tell me what you thought," Annie says, coming forward to pat Dreamy's neck.

"I didn't have great transitions and I screwed up the first canter lead. I think I was better the second direction."

"How would you have improved the transitions?"

"I'm not really sure. She seems so anxious to get going that I couldn't get her to smooth them out."

"Yes, she will learn patience with time. During the first slow gait transition, you had her head tipped to the outside and she read that as a canter cue."

"Ah. I can see that."

"You'll get a better result if you focus on keeping her absolutely straight when you ask for a slow gait. You'll also get a better result with a hot high-headed horse if you keep your hands just half an inch lower. You'll be amazed how much that small adjustment will help. I think you probably could accomplish it by just relaxing your shoulders downward."

Amber nods. "Got it. I was surprised that you didn't ask for a rack."

"I rarely let my big-engined young horses rack. They love going fast and once they do that here at home, it's hard to bring them back and ask them to be patient."

"What else did you see?"

"It went much better than I expected. I agree there is work to do on the transitions. From my view, her biggest weakness is her slow gait. I think that we need to find something that really makes this mare stand out and that would be it. If we could figure out how to get a good old-fashioned slow gait, rather than the slow rack that everyone else is doing, I think we'd be tough to beat."

Amber picks up on the pronoun quickly. "We?"

"You've been doing really well. You work hard and learn fast. Your young horses are on schedule and you're not afraid to ask for help when you need it. I thought it was time for a reward." Annie smiles, "I think you should plan on showing Dreamy this next summer. It's been a few years since Josie showed. I'd like to kick some butt in the four-year-old gaited classes and remind everyone that I can breed and train a top-notch gaited horse."

CHAPTER 35

10 AM March 2, Mountain Ridge Stable, CO

"That was a really nice practice session, Helen. You're really starting to show a lot more confidence with Ninja." Roger is helping Helen out of the cart while Melody holds the horse. "I told Kenny that we would call him today and let him know whether you wanted to keep him."

Helen looks at her husband, who is standing next to the kerosene heater in the center of the ring. "What do you think, honey?"

"I don't think there's even a question about it. You look great driving him and he's gorgeous. I think the smile on your face says it all."

Helen asks Roger, "We radiographed his legs and they were clean, right? Is there any reason to do blood work or anything else?"

"No reason that I can think of. I'm sure his blood is clean because he's been here for two weeks and I certainly know what's been going into his body."

"Do you have any reservations?"

"I don't. I think that we're going to have to keep working him to figure out whether he'll flat walk at a show so that we can put you in a pleasure cart. You're definitely going to be more secure than if you are in a fine harness buggy. So that worries me a little."

Matthew pipes up, "Are you worried that he'll never learn to flat walk? Or do you just think it will take time?"

"I'm fairly certain that he'll eventually walk, but he's a young gelding and doesn't have much show experience, so I'm not sure it will happen this year."

"Do you think you'll have to show him in the Open Division for this year?"

"No. I think he's sensible enough for Helen to drive this year. My recommendation is that we take him to the Colorado Classic and show in amateur pleasure. If he doesn't flat walk, we'll get a low ribbon, but at least we'll know where he's at and how he handles the show ring. I really don't want you to experience that

132

for the first time in a fine harness buggy. I just think we're much better off with you in the more secure pleasure cart."

Melody adds, "Depending on how it goes, we'll either continue with the pleasure route, or we'll start practicing in the fine harness rig so that you get used to being up higher and having a different balance challenge."

"That makes sense to me," Helen says. "I've had five drives with him now, and I'm already feeling a lot more secure. Colorado Classic is the last weekend in April, so we have two more months of practice. I won't say I'm not a little nervous, but I think I can be ready by then."

"I'm sure you'll be ready by then," Roger agrees. "As soon as the weather is better, we'll start practicing outside and Melody will get in the ring with another horse and buggy so that you get some experience passing and being passed. I think that will be important."

"Yes," Melody adds. "Remember that your horse has blinkers on and can't see to his side. So the driver is responsible for all the maneuvering during passing. We'll spend a fair amount of time practicing that so you're equipped to handle it in the show ring."

"So does that mean we own a horse?" Matthew asks Helen.

"Unless you'd rather buy a really nice sailboat, I think it does. Get out your checkbook!"

CHAPTER 36

"I've been waiting all day for you to say it." Jennifer teases her husband and training partner.

"Say what?"

"That I was absolutely right about Blair. Did you hear her ask me to start calling Texas Debutaunt by her new barn name, Debbie?"

He feigns confusion, "And what does that have to do with you being right?"

She playfully punches him in the arm. "That my scheme to get her to spend more time with Debbie would lead to them bonding. Blair even brought bananas to the barn today."

He laughs. "Yes, your brilliant scheme worked, but don't forget that she was on to you from the beginning. I'm glad you're having a good day. While you two were in Debbie's stall, Marianne was giving me an earful."

Jennifer sobers immediately. "Oh yeah? About what?"

"Two things. Evidently she heard that Missy is shopping for a horse and she thinks that it is only to upstage Blair."

"Well, that's kind of dumb. Of course she's doing it to upstage Blair. That's what competition is all about. What did you tell her?"

"Well I certainly didn't tell her that she was being dumb. But I did tell her that Missy was certainly going to try to buy a horse that would fit her, much like we believe Marianne bought the best horse to fit Blair."

"Oh. Nicely done."

"So you see what I did there by turning it into a compliment for Marianne?"

"Impressive. You should go into public relations."

"It would probably pay better," Bobby jokes. "But you haven't heard all of it. Marianne was asking me whether we'd had anyone come look at Vendome and why she hadn't seen him advertised."

Jennifer makes a face to show her unhappiness with this information. "I figured that was coming sooner or later. What did you say?"

"I said that the pool of buyers that could afford a horse of his caliber and also had the talent to ride him as well as Blair was very small and that they didn't need an advertisement to know that Blair had purchased a new horse so Vendome might be available."

"You're right about being suited for a career in public relations. What did she say?"

"She agreed with my point. So that's when I got brave and told her that you and I had been doing some research and thought that Blair might be able to pull off an unprecedented achievement this year. That we thought Vendome will be a force to be reckoned with in Amateur Ladies and that Texas Debutaunt would be at the top of the Amateur division. I told her that with the two horses, a lot of hard work, and a little luck, Blair might be able to rack up wins in both divisions. And that if she did it for the Triple Crown of the Lexington, Louisville, and Kansas City Horse Shows, it would be a feat that had never been accomplished in the entire history of Saddlebreds."

"Wow. Babe, you were on fire today," Jennifer's tone is admiring. "And?"

"And I think she's going to go for it." He delivers the conclusion with a smile, raising his hand for a high five. "We just have to let her think it was her idea the next time it comes up."

"Oh my gosh. You are my hero." Jennifer happily completes the high five. "Now for your next trick, I'd like to figure out what Missy is up to."

"What do you mean?"

"She didn't come out today to ride War Paint. Spring Premier is only a couple of weeks away and it isn't like her to miss a ride."

"Did you call her to make sure everything's okay?"

"She only said something about having a conflict and she would call to schedule something." Jennifer removes the hair clip from her brown ponytail and shakes out her hair. "She feels really distant to me. It almost feels like she's separating from Beech Tree."

"Well, the only thing we can do about it is keep doing our work. She's left before and she's always come back eventually."

"Yes, but I'm getting a little tired of it. Maybe if she leaves again, we should make it the last time."

CHAPTER 37

"Dad? Have you heard anything from Holly about doing the genetic testing on Spy Master?" Jeremy asks as he finishes setting the table for dinner. "My project is due next month."

Kenny sighs. "I haven't. I'll try to call her again right after dinner. Did you ask your Biology teacher what you should do if you can't complete the experiment?"

"Yeah. She said that I'd have to write up the results for both cases. So I would have to do twice the work."

"Honey, I think you should probably get started on that," Angela spoons mashed potatoes into a bowl and then makes eye contact with Kenny. "Holly hasn't answered your emails or your dad's and she hasn't returned any of the phone calls. I think it's pretty obvious that she isn't interested in doing a muscle biopsy or genetic test on Spy Master. And when you think about it, there's really nothing in it for her."

"Except the certainty that Spy Master isn't responsible for the positive PSSM Type 2 results we have in several of our young stock, all of which were sired by him. We tested the mares and they were all negative." Kenny's tone indicates his frustration.

"Yes, but we've talked about this before. The vets all say that there isn't any hard evidence that PSSM Type 2 is genetic. It could be environmental."

"But that's why it's so important that Spy Master be tested," Kenny argues. "If his muscle biopsy is negative, then he still might be a carrier of a recessive gene. But we aren't going to know that unless the research community finds a genetic link, and that might never happen. So if he's negative, we'll have to look elsewhere for why so many of our stock are positive. If he's positive, then I can quit worrying about my water, feed, shavings, training program, and everything else I can think of."

"Honey, I'm not the enemy here," Angela says quietly. "Maybe you should try to call her one more time. Or maybe you should reach out to Eileen. Better yet, you should call her and tell her that you'll give her the rest of the night to call you back or you'll call Eileen in the morning. And do it."

Jeremy adds, "If I were Eileen, I'd want to know if Spy Master had PSSM Type 2 because I'd want to adjust his feed and start giving him the supplements that we're giving our horses. They've improved a lot."

"I'll give it one more try after dinner, like your mom suggested," Kenny agrees. "But if I were you, I'd start writing up the paper for both results."

After dinner, Kenny closes the door of his office to block out the sound of the tv and dials Holly's number. As expected, he gets her voice mail and leaves the message he has already composed in his head. "Hi Holly. I know that you know why I'm calling. If you don't call me back tonight, you've left me no choice but to call Eileen in the morning and ask for her permission to get a muscle biopsy on Spy Master. I don't know if you've even told her about my horses, but I'm going to have to tell her that you haven't been cooperative, so if you don't want her to be blind-sided, you should at least let her know what's going on so that she doesn't hear it from me for the first time. I'm sorry that you and I can't talk about this. I really thought we were friends."

He disconnects the call and sits at his desk to start making notes about what he will say to Eileen in the morning, when his phone rings. He glances at the caller ID and his heart rate elevates when he sees Holly's name. "Hi Holly. I guess you got my message."

Although Holly's voice is slurred, her anger is unmistakable. "How dare you threaten me?"

"You haven't left me much choice. It's important to me to figure out what's causing the PSSM Type 2 result in some of my Spy Master foals. I need to try to rule out Spy Master as a carrier."

"What do you care? You're not even breeding to him anymore."

"I care because it would help me rule out other factors that could be causing it."

"You're just making this stuff up to destroy me because you're jealous."

"Jealous? What would I be jealous of?"

138

"I'm the trainer of a World Champion harness horse. I have a barn in Kentucky that stands the leading American Saddlebred sire," she says derisively. "I have succeeded where you failed. You're a piss-ant wannabe trainer in nowhere Wyoming because you couldn't cut it here."

Kenny is stunned at the level of venom coming from his former friend. "Wow. Well thanks for clearing up what you think of me."

"My pleasure," she slurs.

"Are you drunk?"

"It's none of your business."

"Okay. You're right, so I'll get to the point of my call." He takes a deep breath, "I want you to support doing a muscle biopsy on Spy Master to check for PSSM Type 2. I'll pay for it and my vet can tell your vet how to do it. My vet is willing to do the analysis, but you can have a different vet do it if you want."

"And if I say no?"

"If you say no, I'm going to call Eileen and ask her permission."

"She'll say no, too. There's nothing in it for her. If the test comes back positive, it will ruin Spy Master's value as a breeding stud. If it comes back negative, you'll claim that he's a carrier, anyway. It's a lose-lose situation for us. I read the articles attached to your emails and it's pretty clear to me that you'll just find some other reason to blame me for your problems. You won't be happy until I'm down at your level."

"I can see we aren't getting anywhere," Kenny forces the words out between gritted teeth. "I'll just call Eileen in the morning and ask her permission." He starts to disconnect the call, then adds, "You know, I didn't have to keep my mouth shut about this. I could easily have told everyone I know that I've got more than one Spy Master foal that tested positive for PSSM Type 2. That is all I would have to say to put the Saddlebred trainer gossip machine in motion. But I haven't done that. If it were true that I was trying to destroy you, I have the weapons. To be honest, it sounds to me like you don't need my help and that you're pretty busy destroying yourself. It's a little after eight o'clock your time on a Monday night, and you sound completely wasted. What in the world is wrong with you?"

He is shocked when he hears her start to sob. "Everything is coming apart. All the people here in Kentucky just want me to fail. They're all working together to keep new horses and clients out of my barn. Eileen is paying most of the barn bills and I don't know how much longer she's going to want to do that. I never should have come out here in the first place. And now you want to ruin the one thing that is going right. And you're doing it right in the middle of breeding season."

He listens to her gulp for breath and feels his anger dissipate. "Holly, I'm not doing this to ruin you. I'm just trying to do the right thing for my family and for other breeders."

"But can't you at least wait until the end of breeding season? Then I'll do whatever tests you want to do. Just let me get through this season first."

He hesitates, thinking through the implications of her request, and finally relents. "Okay, but I won't wait longer than the first of June. And you need to get yourself together. Stop feeling sorry for yourself or you won't have to worry about how other people are going to destroy you. You'll do that job all by yourself."

CHAPTER 38

Holly has been waiting in the shadows of the Alltech Arena doorway until she sees Missy leave the stabling area, directly across the paved driveway where several trailers are being loaded with horses at the conclusion of the Kentucky Spring Premier horse show. She times herself to intercept Missy about half-way to the parking lot, and acts surprised, "Hey Missy! You had a pretty good ride on War Paint. I'm sorry the ribbon wasn't better."

Missy smiles half-heartedly, "Thanks. I guess we have some work to do."

"It's particularly hard when your rival wins. Frankly, War Paint didn't look as good as I've seen her look in the past, but the judge gave Texas Debutaunt some slack. He completely turned his back when she missed that last canter."

"That's the way horse shows are. You win some and you lose some." Missy shrugs and sighs dramatically. "And Blair is a stablemate and I'm happy for her. But you're right, it's never fun to get beat."

"Are you hungry? I'm starving and I've been craving the fried chicken at the Old Stone Inn. Do you want to drown your sorrows in mashed potatoes?"

"That sounds wonderful," Missy's smile is genuine now. "Meet you there."

It is nearly 45 minutes later when Holly follows Missy into the parking lot at the restaurant in Simpsonville. She tells the hostess that they're probably going to do as much drinking as eating, and leads the way towards the lively bar, situated at the rear of the building. Missy is slow to make her way across the room as she is interrupted by several people who greet her, and Holly is already seated at the tall top when Missy finally makes her way to the table.

"I ordered an old-fashioned for each of us," Holly jokes, "I figured I'd order something for you that I could drink in case it took too long for you to make it across the room. You must know everyone in this place."

141

"They're almost all horse people. I've known a few of them most of my life." Missy settles into her chair. "I'd be happy to introduce you."

"I'd appreciate that," Holly admits as their drinks arrive. "I still have a few empty stalls at the barn and maybe I could convince them to send me a horse or two."

"The last time we talked it sounded like business was picking up."

"I've been really busy with Spy Master's breeding season. But I just would like to have a few more horses in training. That's what I love to do." She finishes her first drink and waves at the waitress for another. "And I've been meaning to call you to ask if you're still interested in Secret Agent. She is continuing to improve. She looks awesome and I still think she'd make a great horse for you to replace Texas Beauty Queen."

"My hesitation is that she's a little younger than I usually buy them. She's only four years old and she hasn't been shown at all. That's a little too green for my tastes. I don't like getting dumped."

"But it's the perfect age to purchase a new horse. They have enough training so that you can see their potential, but she doesn't yet have the show record that would justify the price that I think she's really worth. And I'm crazy about this filly. She's got a great brain." She leans closer to Missy, "I could possibly drop her price a little if someone like you bought her because it will give me great publicity to sell a young horse to a world-class amateur rider."

Missy toys with her glass, still half-filled with the dark, amber bourbon. "Maybe I should come look at her again."

"Let's do it this week. Can you make it on Wednesday?"

Missy laughs, "Sure. By then the scab will have formed on today's ride and I should be in the mood to see her."

"I know it's none of my business, but if you're open to it, I can tell you what I saw today."

Missy takes a small sip, "What did you see?"

"I've had enough bourbon that I'm probably saying too much, but I think War Paint might need a bridle change. She couldn't get comfortable with her headset. And if I were working her, I'd

142

probably jog her at least twice a week. Maybe they're doing that now, but it seemed like she might have been running out of gas when she was racking the second direction."

"That was probably my fault. I've been slacking on going to the gym lately and I didn't push hard enough with my seat and legs to keep her hind end engaged."

"Or maybe she isn't getting enough conditioning. Beech Tree is a busy barn. In a barn like that, it's hard to give every horse the time it takes for a horse to reach top condition."

Missy glances around nervously to be sure their conversation isn't being overheard and lowers her voice. "I've been very happy at Beech Tree."

"Don't get me wrong. I'm definitely not criticizing them. Their success speaks for itself. But it's just simple math. You can only work so many horses in a single day." After they order their dinners and another round of drinks, she continues. "It is clear to me that Marianne Smithson is the queen bee of that barn and I suspect that her daughter Blair gets all the attention. Don't you get tired of that?"

When Missy shrugs and doesn't answer, Holly continues. "Putting that on top of Bobby's reputation for being a little rough with his horses, I'm just surprised that they have so many clients."

"Wait! What?" Missy's eyes are wide and she is shaking her head. "That's ridiculous. Bobby isn't rough with his horses."

"Oh? Then I must have bad information," Holly says carefully. "You know how horse trainers gossip. I just thought it was common knowledge."

"Who did you hear that from?" Missy demands. "That's the craziest thing I've ever heard. I've been with them off and on for years and I've never seen anything to support that."

"Well," Holly cocks her head to the side, "I'm sure you'd be the last to know. A trainer is never going to mistreat a horse in front of a client. But you're probably right. I imagine it's just gossip. I probably shouldn't even have mentioned it."

Before Missy can respond, the waitress arrives with their food. Missy takes advantage of the interruption to change the topic and they spend the time during dinner discussing movies.

143

When they are in the parking lot preparing to leave, Missy says, "Are you sure you're okay to drive? I could give you a ride home."

"I'm totally fine," Holly laughs, brushing off Missy's concern, "I have a really high tolerance for alcohol. Let's do this again! I've been needing a friend out here and this was really fun!"

"It was fun, but remind me never to go out drinking with you. I switched to water a couple of hours ago and I'm pretty glad of it. I wouldn't even be walking if I'd had four old-fashioneds."

CHAPTER 39

"He feels a little fresh, so you'll need to talk to him to reassure him that he's fine," Roger instructs, helping Helen into the two-wheeled pleasure cart in the practice ring at the National Western Complex in Denver. "It will be better in the ring because you'll have more room. Just remember to give yourself plenty of space. If a horse passes you, just talk to him and keep your hands steady." He helps her settle in the cart, "Lower your hands just a little. We'll let him jog around the practice ring once or twice. The traffic in here is a little tight, so we won't do much. Just enough to get you in the groove."

Helen listens to her trainer's last-minute coaching and nods to show him she understands it. She takes a couple of deep breaths to quell the nerves roiling her stomach and settles herself in the cart, focusing on Ninja's hind quarters. She nods at Melody, holding Ninja's bridle, to show she is ready.

Melody leads Ninja to the rail, looking over her shoulder to make sure Helen is in control and then steps away from the gelding. "Cluck once and let him trot off."

As Helen trots down the rail, she nervously checks the traffic, worrying about the young girl jogging her western pleasure horse on the rail. She nervously uses her inside hand to move Ninja off the rail and holds her breath when he bows his neck to the inside and drops his nose.

"Gently," she hears Roger's command. "Keep him balanced."

She uses her right hand to straighten his head and is rewarded when she sees his hind quarters even out in front of her. She manages to complete a circuit around the ring, barely hearing Roger's direction to bring Ninja into the center and halt. Once she stops, Melody smiles reassuringly.

"Remember to breathe."

"And talk to him!" Roger says. "Let him know you're there to keep him safe."

"He seems nervous," Helen says.

"He's nervous because you're nervous. He figures that if you're nervous, there's something going on that he should be

145

worried about. Just calm down, lower your shoulders, sit straight, and have a little fun." Roger smiles, "There are only four in your class. It's a big ring. We'll make sure that we start you out with plenty of room. Remember that our goal for today is to get a class under your belt."

Helen nods and smiles as Roger adjusts her jacket and uses his towel to wipe the sweat from Ninja's chest, patting the horse reassuringly. They all hear the announcer summon the Pleasure Driving class to the ring, and Helen feels her nerves tap dance in her chest.

"Okay?" Roger asks. When Helen nods, he says "Let's do this thing," and leads her towards the in gate at a jog, releasing Ninja's bridle after they are through the gate.

As Ninja trots into the ring, Helen momentarily freezes, forgetting almost everything she has learned throughout the last several months. Her hands and forearms stiffen, her shoulders rising nearly to her ears. She leans forward, causing Ninja to begin cantering, and then hears Melody on the rail.

"Relax, Helen. Talk to him. Be gentle with your hands."

"Easy, easy," Helen says, "Whup trot." Ninja obeys and begins trotting down the rail. By the time Helen makes it around the other side of the ring where Roger is standing on the rail, she has regained her composure and is focused on the class.

He rewards her as she trots by, "You're doing fine. Just keep talking to him, and try to slow him down a little."

"Easy, easy," she tells Ninja, nervously checking the traffic ahead of her and trying to decide whether she should stay on the rail or move towards the center of the ring to pass the cart ahead of her.

Almost as though Melody can read her mind, Helen hears, "Try to stay behind that horse ahead of you. Match her speed. Balance Ninja up and straighten his head."

Despite Melody's instruction, she can tell that she is going much faster than the driver ahead of her and is uncertain of her ability to slow her speed, so she uses her inside hand to pull Ninja off the rail to pass, giving the other driver a very wide berth and forcing Ninja to execute a sharp turn at the end of the ring. Realizing her error, she uses her rail-side hand to edge him back towards the rail, but overdoes the correction and he rubbernecks, overflexing his neck so that he is imbalanced and leading with his inside shoulder. Helen notices it right away, but it takes several strides before she corrects her cues and straightens him, completely forgetting to use her voice during the process.

As soon as she gets to where Roger is standing, she hears "Talk to him Helen!" almost simultaneously with the ring announcer's command to walk.

Knowing this is their most difficult gait, she leans back slightly and gently pulses the bit in Ninja's mouth to gradually slow his trot, realizing too late that she should have allowed him to complete the next straightaway before attempting to walk, as he is still jogging when he completes the corner in the ring and is looking down the straightaway. Knowing it is too late to change her mind, she continues the transition to the slower gait, still jogging when she passes where Melody is standing on the rail.

"Whoa, walk." Melody says calmly, repeating the cue several times as Ninja passes her.

"Whoa, walk," Helen repeats, mimicking Melody's cadence and tone.

By the time they reach the next corner, Ninja is still jogging, and Helen realizes that she needs to plan her path for reversing direction. She glances around her, realizing that the other horses in the ring are flat-walking, so she is still going much faster than everyone else. Knowing that the announcer is likely to tell the class to reverse and walk, and that she doesn't want to be directly behind another driver in case they halt during the maneuver, she edges Ninja off the rail, knowing that this will make it even less likely that he will flat walk.

Her judgement proves correct as she is directly behind and to the left of the other horse when the announcer tells the class, "Reverse and walk."

Helen allows Ninja to jog slowly past the other cart before moving back to the rail and halting him. Roger has moved up the rail and coaches her through the maneuver. "Take your time. Talk to him. He'll want to trot once you turn so just use the reins and your voice to let him know he should walk."

147

She follows Roger's instructions, executing a jerky turn, but achieving a flat walk once it is completed.

"Good, Helen. Very good. Keep communicating." Roger's tone is pleased, causing Helen to relax her hands on the reins, and Ninja obediently flat walks several steps before again breaking into a jog. Despite her best efforts, she can't achieve the flat walk.

When the announcer asks for a trot, Helen remembers to cluck softly and to slide the bit in Ninja's mouth so that he transitions gently into a forward-going trot. She straightens his body and is relieved to realize that she has plenty of room to trot down the rail in front of the judge. When she reaches Melody, she hears, "Good pass. Keep it up. Gentle hands."

Her driving improves dramatically during the second half of the class and when she is finally lined up, with Roger standing in front of Ninja, she smiles weakly.

"Remember to back up just like if you were riding. Tiny pulses, and talk to him. Work both sides of the bridle to stay straight."

When the ring master asks her to back, she follows Roger's direction and Ninja backs three steps, maintaining a reasonably straight line. She clucks and touches him gently with the end of the long driving whip to get him to step forward, back into the line.

Roger smiles at her. "Well done, Helen."

"I was better the second direction," she answers. "I got rattled and forgot pretty much everything you taught me when I cantered on the first pass."

"That's all right. It happens to pretty much everyone," he says kindly.

Neither of them is surprised when she receives the fourth-place ribbon, as the flat-walk is compulsory in the Pleasure Driving class.

Once they are back at the stalls, Melody helps Helen from the cart and she and Roger unhook Ninja and lead him to his stall.

By then, Matthew has joined them to discuss the class. "You looked great, honey," he compliments. "But you were going a lot faster than everyone else."

"Yes," Helen shakes her head. "It was my fault. I kind of blew it on the way in and had a hard time getting it back together."

Melody and Roger make eye contact, and Roger says, "It wasn't all your fault, Helen. This is just the wrong division for him. I know we were hoping to use the pleasure cart, but he just looks and behaves like a fine harness horse. When you look at his video from today, just picture him in that context."

"It's true," Melody agrees. "He danced down the rail when he was supposed to be flat-walking. He looked stunning, even though he didn't do what we wanted. It's pretty clear that we need to figure out how to get you comfortable in a fine harness buggy. You might be disappointed with today's ribbon, but I saw a lot that I liked in that drive."

"Yep. I think we put him in front of a four-wheeled buggy, we check him up just a teeny bit more, we put an elegant gown on you, and we can let him do his thing," Roger enthuses. "Once we take the pressure to flat walk off you both, we're going to have some fun."

CHAPTER 40

9 AM May 1, Spy Hill Barn, KY

Eileen enters the barn by the side door, balancing a box of doughnuts and two lattes. She notices that the aisle lights are on, but Holly's office is locked and dark. After setting the doughnuts on the shelf in the tack room, she takes the coffees and works her way down the aisle towards an open stall door that is blocked by a wheelbarrow, indicating the stall is being cleaned. She peaks around the stall door, expecting to see Holly, but instead startles a young Latina wielding a pitch fork who quickly removes her headphones.

"Good morning," Eileen says. "I'm Eileen. I was looking for Holly?" She ends the last sentence as a question, unsure of the woman's English skills.

"Holly isn't here. I think she's probably still over at the house."

Relieved that the young woman speaks perfect English, Eileen asks, "Oh no. Is she sick?"

"I don't think so. She usually gets to the barn about now," the woman says, glancing at her watch.

"Oh. Well I put some doughnuts in the tack room. Please help yourself." She looks down awkwardly at the two coffees she is carrying. "Do you drink coffee?" When the woman nods, Eileen hands one of the cups to her. "I hope you like hazelnut."

"Thanks!" The woman reaches for the coffee, beaming. "Do you want me to call Holly?"

"No, don't worry about it. I'm sure she'll be here soon. It'll give me time to say hello to my horses." Eileen begins to explore the barn, looking into stalls as she proceeds, finally finding Sneaky Suspicion. She has just slid the stall door open, when Holly enters the barn, obviously surprised to see Eileen.

"I just noticed your car! I thought you weren't coming until tomorrow. What a nice surprise."

"I was able to catch an earlier flight and decided I could use the extra day of practice for Asheville. I guess I should have called to let you know." Eileen returns the trainer's hug and then stands back to look at the disheveled trainer's thin frame more closely. "Have you been sick? You look like you've lost a lot of weight."

Holly laughs lightly, looking down at her baggy, wrinkled clothes. "No, I've just been working hard. Grace feeds and cleans stalls for me, so I don't usually start working horses until after she's done." She looks around nervously at the barn.

"That must be the young woman working down at the end. I'm sorry that I gave your coffee to her. I was afraid it would get cold before you got here." Eileen hears the note of annoyance enter her voice and smiles apologetically.

"I slept in today because I had a sick mare last night." Holly gestures vaguely at the other end of the barn.

"Let's have a doughnut and catch up. I'm anxious to see the horses and hear what's going on. Asheville is only two weeks away and I'm starting to get a little nervous about it."

"Don't worry! You're going to be really happy with how Sneaky Suspicion looks." Holly says, leading the way to her office.

It is mid-afternoon by the time Eileen is back in her hotel room, thinking through the day's events. She reaches for her phone and dials her best friend.

Karen answers on the first ring, "So? Tell me what happened," she demands. "How are your horses? How is Holly? Did you drive Sneaky Suspicion?"

Despite her glumness, Eileen laughs at her best friend's enthusiasm. "I'm so glad you answered. I need to talk some things through."

"Fire away," Karen says, her tone more subdued. "What's up?"

"I got to the barn at 10 this morning and Holly wasn't there yet. From the reaction of the gal that was cleaning stalls, she doesn't usually get to the barn until 10."

"Wow."

"Yeah. But her excuse was credible. She wants to make sure all the horses have eaten and their stalls are clean before she starts. So I don't think that worries me, but she looks awful. Her clothes looked like she'd slept in them and I bet she's lost 20 pounds."

151

"That isn't good. She didn't have any weight to lose."

"I know," Eileen sighs.

"How are your horses?"

"They seem okay. Maybe a little wild. I saw her work Sneaky Suspicion and my two-year-old and I think they've improved a little since last Fall. Maybe not as much as I'd hoped, but they did get a lot of time off this winter and I know it takes some time for everyone to get back in shape."

"Did you get to drive Sneaky Suspicion?"

"No, but that didn't surprise me. I intentionally showed up a day early and I think she had the workouts planned so that today would be part of her preparation for me."

"That makes sense. I know you were worried about the condition of the barn. How is it?"

"It looks a little dilapidated, but it looks clean. Most of the stalls are still empty though, so that makes it easier to keep the place clean, I'd guess."

"I can hear from your voice that you're concerned."

"Yes. Holly's financial situation doesn't seem to have improved."

"And you're worried that you're going to have responsibility for a failing horse barn?"

"Yes. And I've got a suspicion that she might not be telling me the whole truth."

"Why is that?"

"I think I told you that I'm paying for two grooms?"

"Right," Karen answers. "You told me that you're sending the money directly to Holly."

"Well, she only has one."

"Oh. What did she say when you asked her about it?"

"She said the second one just quit a couple of days earlier."

"Do you believe her?"

"I'm not sure," Eileen hesitates. "The worst part is that I know that I could ask Grace, the one that's still there. But I guess I'm afraid to learn the answer. If Grace tells me that she's been the only one there for a long time, then it will erase any doubt that Holly has been lying to me."

152

"And you're worried that if she's lying to you about that, she might be lying to you about other stuff?"

"I suppose," Eileen responds slowly. "Although I'll admit that I was relieved with how the horses look. I was really worried that they would be in terrible shape. I can tell that she's been putting the work in with them."

"When we had lunch in La Jolla you said that you were concerned that she was drinking too much. Are you still worried about that?"

"I'm not sure what to think. When I talked to her on the phone, it seemed like her voice was often slurred and she seemed a little manic, alternating between happiness and depression. But even though she looked like crap this morning, she was clear-eyed and not jittery or anything."

Karen takes a moment to respond, and then says carefully, "So maybe you were just jumping to conclusions. Maybe she's just an occasional drinker that gets carried away once in a while. Or maybe she's just so stressed out that she isn't sleeping or eating right and it's making her act weird."

"You'd be surprised at how many functional alcoholics there are, though, Karen. My dad was a very successful businessman, but he was a full-blown alcoholic. I don't know if anyone really knew it and we never talked about it outside our family."

"So how did you live with it?"

Eileen's voice softens, "When I was a kid, I used to beg and plead with him to stop drinking and I really believed he would quit if he really loved me. But he could never have just one drink and stop there."

"Gosh," Karen says sympathetically. "It must have been so hard to go through that."

"It was, and I was embarrassed about it as a kid. I never invited other kids over to the house because I was afraid he'd be drunk. I thought he was weak and I hated him for it. I could never understand why my mom didn't make him stop. When I got older, I asked my mom about it and she said that it slowly escalated over time. She said she didn't know when to draw the line and that he would often quit for a while, so she'd convince herself that he wasn't really an alcoholic, but he'd always go back."

"Did he ever quit for good?"

"He did late in life, after I'd finished college. Mom said that he had a particularly bad spell and she threatened to leave him. That caused him to go to rehab and that's where he discovered AA. She said that she felt AA had given her back the guy she married."

"I've never understood why AA works. And I admit that I'm really put off by how religious the people I know that go to AA are. What's the tie between religion and AA, do you know?"

"They teach that alcoholism is a physical craving, not a mental or moral weakness. That made all the difference for my dad. It worked for him because he realized that he was physically unable to stop drinking once he started. He saw it as having an allergy to alcohol." Eileen continues, "I know what you mean about the religious stuff. Before he went to rehab, the religious part of it was always his aversion to AA, too. But he started to think about it as spirituality rather than religion. I think the power of AA was that it let him share his burden with a higher power as well as with all the other people that went to the meetings. He didn't have to fix everything by himself."

Karen lets the silence between them lengthen. "Maybe your experience with your dad is causing you to over-react. You don't spend enough time with Holly to know if she's an alcoholic and butting into her life and suggesting she might need help seems like a dramatic step."

"Yes. I might be being overly judgmental. But I'm worried about my horses. If I were here more often, I could keep a closer eye on things, but I have to be able to trust that my horses are in good hands."

"Yes. You're in a tight spot. I can see that you don't want to just move your horses and abandon her. I do think you owe it to her to tell her what's bothering you and give her a chance to make it right. If she can't do that, you can walk away without guilt."

"How do I even bring the topic up without completely alienating her?"

"I don't know, but the key might be letting her know that you're sincerely trying to help her. I also think you need to make her realize that if she doesn't make some changes, her life might be in ruins before she knows it."

CHAPTER 41

"You had a good ride today, Missy. I think you're ready for Asheville," Jennifer pats War Paint's sweaty neck and hands him off to a waiting groom.

"It's taken nearly five years, but I think I've finally gotten used to her chestnut mare bitchiness," Missy laughs.

"Yes. She likes to do things on her own terms, for sure. And that usually involves a handful of peppermints before we even try to put a halter on her."

Missy suddenly changes the topic, blurting it out quickly. "I went over to see that four-year-old Spy Master filly Holly McNair is trying to sell."

"Oh?" Jennifer says with interest, trying to cover her surprise. "Was she nice?"

"She was," Missy says carefully. "She's big and beautiful with a candy cane neck just like her sire's, and she racks like a maniac. Unfortunately, she also canters like a maniac. I'm not sure she's as finished as Holly thinks."

"She hasn't shown anywhere, I don't think."

"No. She hasn't. Holly said she was slow to grow so they didn't even start her until she was three. Then the move from California set back her schedule a bit. I guess she got sick during the move and she's been convalescing."

"Are you looking for her to replace Texas Beauty Queen? Something that can go to the ring in the Ladies division and win?"

"Yes. I need something young, and she fits that bill. But I'll admit that I'm not completely crazy about her. I'm not even sure why, although she might not be refined enough for that division and there's no way she'd flat walk so that she could be shown in Gaited Pleasure. I've got War Paint in the Amateur class, so I don't really want another horse that only fits in that class."

"Yes, you're a great rider, but even you can only show one horse at a time in a single class," Jennifer smiles at her joke. "Do you want Bobby and I to go look at her? That way, if you decide not to buy her, you could use us as an excuse and you wouldn't jeopardize your friendship with Holly."

"That's why I'm bringing this up. I don't want this to be awkward, but I've gotten to be friends with Holly and she is desperate for some clients. I thought I'd try to help by leaving the filly over there if I bought her."

"I see," Jennifer says quietly. "I won't pretend I'm not disappointed. We've worked hard over the last eight or nine years to make sure you're happy with your horses and that you're getting the results you want."

"Oh! It's not that at all," Missy says quickly. "I've been really happy. I just feel like I should spread my business around a bit to try to help a friend be successful. She doesn't think the Kentucky Saddlebred community has been very welcoming and I'd like to prove her wrong."

"Bobby and I would be happy to go look at the filly anyway, if you'd like that," Jennifer offers. "We value you as a customer and sometimes it just helps to get another set of eyes on one."

"I appreciate the offer, but I think it would be pretty weird."

"Okay, I get that. But the offer is always open. My only recommendation would be to get a really thorough pre-purchase vet exam, but I'm sure you're already doing that."

Missy is about to answer, but they hear a loud ruckus coming from the barn aisle. There is shouting and the sound of a horse's metal shoes scrambling on the cement floor. They both rush to look around the corner to see what is happening.

Bobby is holding the end of a lead rope attached to an obviously frightened young horse. He is jerking on the halter rope, while repeatedly yelling "Back!" As the horse backs away in fear, Bobby follows it, jerking on the halter rope and using a long lunge whip to strike the horse's front legs. The scene is made even more dramatic by the reactions of the other horses in the barn, as they retreat to the far corners of their stalls in fear of Bobby's shouting. Bobby doesn't stop until the young horse is backed up tightly against the barn door at the end of the aisle.

"Holy cow! What happened?" Missy asks Jennifer incredulously.

"It's hard to say," Jennifer says, clearly unruffled by the chaos. "That horse is a bit of a criminal. We haven't had him in here very long but he doesn't have any ground manners at all. I saw him try to strike a groom the other day. Although this isn't fun to watch, he needs to learn that he'll be punished quickly for behaviors that could hurt someone." Seeing the appalled look on Missy's face, she continues, "I'm sorry that you had to see that and I know it's upsetting. Even though the horse is young, he's big and powerful with a brain about the size of a walnut. If we don't fix these behaviors right away, the horse won't be suitable for our client or for anyone else. That could endanger his future far more than a little tough love from Bobby."

Missy shakes her head and makes a quick exit from the barn.

CHAPTER 42

"A day like today kind of makes all the hard work and frustration and sweat worth it," Holly raises her whiskey glass to clink it against Missy's wine glass. They're sitting at the bar in the Hilton Asheville Biltmore Park, avoiding the eye contact of the bartender who clearly wants to close up for the night.

"It was a good night," Missy agrees. "Your client Eileen won the Amateur Fine Harness qualifier with Sneaky Suspicion. Four classes later, you won the Five-Gaited Limit class on Secret Agent. And then War Paint came to the party and took me to a win in my Amateur Gaited qualifier. Three for three! Not bad!"

"Yeah. It was a pretty great night. But I hate it when you only bring two horses to a show and their classes are right on top of each other."

"Why did you decide to show Secret Agent tonight rather than in the Junior class tomorrow night? Wouldn't that have been easier?"

"Maybe, but it's her first show ever and I have learned from experience that the young horses just get more tired as the week goes on. I wanted to get her in the ring and then have her be able to relax the remainder of the week so that she'll learn that horse shows aren't a big deal."

"That makes sense," Missy agrees. "I wonder which class has tougher competition. In the Limit class, you have to deal with older horses whereas the Junior class is full of young stars."

"It probably balances out. The Limit class is full of gaited horses that trainers are trying to sell but are older than four. Most of the horses have been in the ring before, but for one reason or another, they haven't yet sold to an amateur." Holly twirls her empty glass and then motions to the bartender for another round.

"There was a horse in there that I know for sure has had more than six blue ribbons, though. Can't they only show in the Limit class if they've earned less than that?"

"I know which one you're talking about but a couple of those ribbons were in harness and they don't count for under saddle classes."

159

"Oh. That makes sense." Missy takes another sip of wine. "I'm just glad that I didn't have to listen to Marianne Smithson bragging about what a beautiful rider Blair is tonight." She drags out the adjective, mimicking Marianne's cultured southern accent.

Holly laughs. "When are you going to leave that barn? I know you like Bobby and Jennifer, but it has to be hard to deal with the Smithson woman all the time."

Missy looks at her glass intently, "I like it there, but I think you might be right about Bobby mistreating horses."

"Why? Did you see something?"

"After my last ride, I was just winding things up with Jennifer and we heard this commotion out in the barn aisle. Bobby was whipping a horse's front legs. The poor creature was obviously terrified."

"What did Jennifer say?"

"She said something about horses needing to be disciplined so that they don't form dangerous habits and hurt someone."

"And you didn't believe her?"

"It's not so much that I didn't believe her as it just seemed so excessive. It turned my stomach."

"So what did you do?"

"I got out of there as fast as I could. If it had been my horse, I would have lost my mind." She shakes her head. "Jennifer didn't seem fazed by it. That was shocking, too."

"I'm surprised they did that with a client in the barn."

"Me too. And I would never have believed that Bobby would ever mistreat a horse. Jennifer said the horse was a bit of a criminal and her explanation seemed reasonable, but I don't know whether to believe her."

"Missy, you really need to get your horse out of there. How do you know that it hasn't been your horse before? And how do you know it won't be your horse next time? I can promise you that your horse will always be safe with me."

CHAPTER 43

"Nice ride," Annie pats Amber's leg as she helps her dismount at the stalls, removing the championship ribbon from Dreamy's bridle before leading the four-year-old mare into her stall. "I especially liked her the second direction. She used her ears better."

"I had trouble getting her to relax at first," Amber remarks, removing her derby and carefully setting it down on a chair. "She kept looking at everything around the rail and I had to work really hard to keep her straight. She felt like she was going to break into a canter at almost every step in the first trot. I was trying to slow her down with my seat, but I felt like I had no alternative but to get into her mouth a lot."

"That's what it's like when they're young and inexperienced, but I was very happy with the ride. It showed us what we need to work on before we take her to Rock Creek. I expect the competition to be a bit tougher there."

Amber peels off her suit coat and loosens her tie. "Just give me a minute to get out of these clothes and then I'll help you cool her out."

"Don't hurry. I like spending time with my girl, so take your time. We just need to pack everything tonight so we can get out of here bright and early in the morning."

After she changes into jeans, Amber hurries to the restroom to remove her makeup. She pushes the door open, nearly hitting another woman standing at the sink in the small space. After apologizing, Amber jokes about opening the door so quickly, saying, "I just can't wait to wash makeup off my face after a show."

The older woman smiles ruefully, "Well you're lucky. I can only think about removing my Spanx. These undergarments make me feel like they're rearranging my organs."

Amber laughs, admiring the woman's nice figure. "Did you show tonight?"

"I did. In the Amateur Fine Harness Championship."

"I didn't get to see that class. It was the one right ahead of mine. How did it go?"

"Not the way I wanted. I got third. The whole class was just bad. I didn't feel prepared, my buggy wasn't clean, I had different reins than I'd practiced with, and my warm-up was just awkward. Do you ever have a show where everything seems out of synch?"

"I do, but third place isn't bad."

"It is if you're driving the current World Champion harness horse."

"Oh," Amber says slowly, finally recognizing the woman from advertisements and photographs. "You're Eileen Miller. You own Sneaky Suspicion and Spy Master. I'm so sorry I didn't recognize you." Amber quickly introduces herself.

"It's a pleasure to meet you Amber. Since you rode in the Junior Gaited class, I assume you're a trainer? What barn are you with?"

"No, I'm an amateur. I'm riding at Big View Farm with Annie Jessup. We actually have a few Spy Master foals and I've been working one that I'm crazy about."

"I'm so very happy to hear that. Tell me about his breeding and what you like about him."

They chat for several minutes about horses and bloodlines, and then Eileen asks, "So did Annie breed anything to Spy Master this season?"

"She bred her gaited mare, Josephine's Dream, to him. She told me that the stud fee is a really big investment and that she's excited about seeing it pay off."

"Really?" Eileen asks curiously. "I actually thought we were on the low end of the spectrum for his quality. We haven't raised his fee in over five years."

"Oh, I shouldn't have said that," Amber feels her face flush, "I actually don't know anything about it. I probably misunderstood something that Annie said."

"That's okay," Eileen smiles. "Maybe she heard that we were thinking about raising the fee for next season, although I haven't really shared that information with anyone except my trainer."

162

"Like I said, I really don't know anything about it." Amber hurriedly starts washing the makeup from her face to cover her embarrassment.

CHAPTER 44

"Hi honey. How did the show go?" Senator Jim Phillips answers his phone on the first ring.

"Oh Dad, it was awful. I didn't ride well and War Paint wasn't good. I'm so disappointed." Missy tries to keep the tears out of her voice, but is unsuccessful when she hears his familiar baritone.

"I'm sorry I couldn't be there. What happened?"

"I just couldn't get anything right."

"I'm sure that isn't true."

"It is true," she insists. "As an example, I missed the first canter lead." She takes an audible breath and her voice gets tighter, "Do you know how long it's been since I missed a canter lead?"

"Let me guess." He pauses a moment for effect, "Since third grade?"

This elicits a snort from her. "Well, not quite that long, but it's been years."

"Everyone has a bad day, honey. But you don't usually get this upset over an imperfect ride. What's really going on?"

She dabs her tears, trying not to smear her makeup. "I just think it might be time to move on from Bobby and Jennifer."

"Really? You've had a lot of success with them and it seemed like you really respected and liked them."

"I do respect them and like them. At least I thought I did. I don't know what it is, but I just don't feel like I fit there anymore. Maybe I'm just jealous that Blair is doing so well and getting all the attention." When he doesn't respond immediately, she continues, "Gosh, that makes me sound like a spoiled brat when I say it out loud like that."

"Missing a lead and being upset that you're not getting enough attention from your trainer certainly doesn't sound like the Missy Phillips I know. Is something else going on?"

"I guess I'm just starting to doubt some decisions I've made. I probably should never have sold Texas Beauty Queen. She was winning for me and I'm having trouble finding something to

164

replace her. War Paint isn't having a great season. Blair beat us in Louisville last August. Then she beat us at Spring Premier, and now she beat us in Asheville. The last really good ride I had was in Kansas City."

"So what do Bobby and Jennifer say?"

"I didn't even talk to them tonight. I was too upset. I left the stable before they'd even gotten back from Blair's victory pass. I just couldn't stand to listen to Marianne's crowing about what a beautiful rider Blair is."

"You've been shopping for a new horse, haven't you?"

"I have. I've ridden a four-year-old that I kind of like."

"Do your trainers like it?"

She hesitates, then admits, "I haven't even asked them to look at her. I'm considering changing barns and she's over at the new place."

"I see."

"The trainer over there is Holly McNair. She just moved to Kentucky from California. She's really talented and fun and she's about my age. We've become pretty good friends."

"And she's trying to sell you a horse?"

Missy catches the note of concern in his voice and says defensively, "She trained the current World Champion harness horse. So she's no slouch."

"I didn't say she wasn't talented, honey. I'm just cautious about mixing business with friendship."

"I know you've always said that, but I don't know why. Aren't your friends the people most likely to be looking out for your interests? Aren't they the people you trust the most?"

"It isn't that they don't mean well. It's just that things don't always go well in business and having a personal relationship can make it difficult to cope with a business problem as openly as if it were purely professional."

"I hear what you're saying, but I'm friends with Bobby and Jennifer."

"Maybe, but the professional relationship came first, and you only got to be friends after they earned your trust. It sounds like the personal friendship is pre-dating the business relationship with this new trainer."

"Maybe I just really need a change. A new trainer might just freshen me up a bit. And I can always go back if it doesn't work out."

"That's probably true, as long as you don't burn any bridges."

"I guess that there's something else that is bugging me."

"Oh? What's that?"

"A week ago, I saw Bobby disciplining a horse and it just seemed like he was really overdoing it."

"What do you mean?"

"He was whipping the horse's front legs and the poor thing was so scared. I couldn't even watch. I don't think I can be around someone that cruel."

"So now we're getting to the heart of the matter. It seems to me that this might be at the core of why you're feeling so out of sorts. Did you talk to Bobby about it?"

"No. But I did talk to Jennifer. She said that the horse was a criminal and that it probably did something dangerous. She made excuses for him, but I saw a side of him that I'd never seen and I can't seem to get past it."

"I think you ought to confront it. Go talk to him and ask him to explain."

"When I play out that conversation in my head it just sounds like I'm questioning his knowledge or his training techniques. I don't even know how I would start. Especially since it wasn't even my horse and I didn't see whatever led up to the incident."

"So if that's the real reason you want to leave the barn but you don't intend to tell them that, what reason do you plan to give?"

"I'm not sure. I think War Paint and I just might need a change and maybe I'll just tell them that."

CHAPTER 45

"Well that was a thoroughly shitty day," Jennifer tells Bobby as they make their way from the barn to their house. "We lost my favorite client. But I should have seen it coming."

"What do you mean?"

"I should have anticipated it when she told me that she was thinking of buying a four4-year-old from Holly McNair and of leaving it over there at Spy Hill. It just never really occurred to me that she'd move War Paint as well."

"We knew she wasn't happy with her ride in Asheville. It's as much my fault as yours. I should have called her that night to make sure she was okay when we didn't see her at the stalls after her ride."

"I knew she would be upset, but I thought we'd talk about it when she came to ride this week. I certainly didn't expect to find a trailer in the driveway this morning." She runs her hands over her brown ponytail, adjusting the clasp to tighten it. "I couldn't believe it when he said he was there to pick up War Paint. And then she wouldn't even answer her phone."

"We talked about this possibility a couple of weeks ago. It isn't the first time she's left. Honestly, it kind of simplifies things for us. It gives Marianne less to complain about."

"True, but I hate knowing that we have an unhappy customer."

"She was standoffish the whole time we were in Asheville, so I don't think this was a sudden decision." Bobby opens the door for his wife and follows her into their house.

"I noticed that too. I wonder what Holly said to convince her to move."

"Who knows? It could be anything. We can't obsess over it. People come and go all the time."

"True. But she wasn't just any client. She's earned multiple World Championships while she was with our barn. I thought we were closer than that."

"Jennifer, you can't let stuff like this get under your skin."

167

"But it actually hurts my feelings a bit that she couldn't at least talk to us and give us the courtesy of telling us she was moving, rather than just sending a trailer to the barn first thing on Monday morning after a show that didn't go well."

"Honey, it's over. You need to just let it go."

CHAPTER 46

"Amber! Watch this video!" Annie approaches Amber in the tack room, and holds out her phone.

"Who is it?" Amber asks curiously, putting down the training bridle she is cleaning and rotating the device to enlarge the screen.

Annie doesn't answer, but watches Amber's face carefully, nodding anxiously when Amber's eyes widen. "Oh shit. He's a freak!"

"He is. He's every bit as good as I'd heard. Maybe better."

"Holy crap." Amber appears to be at a loss for words.

"Yeah. That's Dreamy's competition at Louisville. We've got our work cut out for us."

"We do. I need to watch it again."

"I've watched it five or six times and I still don't see any real weaknesses. I haven't seen a four-year-old gaited horse that talented in my entire life. He looks like he could win the Open Championship at any show in the country right now."

"Wasn't this his first show ever?"

"Yeah. Which makes it even more impressive. He has incredible presence for a horse with such little experience. He just owns that class. The minute he comes in the gate, you can't even tear your eyes away from him."

"You can tell that from the video. I'm not even sure how many horses were in the class because the people shooting the video couldn't tear their cameras away from this one."

"And did you hear the crowd? They were yelling and screaming for him before the class was even half over."

Annie tousles her short gray hair. "I'm not easily intimidated and I'm not one to back down, but you have to feel like our beautiful Dreamy is competing for second place."

"You're the first one to say that anything can happen in a show season, especially between now and Louisville. Maybe someone will buy him and he won't show. Maybe they'll decide not to bring him all the way out to Kentucky from California." Amber ends the sentence hopefully and then smiles, "But I'll be

169

disappointed if I don't get to see him in person. He looks pretty amazing. What's his name?"

"Rebel Leader."

"Wow. That's a good name. I can already visualize the advertisements."

"It is a good name. I have to admit that I'm pretty glad that we won't run into him before Louisville. We need some time to get Dreamy ready to compete against that powerhouse. We're going to need a strategy."

CHAPTER 47

"That was a great session, Helen! You're really starting to understand how to communicate with Ninja more confidently. That confidence translates through his body, all the way to his ears. Did you notice how he marched up the rail on that last pass? That's exactly what we're looking for!"

Helen smiles at Roger's compliment. "I'm having a good day. I took my medication about an hour before my lesson, and that gave it time to kick in. I'll have to remember that. Also, the grippy sandpaper stuff you put on the floor of the buggy helps me a lot. And changing the cushion to suede also makes me feel more secure. I didn't feel like I was in danger of losing my balance and toppling out over the side of the buggy on the turns."

Melody steps forward with the mounting block to help Helen out of the buggy. "Our outdoor ring is quite a lot smaller than the ring in Estes Park that you'll show in for the Almost Summer show. So you'll be able to take the corners even wider at the show."

"I'm nervous about that. What if a horse cuts in front of me and we have to turn sharply? I'm afraid that if I lose my balance, I'll bump him in the mouth."

Melody smiles comfortingly, "And so what? He'll get over it."

Roger nods his agreement as he releases Ninja from the buggy. "Just do what you do here. Stay calm and collected and keep thinking ahead. Next week, we'll have Melody in the ring with another horse so that you can get more practice passing."

"I'd like that. Do you think that we might be good enough to try to go to Louisville this year?"

Roger looks Helen in the eye. "Helen, you're going to be good enough. Ninja is definitely good enough. The question will be whether you're confident enough so that you'll be able to enjoy it and not stress out."

Helen rubs her hands together, obviously trying to soothe the pins and needles of her neuropathy. "Maybe we can wait to see how the Almost Summer show goes before we make the decision."

"Have you decided what you're going to wear?" Melody asks.

"I'm thinking about some nice black slacks and a fancy jacket. Do you think that will work?"

"I think it will be great for Estes Park. If you decide to go to Louisville, we'll need to step up your game and get two gowns. Or perhaps one long skirt and two jackets."

"I was looking at the photos from the Amateur Fine Harness class from last year. It seems like some of the skirts are so big they could almost catch in the wheels. Doesn't anyone worry about that?"

Melody laughs. "I've noticed that myself. We need to avoid that."

"And if you have a big skirt like that, how do you keep from sliding around on the seat? If the fabric of the dress is silky, wouldn't you have trouble sitting square and still?"

"My goodness, you've been thinking about this a lot, haven't you?"

"You have no idea," Helen admits ruefully. "I've been wondering if they make a suede gown, so I'm anchored onto the suede cushion." When Melody laughs, she says, "I'm not really joking. It's causing me a lot of anxiety."

"We'll go shopping after the Almost Summer show. There are some great consignment shops in Cherry Creek and we'll figure something out. Don't worry about it."

"Easy for you to say," Helen jokes. "You're not the one who could fall out of the buggy in front of the crowd at Freedom Hall."

"We'll make sure you have a high neck to keep the dirt out of your bra and just be sure to wear pretty underwear," Melody giggles. "If you topple out, it would be embarrassing for people to see granny panties."

CHAPTER 48

"She's feeling fresh today. It's a cool day and she's noticing everything, so just push her through it. Even though she's six years old, she doesn't have much experience so you have to ride her like a young mare and expect her to gawk at stuff." Jennifer helps Blair mount Texas Debutaunt and waits for her to gather her reins. "Let her walk around once and then let her trot, Blair. Just an easy park trot, if you can."

Jennifer watches Blair maneuver the horse up the side of the ring, posting high as the mare picks up speed. "Lower your post and use your elbows to slow her down," Jennifer shouts, but it is already too late. Texas Debutaunt notices an unfamiliar sunspot on the ground and hesitates, then flinches away from it. Blair is at the top of her post when it happens, and loses her balance, pitching forward over the mare's right shoulder. Her arms start to go around the horse's neck, which causes the mare to jump sideways, easily unseating the woman.

Jennifer watches helplessly as Blair hits the ground, letting out a sharp cry. She glances quickly at the mare, who is galloping towards the far end of the ring, reins and stirrup irons flapping, before running to assist Blair. "Are you okay?"

"I think so," Blair's voice is shaky, but she's already sitting up when Jennifer reaches her. "What happened?"

"She's just feeling good and she found something to shy at," Jennifer helps her client to her feet. "Are you sure you're okay?"

"Yes," she says uncertainly. "I'm just a little shaky. It was so sudden. I don't know what caused her to do that and I didn't want her to run off with me, so I bailed off."

After convincing herself that Blair is fine, Jennifer helps her brush the dirt from her clothes. "Bailing off a horse is almost always a bad idea unless they're going to fall on you. Your job is to stay on and it doesn't matter how undignified you look. Grab mane, grab saddle, do whatever you have to do to stay in the saddle."

"But I didn't get hurt and I thought it would just be simpler to bail in case she was going to do something worse."

"I'm really glad you're okay. But now the mare knows that she can dump you and she will remember how scary this was. So, we're going to have to work hard to erase this from her memory. It's always better to try to avoid that." Although Jennifer's voice is gentle, it is very serious. "When you're riding a young horse, keep your heels down, your weight back and deep in the saddle, and keep your post low and tight. If you do that, you're far more likely to stick with them when they do something silly."

Evidently, the noise from Texas Debutaunt's gallop around the ring caught the attention of Bobby and a groom. Once they have successfully caught her and led her back to the women, Bobby tries to lighten the mood, "I found a fancy horse without a rider. I think she must belong to one of you. What happened?"

Jennifer takes the reins, "She spooked. I was just giving Blair some pointers on how to stay on a horse when they do silly stuff like that."

Bobby looks at Blair with concern, "Are you okay?" After she nods, he says "Did Jennifer tell you that if a horse tries to buck, you need to keep their head up? They can only buck hard if they get their head down between their knees. That's when the trouble starts," he laughs.

"You're not helping," Jennifer says seriously, but her quick smile shows she is amused. "Debbie didn't buck, she just spooked." Jennifer checks the mare's girth, pats her on the neck and talks to her quietly and calmly. She asks Blair, "Wanna try that again?"

"No." Blair answers without hesitation, removing her gloves. "I've had enough for today."

Jennifer tries to hide her surprise. "I tell you what, let me work her and see how it goes. Then you can decide if you'd like to get back on today."

"Nope," Blair is definite. "I'll watch you work her, but I think she's too much for me today."

Thirty minutes later, Blair has left the barn and Debbie is back in her stall. Jennifer removes her saddle while Bobby watches from the stall door. "You were a little obvious in showing that you thought Blair should get back on."

Jennifer turns to him, her frustration evident. "She should have. I hate that she is so timid. We're going to have to do hours of work to put this team back together, and we're at the front end of show season. She's completely freaked out that Rock Creek is next weekend. She even suggested canceling since it's an outdoor show and at night. She's worried that her horse will spook at the lights and the hot dog stand. Of course she'll try to spook! She's a young show horse. That's what they do!"

"Is there a chance that you're feeling a little guilty and you're taking it out on Blair?"

"What do you mean?"

Bobby's voice is gentle, but he looks her directly in the eyes. "We know that Blair is a timid rider. And we know that today is cool and we only gave the mare light work the last two days. We should have seen this coming."

Jennifer narrows her eyes, "So you're saying I'm to blame?"

"No. I'm saying we're both to blame. We probably shouldn't have put her up on Debbie when the mare was so fresh. I could have lunged her this morning, and I didn't. It's my fault, too."

"The mare is a show horse. They're supposed to be fresh. Blair is 38 years old. She's been riding since she was a kid. I don't think it's too much to expect for the woman to be able to ride a show horse. I can't believe that she admitted to bailing off. I would never bail off a horse unless I thought it was going to kill me."

"I know," he says, his voice soothing. "But you don't know how lucky you are that you've never been afraid of a horse. Blair is a competent rider, but I can tell that she's afraid."

Jennifer cocks her head, "I've never heard her say she's afraid."

"Of course not. She can't admit it out loud. Especially with that mother of hers telling everyone what a beautiful rider she is. But that's why she loves Vendome so much. She has come to trust that he won't hurt her. She's learning to like Debbie, but she's afraid that the mare is going to hurt her. You said she bailed off. That's a fear response, plain and simple."

Jennifer sighs, "As usual, you're right. But just think of all the work we have to do to fix this."

175

"That's why we call ourselves horse trainers, babe. That's what we do."

CHAPTER 49

"Oh man, I wonder if this is what I think it is," Kenny says aloud, looking at his phone display when it rings. He hesitates to answer before finally saying, "Rivers Ranch, Kenny here."

"Kenny? This is Eileen Miller."

Kenny intentionally warms his voice and tells a small lie, "Mrs. Miller! I saw the California area code but didn't realize it was yours. How are you?"

"Kenny! It's so great to hear your voice. And please, call me Eileen."

"It's wonderful to hear from you, Eileen. I don't think I ever congratulated you on your fine harness World Championship last year. I didn't get to see it in person, but she was spectacular on the video."

"Thank you, Kenny. She's a nice mare, although our class in Asheville two weeks ago wouldn't have convinced anyone of that."

"I'm sorry to hear that. Everyone has a bad show every now and then. I'm sure you'll get back on track."

He hears the woman draw a slow breath and then say, "Have you talked to Holly lately?"

"Not since March, actually. That wasn't a very good conversation, I'll admit."

"Can I ask why?"

Kenny pauses, wondering whether Holly has told Eileen of his PSSM Type 2 concerns, and then answers carefully, "I think the stress of moving to Kentucky threw her for a loop. She hasn't been the same gal that I used to know."

"Kenny, I'll make this easier on both of us. I'll tell you what I know and what I suspect, and then I hope you'll do the same. I think Holly is an alcoholic."

This is not the way that Kenny thought the conversation was heading, "Oh?"

"I won't lay out all the data for you, but I lived with an alcoholic father, and I'm recognizing the same behaviors. I'm worried about her and I know how close you are…" Her voice trails off.

"We aren't that close anymore," he admits. "I talked to her in March and we disagreed about something big. In fact, I thought that's why you were calling."

"What do you mean?"

"It's a long story, but I'll try to make it fast. In March, I threatened to call you because I wanted her to test Spy Master for a disease called PSSM Type 2. Have you ever heard of it?"

"No. What is that? And why Spy Master?"

"It's a problem with how a horse's muscles store sugar." He takes a deep breath before continuing, "I think you know that I was breeding all of my mares to him, so I've got a pasture full of Spy Master offspring. We started noticing that a few of them seemed kind of stiff and sore before workouts and we ended up getting some genetic testing and muscle biopsies done. Long story short, a number of my horses tested positive for PSSM Type 2. The vets aren't sure whether it is genetic and are still doing research."

"And you think it might have been passed down from Spy Master?"

"I'm not sure. It could be environmental." He pauses and says reassuringly, "I called Holly and asked her to get Spy Master tested and I told her that if she didn't tell you about it, I would. I thought that you were calling because she'd finally said something to you."

"No!" Eileen's voice wavers between anger and surprise. "She most certainly didn't tell me about it."

"When I talked to her in March, she begged me to wait until the end of breeding season and I told her that I'd wait until June before I called you and that she'd better get to you first."

"No," Eileen repeats. "She didn't tell me a thing about it. How serious is it?"

"There's good news there," Kenny answers. "I'm managing it pretty successfully in my horses with a low-carb diet and a change in training. I'm taking a lot longer to warm the horses up and I'm working them every day, even if it's just to give them a turn out. It's working pretty well."

178

"Why did Holly refuse to do the test? Why wouldn't she tell me about this?"

"She probably didn't want to put you in a bad spot about deciding what to do. And I think Spy Master's breeding fees are keeping her afloat. It might not be so easy to get those high fees if people start worrying that PSSM Type 2 is genetic."

"You're the second person that has mentioned how high his fees are," Eileen says carefully. "Just out of curiosity, how high do you think they are?"

This question surprises Kenny. "She quoted me $9,500."

"$9,500?" Eileen says disbelievingly. "It's $6,000! She must have been quoting you the mare care price."

Despite his certainty that the quote was just for semen, Kenny answers carefully. "Maybe you're right. She told me it went up to $9,500 this season and I assumed we were talking about the same thing. I didn't use him this year because of the PSSM issue, but I couldn't have afforded him even if the PSSM thing hadn't come up."

"What? How long have you known about this disease?"

"We did the testing in December and got the diagnosis in January."

"January? And I'm just hearing about it now." Kenny hears Eileen take an unsteady breath. "How long has Holly known?"

"I told her that I suspected something in January. The last time we talked about it was March. As I said, she told me she was going to tell you."

"Well, she didn't."

"I'm sorry," Kenny says sincerely and listens to Eileen take another deep breath. "I know this is a lot to take in."

"I just can't believe it," Eileen says shakily. "I trusted her without question. I don't think she's ever done anything like this before. Why would she hide this from me? I don't even know what to say."

"I'm sorry," Kenny repeats, at a loss for anything different. "Is there anything I can do to help?"

"Oh my gosh. I don't know what to do. It's probably a good thing I'm not in Kentucky right now. I'd go over to the barn and…" Her voice trails off. "I loved her like a daughter."

"I know you're angry right now. And maybe Holly didn't tell you about the PSSM because she thought it would go away. I'm sure it doesn't seem this way to you, but she has staked her business on Spy Master's reputation so she is motivated to keep an issue like this quiet." He pauses, but when she doesn't respond right away, he goes on, "You certainly don't need advice from me, but I'd counsel you to try to focus on the big picture. Spy Master is a huge investment for you and he is important to the Saddlebred breed. However you decide to punish Holly is completely up to you, but I hope you'll consent to getting a muscle biopsy from Spy Master to clear up whether he could potentially have a genetic issue. I know this isn't about my concerns, but I'm in an ethical dilemma. I haven't told anyone about the PSSM Type 2 results in my horses, but the veterinary school at CSU did the testing. It's possible they may publish the results. I think we need to get ahead of any potential bad press and get Spy Master tested. He might be negative and then this part of the story will go away and I'll need to look elsewhere for the culprit. But if he tests positive, deciding on your next step could be complicated."

"I don't know if I'm mostly mad or mostly disappointed. I feel betrayed."

"I understand."

"And to think that I called you because I was worried about her and was trying to find a way to help her. She's been so erratic lately that I've convinced myself that she might be an alcoholic."

Kenny is silent for a long minute, and then says slowly, "That actually wouldn't surprise me too much. Erratic is exactly the right word for how she's behaving. I guess I didn't put two and two together."

"I knew you have known each other for a long time and I was going to ask you if you thought it was a possibility."

"Yeah. We dated in college. I wouldn't have described her as an alcoholic, though. Sure, she would binge-drink occasionally, but what college student doesn't? The last couple of times I've talked to her on the phone I've suspected that she was drinking. In fact, I think I even asked her about it when we had the big blow up in March. She got really mad."

"Well, it's kind of water under the bridge now. Even if she is an alcoholic, it doesn't excuse the fact that she's been lying to me."

"I totally understand. What's your next step?"

Eileen sighs. "I don't know. There's a lot to process."

"Yes. It is a lot to process. But it seems there might be at least two separate problems and maybe we should tackle them separately."

"What do you mean?"

"I know that they are connected through her breach of your trust, but the PSSM Type 2 potential is separate from the fact that you can't trust her." He deliberately avoids mentioning the very real potential that Holly is stealing from Eileen. "I know you need time to think about it, but I really hope you'll have Spy Master tested. It's a pretty simple muscle biopsy. The vets I used at CSU could process the test."

"I need to think through the implications," she responds.

"Yes. We can hope that he tests negative and then one big worry is off your plate."

"Right, but what if he tests positive."

"If he tests positive, there are some potential implications for the breed and for equine research. It would be a signal that Saddlebreds can get the disease but that it can be managed very effectively through diet and training. But more importantly, it would be a clue that PSSM Type 2 might be genetic and could help the research community to identify the gene sequence that is involved. That would be a big deal for all breeders, not just in Saddlebreds but across all the breeds."

"But it could destroy his value."

"I've been thinking about that and I'm not sure I agree. He's the leading sire in our breed. If he carries PSSM Type 2, it certainly didn't happen yesterday. He's had it all along. Yet look at how his foals perform. I think it all depends on how you handle it. If he tests positive, I think you just need to point at his record and explain how to treat any horse that also tests positive."

"But if it's genetic, continuing to breed him would increase the incidence of the genetic defect across the breed."

"True. And that's a potential problem. But who knows how many Saddlebreds have this already? By increasing awareness, we can help trainers and owners manage the disease. It's not like it's a fatal problem, or even an expensive one. It can be dealt with economically and successfully. I can demonstrate that with my experience."

"Let me think about it, okay?"

"Of course. I did tell Holly that I would call you on the first of June if she didn't tell you first. Maybe I should send her a note reminding her of that and maybe it will cause her to reach out to you."

"Ok. Wait a couple of days to give me time to think through my next move, ok?"

CHAPTER 50

"Does it always rain during Rock Creek, or is it just my imagination?" Bobby asks Jennifer.

"At least it quit for now," she answers, handing him a fresh towel. "Maybe we can get Vendome and Blair through their class before it starts to pour again. Is he ready to go?"

"All bridled and ready. I thought I'd warm him up over in the aisle of one of the old barns to try to keep him clean and dry. Maybe we can put her on over there so that he'll be clean when he hits the ring."

Jennifer laughs, "I don't think it will make much difference. He'll be a muddy mess after the first pass, anyway. We'll follow you over to the barn when you're ready."

Jennifer heads to the dressing room where Blair is waiting, nervously pacing in her suit, holding a clear plastic raincoat. When she sees Jennifer she says, "I can't decide if I should put this on. I don't think it will rain on us, but I don't want to get covered in mud."

Jennifer laughs, "Blair, you're going to get covered in mud regardless of what you wear. I hope that's an old suit."

Blair nods, setting the raincoat aside. "It is. Do you think the ground will be slick?"

"I don't. It doesn't really get slick here. I'd just stay away from that low spot near the announcer's stand. Cut that corner a little short. I'd also stay off the rail. The ground slopes slightly towards the rail, so it will be a little drier if you stay a couple of feet off it. And keep pushing him with your legs. He's going to get tired faster in this mud, especially the second direction racking. You're really going to have to work hard to keep him together."

Blair nods, stepping back to give Bobby room as he leads Vendome Copper past them. He looks at her and jokes, "You look like a rider that's ready to get muddy. I'll be disappointed if you come out of the ring without at least some mud on your face."

183

Despite her obvious nervousness, Blair smiles. "I'll try not to let you down."

Bobby mounts and Jennifer gathers up an armful of towels before she and Blair follow him to the warm-up area. When they get there, they're surprised to see Bobby dismounted, holding up Vendome's left front foot.

Jennifer hurries over to him, "What's wrong?"

"He's lame. I was hoping to find a rock or something, but his feet are clean."

"How lame?"

"Bad. I noticed he seemed a little off when we were walking over here, but it's really obvious at the trot, and got worse fast."

"Oh no. What do you think it is?"

"It's definitely in the foot. We'll need to get a vet, but my guess is an abscess. This wet weather probably played a hand in it."

By now, Blair has joined them, "What's wrong?"

"He's got a sore foot, Blair," Jennifer answers. "He's not going to be able to show."

Blair reaches out to rub the horse's muzzle with obvious concern. "Poor baby. Do you think it's serious?"

Bobby answers her, "We'll get a vet over to the stalls right away. I can't be sure, but I'd guess it's an abscess. It sometimes happens when there's wet weather like this. Bacteria can get into a foot through tiny cracks." He notices Blair start to tear up, and says comfortingly, "Abscesses are pretty common, Blair. It takes time to heal, but he'll be okay. We just need to get him back to the stall, see what the vet says, and make sure he's comfortable."

"I'll let the management know we're scratching," Jennifer says, giving Blair a small hug.

CHAPTER 51

Bobby is sweeping the aisle in front of his stalls at Rock Creek, listening to the faint music from the band playing in the clubhouse when he hears a soft voice behind him.

"Are you mad at me?"

He turns to see Missy, standing at the end of the aisle with her hands stuffed deeply into the pockets of her brightly colored skirt.

"Of course not," he replies with a small smile. "Although, Jennifer might give you the cold shoulder the next time or two that you run into her."

Missy smiles ruefully. "I owe you both an apology. I acted like a child. I didn't get the ride I wanted at Asheville and instead of looking at what I had done to cause it, I blamed someone else. I've been at this long enough to know better and I'm sorry and ashamed."

"Missy, it's okay. It happens. We get it." Bobby notices the tears in her eyes and softens his voice. "I appreciate the apology, though."

Missy dabs at her eyes, which are welling with tears. "Why do you have to be so nice? If you had been mad and told me to go away, I wouldn't feel half as bad."

He laughs and reaches into a nearby cooler for a soft drink, handing one to her before taking another for himself. "So tell me what's up."

"I know you saw me show War Paint tonight because Blair was in my class. I got my butt kicked."

"Yeah. I did see that." Bobby takes a long drink of his soda. "Neither one of you had a good ride."

"I was too busy with my disaster to see what happened to Blair. She got third to horses that she's already beat this year. What happened?"

"I'm not sure if you heard, but she took a spill off Texas Debutaunt a couple of days ago. It threw her for a loop. She rode tonight as if she expected to hit the mud at every stride."

"I'm sorry to hear that. I bet her mother was fit to be tied."

185

"I don't know if she knows why Blair was riding like that. I certainly didn't tell her that Blair came off Debbie in the barn during her last lesson. I'm not sure if Blair told her. We blamed it on the mud hitting the mare's belly, but a week ago it wouldn't have bothered her at all. The horse could feel Blair's uncertainty and was uncertain herself because of it." He takes another drink. "On top of that, Vendome has a hoof abscess. Poor Blair is worried sick about him, although I know he's going to recover. It will just take a little time."

"I'm sure you'll get it all put back together. The season is really just getting started. I'm sure Blair will be fine and will be back to her winning ways in no time."

"You didn't come over here to talk about Blair, did you?" Bobby waves her toward one of the chairs in the empty lounge area, settling into one himself.

She accepts his invitation and after perching on the edge of a chair says, "I regret not buying Texas Debutaunt. I don't really even know what I was thinking."

"I think she's capable of becoming a World Champion," Bobby agrees. "Once Blair starts to trust her, she's going to be tough to beat." He tilts his head and says gently, "Missy, I know you didn't come over here to talk about Blair's horse. Why don't you quit beating around the bush and let me know what's on your mind?"

She sighs heavily and then pretends to wipe an imaginary spot off her soda can. "I think I'm in a mess and I don't know how to get out of it."

"What kind of mess?"

"My horses look awful, and while I can take some of the responsibility for War Paint not showing well tonight, you probably noticed that my four-year-old, Secret Agent, didn't even make it onto the trailer."

"I didn't notice that. She would have showed tomorrow, right? What happened?"

"She isn't progressing. I don't really know why. I've asked Holly to wait to work her until I can get to the barn, but something always gets in the way and by the time I get there, she's already been worked or is getting the day off for one reason

186

or another. I've only seen her working under saddle a couple of times since I bought her."

Bobby says carefully, "Do you suspect that she's not actually getting worked every day?"

"I'm not sure what's going on. I can't assess her progress because I don't see her under saddle. I've seen her in the long lines, but I haven't seen her slow gait or rack. I kind of thought that she'd show here and it would be my first opportunity to see her along with everyone else's."

"Have you talked to Holly about it?"

"I probably haven't been as direct as I could be. We're friends and I know that she has a lot of financial worries with the new barn and her move to Kentucky. I don't want to put more pressure on her."

"Ah." Bobby leans back in his chair. "You know what they say about mixing business and pleasure."

"Yes, but in my defense, I had good intentions. I know she's a good trainer. She trained Spy Master and Sneaky Suspicion, after all. And I wanted to help her out and give her some support here in Kentucky."

"I understand that you had good intentions, but I imagine you're going to have to make some hard decisions." Bobby's voice is earnest, "Are your horses safe, well-fed, and well-cared for?"

"Yes," she says emphatically. "I'm not at all worried about their welfare. But I want to show them both at Louisville and I'm afraid that Holly won't be able to get me there. I'm wondering if you'd be willing to take me back and if you have room for both my horses, Secret Agent and War Paint."

"I'd need to talk to Jennifer about it. And whether we can help you be successful at the World Championships is hard to say. I know War Paint well enough to believe that we could probably get her in the ring if we got her back by early July. But I don't know anything at all about Secret Agent. I can't make any promises."

"I understand," Missy nods, clearly uncertain. "I want to win and I'm not sure that Holly can get me there. But I also don't want to abandon her. I feel like she needs my help and support."

"You have some time to figure out your next move. I'd encourage you to be honest with her."

Missy looks at the ground and then nervously rubs her hands on her thighs, as though she were trying to rub out wrinkles in her skirt. "In the vein of being honest, I have a confession to make."

He leans forward and arches his eyebrows, waiting for her to go on.

"My poor showing at Asheville wasn't the only reason that I left Beech Tree. You might not even remember it, but I saw you discipline a horse one day in the barn, and that's really the biggest reason for why I moved. I thought you were being mean and cruel. That poor animal was so frightened and you kept yelling at it. I just couldn't..." Her voice trails off.

Bobby nods slowly, "I remember that. It was that colt I'd gotten from up north. He hadn't been taught anything as a youngster. He struck out at one of the grooms." He says the words softly, remembering the incident. "I'm sorry you had to see it, but I'm not sorry I did it. If a horse like that isn't punished, he could seriously hurt one of my employees. If he can't be made safe, then he will end up at a sale and the life he might have had as a pampered show horse will be over. I owe it to him to try to fix him."

She wipes away a tear, "I didn't understand that. As long as I've been around horses, I don't think I've ever seen anything so upsetting."

"I'm sorry you feel like that. What I find upsetting is when a horse with such potential ends up in a sale ring because he can't be trusted and he isn't safe to have in a barn like ours. And it isn't his fault. He just was never taught any better."

Missy sniffles. "It was awful."

"I wish you had said something then. I had no idea that was the trigger that caused you to leave."

"I'd been told you were hard on your horses and I didn't believe it until I saw that."

Bobby becomes perfectly still, not believing what he just heard. "What? Who said I was hard on my horses?"

Missy is suddenly evasive, clearly realizing the seriousness of her statement. "I don't want to say. I shouldn't even have listened to gossip."

He is on his feet, his face reddening with a mixture of anger and disbelief, "That is slander, not just harmless gossip. Why would you ever believe such a thing?"

"I shouldn't have, and I didn't. But then I saw you with the whip yelling at that horse..." Her voice trails off.

His voice is loud and strained, "Whoever told you that is a vicious liar and they deserve to be confronted. Who was it?"

Missy is also on her feet now. "I'm sorry I shouldn't have said anything and I should never have believed it. I'm not going to tell you who it was, but I will..."

He interrupts her, "Is this rumor going around? Have you heard it from more than just this one liar?"

"No!" She is adamant, "Of course not. You have a great reputation."

Bobby shakes his head in disgust. "I'm floored by this. I have never in my life mistreated a horse. The event you saw was necessary for that animal's future well-being and for the safety of my employees and customers. I do not lose my temper with animals. Ever."

"Please calm down. I'm sorry I said anything. I won't tell you who said it, but I will go back to them and tell them how wrong they were."

Bobby paces the lounge area in frustration. "This kind of crap is why it is so hard to be a horse trainer in Kentucky. I can only guess that whoever said it was trying to damage my business." He makes eye contact with Missy, "I know you're not going to tell me who said it, but this kind of rumor could ruin Beech Tree. I'm trusting you to go back to whoever you heard it from and tell them it's baseless."

"I will, Bobby. I know that I owe you that."

189

CHAPTER 52

Holly uses her thumb to scroll through her emails on her phone while she sips from the hot coffee she has just purchased from the only open concession stand on the show grounds. She pauses when she sees Kenny's name go by among the multiple offers for debt relief, credit cards, and other spam.

She waits until she is back at her stalls to read Kenny's email, and her heart pounds when the opening sentence tells her that he is disappointed that he hasn't heard from her and that he intends to call Eileen this evening to request that she have Spy Master tested for PSSM Type 2. Cussing under her breath, Holly checks her watch and subtracts three hours to calculate the time in California.

After pacing around her stalls for several minutes, she finally goes to her truck, closes the door, extracts a small whiskey bottle from beneath the passenger seat and pours a healthy portion into her cooling coffee. She drinks from the cup, then closes her eyes, leans back in the seat, and plays through the conversation she has been avoiding for months.

Her coffee cup is nearly empty when she finally dials her cell phone, hoping in vain that Eileen won't answer.

"Hi Holly."

Eileen's voice is subdued and Holly takes a deep breath before plunging in. "Hi Eileen. I'm sorry to bother you but I have something serious to tell you."

Eileen doesn't interrupt Holly, so it only takes a couple of minutes for Holly to tell Eileen that Kenny Rivers suspects Spy Master might be carrying a genetic disease. When she finally finishes, her client is silent, prompting her to say, "Eileen? Are you there?"

"How long ago did Kenny first contact you about this?" Eileen's voice is low and serious.

"I'm not exactly sure. It was after the first of the year."

"And you didn't think that I should know right away?"

Eileen's anger is now apparent to Holly, and she hears defensiveness creep into her voice when she responds. "I really thought it would go away. From what Kenny said, it isn't even clear that it is genetic. It probably isn't even coming from Spy Master. It might be coming from something he's feeding, or even his water supply. And if it is genetic, it's probably coming from his mares." Holly looks at her empty coffee cup with longing. "I can't imagine anything is wrong with Spy Master. Just look at how well his foals are doing."

"If you believe that nothing could be wrong, then I don't understand why you would hide this from me."

"I didn't want to worry you. I know how much you've invested in your horses and in helping me transition to Kentucky. I didn't want to cause you more stress."

"I'm a big girl, Holly. I'm fully capable of handling stress. I'm not so sure that I would say the same thing about you, though."

"What do you mean?"

"I don't want to have this conversation now, but I have to say that I'm very disappointed in you. I thought I could trust you completely, and now I learn that you've been withholding important information about my horses."

"I know it looks bad, but I really did think it would go away."

The silence on the line is long and uncomfortable and then Eileen speaks, "There's one thing I've learned about life, Holly. And that is that bad news doesn't get better with age. I want you to get Spy Master tested immediately. I want you to have the test done as quietly as possible. And I want you to have the vet call me directly with the results."

Before Holly can respond, Eileen disconnects the call.

CHAPTER 53

"Are you ready to go?" Annie asks Amber, glancing over her shoulder to see her protégé pacing in the stall aisle outside of Dreamy's stall.

"More than ready. I've been having trouble hearing the announcer but I think we only have three classes before Dreamy's. Do you have any last-minute advice?"

"Just ride her like you've been riding her at home. She hasn't shown outdoors before, so expect her to look at everything, especially that corn dog stand next to the rail." Annie smiles, "But you've been showing in this ring your entire life. You probably know more about it than I do. Just stay calm, remember that she's young, so don't react too quickly. Expect her to make some mistakes." Annie reaches back to double check the young mare's bridle as she talks, making sure the bits are seated comfortably in her mouth by working the shaft of the curb and then pulling gently on the snaffle rings.

"I wonder how she'll like the wet ground."

"I'm pretty glad we didn't have to show her yesterday or the day before. It's much drier now. She might still kick some mud up on her belly, so expect her to be a little jumpy until she gets used to it. But I imagine she'll be so busy looking at everything that she might not even notice it."

Amber readjusts the Velcro straps on her gloves for the twentieth time.

"Go in and have fun. This is the first real competition she's seen this year and just get the very best ride you can. Who knows? Someone with deep pockets might see her and decide they can't live without her."

"No pressure," Amber jokes weakly, hearing the announcer call the class ahead of hers to the ring, and standing back while Annie leads Dreamy from her stall.

Amber mounts quickly and they walk Dreamy to the narrow alley behind the show ring. It is as chaotic as usual, with several trainers warming up their four-year-old gaited horses, passing each other and maneuvering around spectators in the congested

192

space. Amber's nerves flare when she recognizes several famous trainers among the riders, and she looks down at Annie as one of them racks by her, spraying wet gravel every direction. "I guess they didn't come here to play," she cracks.

"Neither did we," Annie replies, patting Amber's leg. "You can ride with any of these trainers. Just sit deep, help your horse be calm, and try to stay clear of the traffic. Put your game face on and go trot." She gives Amber's leg a small slap and steps back.

Amber gathers her reins and nudges Dreamy into a trot, using strong legs and seat to keep the young mare's body straight, and working her fingers gently on the top rein to slide the snaffle in Dreamy's mouth. She feels the mare focus almost immediately and settle into a forward-going trot. Amber lets her go to the end of the alley, then halts her. After she has settled for a few seconds, she carefully turns her to the left and trots back towards Annie, picking up speed and confidence as she goes. When she gets to her trainer, she halts again.

"Very good," Annie says. "Do it again and then we'll let her slow gait."

Amber repeats the trotting passes, driving the mare with her seat more aggressively as she starts to relax. The mare's ears are up, her head is high, and she is very light on the bit. Amber uses her little fingers to maintain a gentle communication with her horse.

"Very nice," Annie compliments when they pause again in front of her. "Ask her to slow gait. Just keep her as slow and straight as you can. Make sure she's paying attention to you."

Amber follows Annie's instructions and eases the mare into the four-beat gait, using her little fingers to work the snaffle in alternate directions very slightly. The mare's gait evens and she works smoothly down the alley. As with the trot, Amber halts her at the end and then pivots her and returns to where Annie is standing. When she reaches the trainer and halts again, she asks. "Good?"

"Pretty good," Annie says, coming forward with a towel to wipe the mud splatters from the mare's coat. "Try to keep your hands just a little lower, and maybe use just a touch more of the curb rein to keep her nose in a little at the trot. She's fine at the slow gait."

Amber nods, listening nervously as the ring master summons her class to the ring. Annie touches her leg. "We'll go in last so that you get a nice clean pass in front of the judges with no one pushing you. Be aware of your ring placement and don't let any of these trainers bully you. You're every bit as good a showman as they are and your horse is as good as they come. Try to have a little fun." Annie watches the traffic into the ring and finally nods at Amber, "It's time. Go get 'em."

Amber nods nervously, adjusts her reins, and heads to the ring at a trot.

Fifteen minutes later, Annie is wearing a broad smile as she walks back to the stalls with Amber, admiring the first-place ribbon attached to Amber's suit coat pocket. "Damn, girl. You looked right at home in that class," she effuses. "You were on the money from the first pass on. The judges couldn't take their eyes off you on that first racking pass."

Amber smiles happily. "She was so easy to ride. She was bright and was listening to me the entire way. She didn't even get rattled when that other horse bumped her on the canter. I'm so proud of her."

"I'm proud of you both!" Annie says. "All I've been hearing about lately is that four-year-old gaited stud from California and how he's going to come to the Championships and show us all how it's done. Well, he might not find it all that easy if Dreamy shows like she did tonight."

"She really seemed to like the outdoor ring," Amber says as she dismounts at the stalls, giving the mare a confident pat. "It gave her a lot to look at and she was really soft and light. She was much easier to ride than she is at home."

"Some horses are like that," Annie talks over her shoulder as she leads Dreamy into her stall and begins to remove the bridle. "Sometimes they get a little bored with the same environment all the time and need a change of scenery to brighten up. I always used to say that those horses showed over their heads."

Their conversation is interrupted by a well-dressed couple coming by the stalls. They loiter a moment, obviously looking to speak privately with Annie, so Amber ducks into the dressing room to remove her suit. She tries to listen through the canvas walls to hear their conversation, but she can only discern a murmur of voices. By the time she has changed her clothes, replaced them in her suit bag, and emerged from the dressing room, the couple has left. Unable to contain her curiosity, she asks, "What was that about?"

"Our first real offer to buy your ride," Annie answers. "They want to buy Dreamy."

"Oh!" Amber can't hide the disappointment in her voice and her voice trails off.

Annie laughs. "Don't worry. We're taking her home with us. Your ride tonight just increased her price tag and I think it was too high for them."

Amber tries to act casual as her heart rate returns to normal. "I won't lie. I'd be disappointed if you sold her. She might be a World Champion in the making."

"Your ride tonight has made me think you might be right, but we can't forget about that Rebel Leader horse from California. His videos are breathtaking. Even with a perfect ride, he will be tough competition."

CHAPTER 54

7:00 PM June 3, Rock Creek, KY

"They've called the show off for tonight and will run tonight's session in the morning," Bobby tells Jennifer after he returns from the emergency trainer's meeting in the clubhouse. "The lightning in the area is making everyone jumpy and the storms are supposed to continue all night."

"I get it," she responds. "And the ring is soup, anyway. It would be absolutely miserable to put horses and riders in the ring tonight. Blair already told me that she didn't want to show in the championship, and I'm glad because she needs some quiet, controlled sessions with Debbie before we get into the ring again."

"Yeah, most of the trainers said they're going to load up and pull out tonight. The only ones staying are those that need a qualifying class for Louisville. We don't have any horses or riders in that category."

"Why don't you check with the riders we have that were going to show tonight to make sure no one will be too devastated if we head home, and I'll get started on packing up?"

Bobby nods, "This is usually my favorite show of the season, but it certainly has been disappointing this year. I hope it isn't a sign for the rest of the season."

Jennifer looks at him in surprise. "Babe! You're usually the optimistic one! I agree that this hasn't been a good show for us, but it's just one show. We have plenty of time to recover before Louisville."

CHAPTER 55

"That was so much fun!" Helen gushes as she exits the show ring at the Almost Summer Horse Show. "I can't believe we won! Ninja was such a good boy."

"Well done, Helen," Roger agrees, jogging alongside the harness gelding as they turn towards the stabling area. "You made great decisions in there and you kept him at the perfect speed. I'm proud of how well you maneuvered during the reverse. You let him know what you wanted from him and he responded to your confidence."

"Awesome drive, Helen!" Melody agrees as she jogs along on the other side of the buggy. "That's the best I've ever seen you drive him. I'm so proud of you."

Helen beams her thanks at her trainer and accepts their help getting out of the harness buggy once they reach the stalls. Matthew hands her a cane and hugs her once he is certain she is securely balanced. "Great job, honey. You looked awesome."

Helen beams, makes her way to a chair in the waiting area, and carefully sits down. "All the changes we've made helped a lot. I am not having any pain at all today, I thought my balance was pretty good in the turns, and it just felt comfortable. I felt like Ninja was really taking care of me. I finally understand why some people like driving so much."

Melody sits next to her while Roger puts Ninja in his stall. "It was a wonderful sight to watch, Helen. You just kept getting better and better."

"Does this mean we're going to Louisville?" Matthew asks, returning from feeding Ninja a handful of peppermints.

Helen hesitates, looking at Melody. "Do you think we're good enough?"

"Hell yeah, you're good enough," her trainer laughs. "I think you might even surprise some people. They'll think you came out of nowhere."

Helen looks at her husband, "I know we entered so that we could make the deadline just in case we decided to go. But the real expense is in shipping and travel and lodging. Are you sure you want to spend the money? It will be expensive."

"Honey, you only live once. We may not get this opportunity again, so we shouldn't even hesitate. Let's go!"

"I guess we need to get serious about finding some Louisville-worthy clothes then," Helen laughs.

CHAPTER 56

Kenny's phone displays Eileen's name when it rings on a sunny mid-afternoon, and he hurries to answer it. "Hi Eileen, Kenny here. Did you get Spy Master's results?"

The woman's voice is low and soft. "I did. He's positive."

Kenny reaches behind himself to make sure the bale of hay he just moved is there, and sits down heavily. "Damn. I'm sorry."

"I'm not sure what it means Kenny." She sighs, "I mean that I know that it means he has PSSM Type 2. And I have read everything available about the disease. Particularly the part about how uncertain researchers are about whether it is genetic. And I know that it can be treated pretty successfully with diet and exercise. What I don't know is what my obligations are to disclose it to the public."

Kenny removes his sweat-stained ballcap and runs his fingers through short hair. "I understand what you're saying, and I've been thinking about it a lot. I have a suggestion if you'd like to hear it."

"Of course! That's why I called."

"Breeding season is over until February or so. Agree?"

"Yes. Definitely."

"And we're right in the middle of show season."

"Yes." Her voice betrays her curiosity at where the conversation is leading.

"I've been watching the show results and Spy Master's foals continue to dominate the best placings at the biggest shows."

"Right."

"So I don't think you should disclose anything until after the World Championships in late August." He waits for her to respond, and when she doesn't immediately comment, he continues. "My logic is that if you say something now, it could bias the judges in Louisville against Spy Master-bred horses. That could devastate your customers, and it would be unfair because they are obviously of high quality. For evidence of that, just look at how well they've done in previous years and continue to do this year. That isn't an accident. It is solid proof that even if more horses have PSSM Type 2, whether they got it from him or from another cause, they're performing well."

"Yes, I see your point, but won't I be criticized for not disclosing something like this?"

"I'm sure there will be plenty of competitors that will have a lot to say about it, but what would saying something right now accomplish? If you quit breeding him as soon as you know about it, and then disclose before you open up the next breeding season, then you have a solid defense that you did not knowingly breed him without disclosing it."

"But what will happen next season?"

"People can make up their own minds. If his foals continue to perform well, my guess is that you'll have a lot of people that will continue to breed to him."

"And maybe I could generate more goodwill by donating a portion of his stud fees to research?"

"That's a really great idea," Kenny says enthusiastically.

"It also gives me some time to figure out what to say."

"It does. And I'd honestly be curious about whether PSSM Type 2 is lurking in other bloodlines as well. We only tested Spy Master because of my suspicions. But we don't know that other Saddlebreds wouldn't test positive for it. You hear trainers talk about horses that require longer to warm up than others all the time. And trainers are using acupuncture, massage, magnets, chiropractic, injections, and other treatments to relieve muscle stiffness. I have started to wonder whether we're really looking at an inability of the muscles to store sugar properly and more horses would benefit from a low-carb diet."

"Yes. I agree." Eileen's voice has brightened. "I need to think it through more carefully, but I really appreciate your suggestions. They make sense to me."

"Have you talked to Holly yet?"

"No. You were my first call. She's on my list."

"Will you tell her?"

Eileen doesn't respond immediately. "Honestly, it hadn't occurred to me not to tell her. But now that you've mentioned it, I guess I need to think about that."

"I didn't mean to influence you one way or the other. It's just that I wanted to be sure I didn't say something out of turn."

"Well she knows that the vet did the test on Spy Master, so she'll be wondering how it came out. And I want to adjust his feed, so I don't think I have a choice."

"Right. I just would say that it is really important for you to control the narrative on the story. You could tell her that the test was inconclusive and that you want to change his diet as a precaution."

"I could."

"From our last conversation, it seems like you might have reasons to not fully trust her and if for some reason you were to decide to move your horses or change trainers, you wouldn't want her to be able to sabotage you."

"I hadn't thought about it that way, but you're right. I'm headed back to Kentucky for the Lexington Junior League show next month and that will give me a chance to evaluate how things are going. Putting off telling her until at least then makes a lot of sense to me." Eileen's voice brightens as she thanks Kenny for his advice and says goodbye.

CHAPTER 57

Eileen and Holly are sharing a late dinner at Ramsey's in Lexington and happily talking through Eileen's class with Sneaky Suspicion. After ordering fried chicken dinners, Eileen breaks apart a fresh biscuit and slathers it with butter. "She felt great, Holly. I can't even begin to tell you how much confidence it gave me to have a drive like that. It won't surprise you to hear that I was a little afraid that this entire idea of transitioning to Kentucky was a big mistake, but the class we had tonight might be my favorite experience in a show ring ever. She positively glided through it."

Holly smiles, and takes a long drink of her sweetened ice tea. "I'm pleased that you had a good drive. We all knew that it was there. She is the defending World Champion, after all, but I agree that the transition has been tougher than we expected. It has taken me awhile to get my feet on the ground."

Their conversation is interrupted by the waiter bringing steaming plates of freshly fried chicken and refilling their tea glasses. "I don't often eat this kind of food," Eileen admits, "but I do believe this is my favorite restaurant in the world. I never miss an opportunity to come here whenever I'm near Lexington."

"I can see why," Holly agrees, taking a bite of her fried okra, "everything looks delicious."

"Why didn't you show Missy's four-year-old tonight?" Eileen asks. "She hasn't been shown at all yet, has she?"

"No, but I'm not particularly worried. We've got a couple of county fairs coming up that we can catch, and we'll definitely show her at Shelbyville. I think she'll be okay. This ring is awfully big for a young horse that doesn't have much ring experience, and since Sneaky Suspicion was in the very next class, we had some logistical challenges. So I didn't encourage Missy to do it."

"You have both of Missy's show horses, don't you? How are they doing?"

"They're both good. War Paint is a tense mare. She is hard to please and has days where she argues with every little thing, much like I'd imagine a teenage daughter would."

Eileen laughs, "Maybe she needs help adjusting her hormones."

"Yes, I just haven't been able to find a way to keep her moods evened out. I've been experimenting with different supplements, but it takes a long time to see if they're making any difference. Just when I think something is working, she'll have a bad day and send me back to the drawing board."

"Too bad they can't talk and just tell us what's bothering them." Eileen takes another bite and changes the subject, "So tell me about how you're doing. Are you making friends here? Are you happy?"

Holly shrugs lightly, "I really haven't been getting out much. There's so much to do at the barn. I've gotten to know Missy and I thought we were getting to be friends, but since I've had her horses over at Spy Hill, she seems to have backed off."

"It's hard to balance friendship and business, especially if the results aren't what she wants. Missy is used to winning world championships. It seems to me that she might not be pleased with anything less."

Holly shrugs again, "Maybe, but we really haven't been showing much. Rock Creek was a disaster. The weather was awful and we just had a terrible show. But we all know that happens to everyone."

"How about you, though? Are you happy here?"

"Mostly, yes. I underestimated how long it would take to be part of the community. It's a little lonely. And I admit that I didn't handle it very well."

"What do you mean?" Eileen keeps her voice casual, but her interest is piqued.

"I got used to having a bourbon every night, and then, on particularly bad or lonely nights, it got to be two or three bourbons." Holly looks up from her plate. "I realized that I had to cut down."

"Good for you," Eileen says sincerely. "It takes a lot of wisdom to recognize that you have to make a change like that."

"After show season, I need to find a way to develop more hobbies. Maybe I'll start going to a gym or learn to rock climb or something. I need to find a way to meet people and socialize in someplace other than a bar."

Eileen nods, "I understand. But you could always move back to California, you know. If you aren't happy in Kentucky, I don't think you should feel obligated to stay."

Holly looks up in surprise, "But I thought you were committed to this."

"I am, but not at your expense, Holly. I love you like a daughter and I've been worried about you. You haven't seemed yourself and I have felt like we've lost the connection we once had. Frankly, I miss it."

Eileen notices with surprise that tears suddenly fill Holly's eyes and the younger woman says, "I've felt that too. I've felt that you're angry or frustrated with me."

"No, not angry or frustrated. I'm not sure how I'd describe how I'm feeling. You have seemed distant and I haven't known what to say to close the gap. I'll admit that the money concerns with the barn not filling up like we've needed have complicated things. I didn't anticipate how hard it would be."

"Nor did I," Holly says fervently. "And I appreciate all you've done and I will make it up to you."

"I know. But there's something I need to tell you and I need you to keep it between us."

"Of course!"

"When I told you that Spy Master's PSSM Type 2 test was inconclusive, I wasn't being honest. It came back positive."

Holly pauses in mid-bite to stare at Eileen. "Oh no."

"Yes. I needed some time to digest the news and figure out how best to handle it before I shared it."

"Oh no," Holly repeats. "What now?"

"Well, I've decided that I'm going to keep it quiet until after the Louisville show. I don't want to risk any bad press that his foals would get going into the show. His offspring dominated the show last year, and there's no reason to think they won't do it again this year. If they do, then it changes our message when we decide how to disclose this news."

"You will disclose it then? Even though there isn't any evidence that it is genetic?"

"I've thought through that and decided that I'm ethically obligated to share it because it might inspire owners to get their horses tested. Horses with this diagnosis can be easily and successfully treated, and I owe it to the industry to educate them. And this might not be Spy Master-related. It could be far more prevalent than anyone realizes."

Holly nods, "That makes sense."

"But I need to manage this information carefully. I'm trusting you to not share it with anyone until I'm ready. Agree?"

"Agreed."

CHAPTER 58

"I'm so disappointed we couldn't show Vendome here," Blair tells Jennifer. "I really thought a month would be enough for him to be ready."

"Bobby said he might have been ready but wanted to err on the side of caution," Jennifer is gently inserting the two bits into Texas Debutaunt's mouth, and then slowly slides the headstall over the mare's ears, making sure it fits flatly and perfectly on the horse's face. "Don't worry, Blair, you can ride Vendome in your sleep. You'll be ready to go in time for Louisville."

The woman changes the subject to her upcoming ride. "Did you work Debbie in the ring yesterday so that she won't shy at anything today?"

"I did, and she was a perfect lady. I don't think you have anything to worry about. We'll send you in after several others are in the ring so that she has someone to follow, but I don't think you're going to have any trouble. She was all business when I worked her."

Blair's relief is palpable. "I know you think I'm being a chicken…"

Jennifer interrupts quickly, "I understand that it isn't fun to worry about coming off. But you can do this. Just keep your thighs tight and your post low. Don't get ahead of her, and watch her ears. A horse always telegraphs their intent with their ears." She doublechecks the bridle keepers as she talks, and then pats the mare's neck. "Most of all, ride confidently so that you give her confidence. Remember that a horse can feel a small fly land on their hide. She'll feel every move you make. Make her feel secure."

Blair nods and fidgets with her gloves.

"I'll warm her up for you just like usual, but we'll put you on so that you have plenty of time to get used to each other." Jennifer slides back the door of the stall, checking to make sure the latch is fully retracted and that it won't catch on the horse or tack as she exits the stall.

206

Bobby appears to help and raises his eyebrows curiously at Jennifer, nodding at his watch.

"I know we're a little early," she responds, reacting to his signal, "but I want to make sure Blair has plenty of time to get comfortable. I'd rather she be a little tired than too edgy."

Bobby gives Blair a reassuring smile, "Are you ready to kick some butt?"

She smiles weakly, "I'll try."

"You'll try?" he teases. "That's not the answer I want! You can do better than that!" He raises his voice, mimicking a boxing announcer. "Are you ready to rumble?"

This earns a laugh from Blair and she answers more energetically, "I am!"

"That's more like it. Let's do this thing!" He picks up clean towels and a comb, and he and Blair follow Jennifer to the warm-up ring.

Bobby keeps up a stream of banter to lighten Blair's mood, and by the time they are warmed up and ready to enter the ring, she looks calm and comfortable.

The class goes quickly and it is apparent to Jennifer that Missy Phillips on War Paint is winning it easily. She is relieved when Blair is awarded the second-place ribbon, and Blair seems satisfied as they return to the stabling area.

"Nice ride," Bobby compliments her as they walk up the gravel path to the barn. "I thought you handled the ring well and found ways to stay out of the traffic."

"Thanks, Debbie was good. She didn't spook at anything."

Jennifer waits until they are back at the stalls and Blair has dismounted to say, "Your Debbie is a nicer horse than War Paint. The only reason Missy Phillips beat you today was because she rode more aggressively. It was impossible for the judges to overlook how badly she wanted the win. I know that you needed to get a smooth ride under your belt so that you could get back to trusting Debbie, but you can beat Missy every time you enter the ring if you just ride more aggressively."

"I felt like all Debbie's gaits were a little fast," Blair says defensively.

"Ah, but I don't mean that I want you to go faster when I say that I want you to be more aggressive. I want you to go bigger. There's a difference." The trainer softens her voice. "When you come back in the championship, I want you to be a bigger force in the class. I want you to take control of the ring. Enter it like you own it! On every end, prepare your horse to strut down the rail! Demand that the judges pay attention to you!" She pauses to see if Blair looks receptive. When her rider acknowledges Jennifer's point, she continues. "You are among the most experienced riders in the ring. I believe you have the very best horse. I want you to ride like you believe it, too."

"I'm just worried that we'll make a mistake, so I'm being careful."

"She's a little inexperienced and she'll definitely make mistakes. There's no doubt of that. She's a very exciting ride and that can be a little intimidating. But when you're being overly careful, you dull her. Do you know what I mean?"

Blair nods slowly. "I do. I hear you."

"Good. In the Championship, we're going to have you come in a little fresher. You're going to ride like you want it worse than Missy Phillips, and we are going to take control of this Amateur Gaited division, right?"

"I'll try."

Bobby has stood by quietly during this conversation and he says, with a broad grin, "What? You can do better than that!"

"Yes!" Blair shouts back, returning his smile. "We are going to take control!"

CHAPTER 59

Melody's phone rings, and she glances at the caller ID. She looks across the family room to Roger and says, "I'll give you three guesses who it is and the first two don't count."

"It's Helen. She's seen the Fine Harness Championship from Lexington and she's freaking out," he predicts.

Before Melody even has time to say hello, the voice on the line says, "I'm sorry to call so late, but I'm sure you are watching the show in Lexington. Did you see that horse that won the Fine Harness class? Wowza!" Helen is nearly breathless with excitement. "If that's the kind of horse that will be in Louisville, maybe we should change our minds and stay home."

Melody laughs, "Well, that horse is the reigning World Champion harness horse. And she's only five years old. There aren't many, if any, out there like her."

"She's gorgeous!"

"She is gorgeous. And she will definitely be tough to beat. But that doesn't mean that it's impossible."

"Did you see that woman's dress? It was covered in sequins. And the sleeves just billowed out behind her. She looked like she was flying and that dress looked like it fit like a glove."

"Now Helen, don't let yourself get psyched out. We're getting your jackets tailored and you are going to look phenomenal. You'll look every bit as good as her." Melody looks across the family room at Roger as he rolls his eyes at her. "Seriously, Helen, you're going to do great. We're going to have fun and do well." She changes the topic to divert Helen, "Did you see the proof of Ninja's new advertisement? I think it turned out great."

"I did see it! It's amazing!"

"I think we need to start advertising with email blasts, through social media, and in print at the end of this month. We want the judges to be looking for you when Ninja trots into the ring."

"Oh my. I really hope I don't embarrass you all."

"Go do some meditation Helen. Relax. We're going to have fun." Without giving Helen time to respond, Melody disconnects the call.

Roger's deep voice is calm, "I love that lady, but she can worry the spots off a leopard."

9:00 PM July 9, Kentucky Hor

"Hot damn, girl! I knew y
meet Blair in the center ring
Amateur Gaited Champior
to beat somebody and yo'

Jennifer chimes in, r
pocket. "That was awesome, ⌐

Blair smiles at them, "I goofeᴅ ᴄ,
the inside instead of the outside."

Bobby laughs, "Really? You just won your ⌐
new horse and all you can say is that you reversed wɪᴄ.
you need to let up on yourself!"

Blair poses for the picture as the other ribbon winners are announced and leave the ring, noticing that Missy Phillips got second place. She makes her victory pass, uncharacteristically smiling widely as she exits the ring.

After dismounting back at the stalls, Blair removes her derby and peels off her sweaty gloves. "Oh man, I need a shower."

Jennifer laughs, "I don't think I've ever seen you sweat before."

"I don't think I even remember most of it. I was just concentrating on getting my gaits and getting around the ring."

"That's what made it so great, Blair. You freed her up to do her thing. I especially loved when you passed Missy Phillips on the outside! That was gutsy!"

Blair laughs, "It wasn't deliberate, believe me. Debbie just was pointed in that direction and I wasn't brave enough to try to change her mind."

"Well, it was the best ride I've ever seen you make. It showed courage and determination and spirit. That's the rider I want to see for the rest of this season."

CHAPTER 61

0, Spy Hill Barn, KY

s to decide whether to return Kenny's call as she
oicemail he left once more. "Holly, It's me, Kenny. I
assume that you're ducking my calls since you haven't
d the last 10 or so." There is a lengthy gap before he goes
was happy to see you did well at the Lexington Junior
gue show. That's a tough one, and it's great to see you've got
ur mojo back." There is another gap and he says, "I really need
to talk to you about Spy Master's stud fee. I think there might be
a discrepancy between what you quoted me and the price that
Eileen thinks she's getting. I wanted to talk to you about it…"
His voice trails off, then "Look. Just call me. We need to talk. It's
important."

Holly drums her fingers on the desk in her office, anticipating
the topic behind Kenny's call and wondering how to react. After
many long minutes of thought, she dials his number.

He answers without greeting her, "I'm surprised you called
me back."

"How could I not, after the message you left?" She returns his
brusque tone with one of her own. "What's on your mind?"

"I wanted to let you know that I believe you've been
skimming money from Spy Master's stud fees and I won't be the
one to tell Eileen about it, but I imagine she isn't very far from
finding out."

She purposefully injects a defensive tone, "How dare you
accuse me of that? You don't know anything about it."

"Well I know that you quoted me $9,500 and I know that
Eileen believes his stud fee is $6,000." He makes the statement
quietly.

"How do you know what Eileen believes?"

"Come on, Holly. Is this the way you're going to play it? She
called me about the PSSM Type 2 diagnosis and we were talking
about Spy Master's future as a breeding stud. I mentioned that I
thought his fee was too rich for my blood, and she was surprised
because she said the price was the same as it had been the last
three years. You and I both know that isn't true."

212

"What did you tell her?"

"I made some sort of excuse about how I must have misunderstood, but I know I didn't. I thought that maybe you had just quoted me a special higher price because you were angry with me, so I called a friend who told me that they paid $9,500 this season." He pauses, but she doesn't respond. "I don't even recognize you anymore, Holly. You owe a lot to Eileen and you're repaying her by stealing from her. You have to assume that she will find out. You're playing a dangerous game that could get you arrested for embezzlement."

"Kenny. Do me a favor and butt out of my life. You have no idea what it's like to be under the pressure I'm under."

"Oh really? Have you forgotten that I had a barn just a few miles from where you are now? I know exactly what it's like to compete with the big, successful barns in Shelby County, Kentucky. It's tough. But I didn't lie, cheat, and steal to make it happen."

"Are you calling me a liar and a cheat?"

"I am, Holly. You know it's true. I'm not going to waste any more time worrying about you. I'm sorry that we can't be friends any more. This may be the last time we ever speak to each other. I'm trying to do you a favor and tell you that you need to confess to Eileen and hope she forgives you. If she learns what you're doing from someone else, you will be finished. Not just in this business, but if she presses charges, you will be convicted of a felony. This is not a joke. Good luck."

Holly hears the line disconnect, and is left holding her phone next to her ear.

CHAPTER 62

"Nice ride, Amber. She's looking really solid."

"Do you think we need to change her bits at all? It seems like I have to use the curb more than I used to."

Annie cocks her head to one side, obviously thinking about the question. "Maybe. I think I'd like to wait until after the Shelbyville show to decide. Let's see how she does in front of the crowd."

Amber nods and dismounts, patting Dreamy's neck. "I hope the weather cools off before then. This summer has been really hot." She runs her stirrups up the leathers before turning Dreamy towards her stall. "Do you think we're going to see big classes in Shelbyville?"

"It's hard to say. It's so close to the Louisville show that some people like to rest their horses and let them freshen up a little before the championships. I just feel like we need to give Dreamy a little more ring experience. She's in great condition, so I sure don't think it will hurt any. And two out of the three Louisville judges will be there so it will be nice to make a splash."

"Did you see this week's *Saddlehorse Report*?"

I did. And before you ask, yes, I noticed the ad for Rebel Leader, that four-year-old from California. He's a stunner."

"Do you think we can beat him?"

"I don't know, honestly. We're definitely going to have our hands full. I'm pretty happy we're only competing against the mares in the qualifier."

"Would you consider showing Dreamy in the Amateur division?"

The older woman stands back while Amber leads the young mare into her stall and turns her to face the hallway. "I hadn't seriously considered it. Why do you think that's a good idea?"

Amber looks away from her mentor, focusing on removing Dreamy's bridle and putting on her halter. "I just thought that it might be an easier path to the World Championship this year."

"Go on," Annie encourages. "Talk me through your logic. The Amateur division is full of experienced horses and is likely to be a much larger class than the four-year-old class."

"Maybe, but you said yourself that the stud colt from California would be tough to beat. I don't see anything in the Amateur division that we don't have a good chance of beating."

"In the mare class you've got Texas Debutaunt, War Paint, and several others."

"True," Amber agrees. "But Texas Debutaunt used to be mine. I know for a fact that Dreamy is more talented."

"I won't argue with you that on her best day, Dreamy is better, but Texas Debutaunt has more experience. Dreamy could get rattled by the Freedom Hall environment.

"I don't think so, Annie. She's never gotten rattled anywhere else. She's bold and brave."

Annie is obviously giving the idea some thought. "What about War Paint? Missy Phillips is a tough competitor."

"She is, but I've been watching the results since she changed trainers. They haven't been that good. Texas Debutaunt beat her in the championship at Lexington Junior League."

"It's an interesting idea and maybe worth thinking about. But I'm biased towards staying with the four-year-olds. The older horses are going to be bigger than her and will be carrying more muscle. I just think that young horses are better off staying in their year so they don't look undersized."

Amber shrugs, removing her saddle from the sweaty horse. "Ok. I just thought I'd mention it."

"I'm not saying that it isn't worth thinking about. But from what I know now, I think we're better off with the young horses."

CHAPTER 63

"We have time before we have to show that country pleasure horse, so I'm going to go up and watch the Amateur Gaited class. Do you want to come along?" Bobby asks Jennifer. As they walk up to the ring from the stabling area, he remarks, "I will never understand why they make the Amateur Gaited horses show in the first class of this horse show. It is almost always blazing hot. And it's only two or three weeks before Louisville. That isn't the best time to be working a horse to exhaustion."

"I asked why they did that and was told that it was to get the crowd to their seats. This show goes so fast that they needed to get people here early or they'd miss all the fun!" Jennifer pulls her pony tail up off her neck, quickly knotting it on top of her head.

"Not much chance of that," Bobby says dryly, gesturing towards the lively crowd partying in the large covered structure at the end of the ring. "They aren't here for the horses anyway."

"I'm glad we talked Blair and Marianne into leaving Debbie and Vendome at home. They'll be a lot fresher for the championship than they would have been if they had come here."

They find a spot in the shade and lean back against the weathered boards of the grandstand. Bobby leans back, trying to keep his tall frame out of the sun. "Blair is still insecure on Debbie, but it's getting better every day. Having that mare trot up towards the noise and clinking glasses at the end of the ring just didn't seem like a scenario that would be good for her confidence, anyway. And we haven't shown Vendome since before Rock Creek, but he is really on the money at home. We'll probably surprise some people with him at Louisville, since he's not been showing this season."

"And Blair can ride him in her sleep. I think that between now and Louisville, we just do whatever it takes to build up her confidence. What would you think about letting her have a session or two on Debbie where they just kind of dink around in the ring and do whatever they want? Maybe we could get some of the love connection between them going again?"

He tilts his head, thinking about her suggestion. "It probably isn't a bad idea. It would be good to get them back to where they were before she fell off."

"Yeah. I wish she were more resilient. That pep talk you gave her before she went in the ring at Lexington for the Championship really did the trick, too. You should definitely repeat a version of that. What did you tell her anyway?"

"I just told her to toughen up and that she owed it to her horse and to the team at the barn to do well. That they all work hard and a big part of their reward is having blue ribbons hang from the curtains at a show when all their friends are around. And that Debbie works harder than anyone and deserves to win."

"Interesting strategy. I wouldn't have thought that making it about what she owed the horse and the barn crew would work so much magic. She was a completely different rider. And she even cracked a smile on her victory pass. I don't think I've seen that before in all the years that she's been with us."

Bobby laughs, "Well, I won't take credit for having thought through the psychology of what I was going to tell her. I was just frustrated that I believed we had the best horse in the ring and we were getting beat by War Paint. I've never liked that horse, if you want to know the truth. I don't miss working her. She was a major bitch in the barn, always trying to bite the grooms and kick the farrier."

"Speaking of War Paint, here she comes." Jennifer says quietly, watching Missy ride the tall chestnut mare up the alley, under the crow's nest serving as the announcer's stand, and then make the sharp right corner into the ring. Holly jogs in front of them, making her way to the far side of the ring to coach her rider.

"Is it me, or does she look like she just got out of bed?" Jennifer whispers to her husband.

He nods once, keeping his eyes glued on Missy and her mare as they make their first pass. "She looks uneven, look at how she's throwing the front right leg out in front of her," he says under his breath. "They need to get some help from the farrier." He continues watching until the class begins to slow gait, then leans over to Jennifer, "I can't watch another minute of this disaster. I'm going back to the barn."

It isn't until the show is over for the night that they have time to talk about the class. "I bet Missy is disappointed," Jennifer says. "She got a fifth-place ribbon, but that was a mercy placing. I probably wouldn't have given her a ribbon at all. War Paint was pacing and this judge actually cared. Love the mare or not, she's always had a solid, four-beat rack."

Bobby shakes his head in disgust. "I bet you could fix it all with a good farrier and some hard work in the long lines. She was good in Lexington and that was just three weeks ago. She trots sound, so I bet it's just a shoeing issue."

"Holly looked awful. Did you hear her yelling at Missy from the rail? Missy can outride anyone at the fairgrounds, trainers included. She doesn't need to be told which rein to use to get a canter lead. I'm surprised Missy stays there."

"Would you take her back?"

Jennifer looks up from the saddle she is carefully placing in a tack trunk. "Why? Did Missy say something to you?"

"No. But when we talked at Rock Creek, she hinted around about it. I haven't really talked to her since."

"It's the oddest thing, Bobby. She did really well in Lexington, but she didn't even deserve to be in the ring tonight. How could things go south so fast?"

"My guess would be that she has a drunk for a trainer. And I'd imagine that when she's sober, she's a great trainer. And when she drinks, she's no trainer at all. And that she's drinking now."

"That would make sense. And I feel bad that Missy is in the middle of it, and I feel even worse for the horses. It may be true that War Paint isn't a peach to work with, but she deserves good care and the opportunity to be the best horse she can be."

"You haven't answered my question."

"You mean about taking Missy back?" Jennifer returns to packing the saddle. "I don't know. I don't miss the friction between her and Marianne. And we have a completely full barn. We'd have to kick out two of our young horses to make room for her, assuming she'd bring War Paint and her four-year-old. And

218

she didn't exactly leave us gracefully. I'm not sure I want her back."

Bobby doesn't respond right away, and when he does, his voice is low. "I guess I agree with you, although I hate seeing what we saw tonight."

"You're a fixer, honey."

"I don't even think it would be that hard to fix, Babe. We have access to some of the best farriers in the world here in Shelby County Kentucky. If War Paint were in our barn, I'd beg them to be at the barn tomorrow morning to help me."

"If War Paint were in our barn, it wouldn't have gotten to this point in the first place."

CHAPTER 64

"We'll wait until the first class in the ring turns around to get her out of her stall," Amber can hear Annie's gravelly voice coming from Dreamy's stall. She checks her hat one final time in the dressing room mirror, takes a deep breath to calm her nerves, and steps out into the aisle of the barn.

Annie continues, her own nervousness apparent in the tone of her voice. "Remember what we talked about. Don't let those trainers in there bully you. Just do your best to stay clear of the traffic. I watched the judge for the last two nights, and she watches the horses come in, but after that, she turns her back to the sun and focuses on the back rail. So that's where you're going to want to make your best passes. It'll be especially hard to set up a young horse near the pavilion on that end where the crowd is partying, but don't cut that corner too short or you won't give Dreamy time to get square before she's in front of the judge. Try to go as deep as you can."

In spite of her nerves, Amber smiles to herself, never remembering a time when she's heard Annie give such a long speech. She can't resist the urge to tease her, "Don't be nervous Annie, you always tell me it's misplaced energy."

She is rewarded when Annie laughs. "Nervous? I'm not nervous. You practically grew up showing in this ring. I don't know why I'm giving you advice. You know this ring better than anyone."

Amber listens to the announcer call for the class in the ring to reverse and says, "That's our cue," standing back as Annie carefully leads the young mare from her stall.

The indoor warm-up ring is stifling hot, and Amber waits for a break in the traffic before coaxing Dreamy into the ring. It takes the young mare two complete circuits of the ring before Amber feels her relax. She glances at Annie for approval, and the trainer motions her into the center. "How about a short slow gait and then we get her out of this oven into the fresh air?" Annie wipes the mare's sweaty coat as she talks.

Amber agrees and again waits for a gap in the traffic in the busy ring before cueing Dreamy to slow gait, separating her hands and applying leg and seat to keep the gaited horse collected and slow. They make one and a half rounds before she hears Annie's "That's good."

They find a quiet spot to wait for Dreamy's class to be called, and Amber has time to look around at the four-year-olds waiting to enter the ring. There are at least 10 of them, and Annie scans the riders' faces, noting that all but one are well-known trainers or assistants. The only non-trainer other than herself is Missy Phillips. Missy is mounted on a leggy, long-necked chestnut mare with no white at all. Her typically friendly face is tense, and her horse looks equally tense, fidgeting in the bridle as they wait.

Amber's attention reverts to Dreamy when Annie touches her leg and says, "I watched everyone in the warm-up ring. Quite a few of them look tired already. We'll put you in last, so try to get a nice fresh trot on your first pass. Then save a little punch for the second direction. Dreamy has enough engine that I think she can smoke 'em in the second rack."

Amber hears the bugler and waits impatiently for the other horses to trot up the hill and into the ring, spacing themselves so they don't reach the in gate at the same time. When the other horses have all gone, Amber clucks at Dreamy, the mare pricks her ears forward, and they confidently trot into the show ring.

Her first pass goes well, with Amber having the rail all to herself until near the end, when a young horse passes Dreamy on the inside, forcing her to go nearer the lively crowd at the end of the ring than she prefers. She feels Dreamy hesitate, stutter-stepping and flinching towards the center of the ring, laying her ears back at the young horse pressuring her on the inside. Amber applies her left leg and uses the little finger on her left hand to gently tweak the inside corner of the mare's mouth, diverting her attention from the distractions. Amber clucks once, driving hard with her seat to get the mare's hind end engaged around the corner and glances over her shoulder to make sure there is room to move off the rail a couple of feet. Unfortunately, several of the horses that entered the ring before her have cut the end of the ring

221

short and are now positioned to pass her on the inside, blocking Dreamy from the judge's eyes.

Amber sits two strides of the trot, shortening Dreamy's stride and giving the crowd behind her time to pass, then begins posting and applies a strong rail-side leg and hand to neatly move off the rail to catch the judge's attention as she trots by her.

Annie's voice comes to her as she completes the pass, "Good speed. Don't get covered up on this side."

She settles into the class, enjoying her horse's rhythm and the strategy involved in maneuvering Dreamy and timing her passes so that she has room around Dreamy when she passes in front of the judge.

When the announcer calls for the first canter, Dreamy is facing the pavilion and Missy's horse is ahead of her on the rail. Amber waits for Missy to get the canter, but quickly notices that Missy's horse is balking, refusing to go forward and threatening to spin to the inside of the ring. Amber can hear horses cantering up behind her and passing on the left, and quickly decides to risk cutting them off in order to avoid colliding with Missy. She applies a strong right snaffle rein to Dreamy, bending the mare's body to the rail to ensure she gets the correct lead and clucks to her to cue the canter gait. As soon as the mare steps off, Amber sits deep on the right side of her saddle to keep the mare in the correct lead as she swerves around Missy's horse, which is now shying towards the center of the show ring. Amber focuses on the path forward, managing to avoid traffic and keep Dreamy in the correct lead and gait.

Once the class reverses, Amber can feel Dreamy get stronger, and she moves confidently off the rail, passing horses easily as they trot, slow gait, and then rack. Sweat runs from under her hat band and down the sides of her face as the heat and the effort from the ride take their toll. She can barely hear Annie's comments over her own breathing, and realizes that her sweaty hands have soaked her gloves, making it difficult to keep the reins from sliding through her fingers. She feels pure relief when they announcer finally calls for the class to line up.

In the line-up, she reaches down to pat Dreamy's foaming neck, loosening her reins and feeling the mare's sides heave as she catches her breath. Missy is next to her, and Amber smiles when she catches her eye. "How was your ride?"

Missy grimaces, "A disaster. Embarrassing." She shakes her head, but reaches down to pat her exhausted horse.

"It was a tough class," Amber says, comfortingly. "So hot."

"Yes, I felt like I was riding one of those balls in a pinball machine, careening from one thing to another with little control." Missy rolls her eyes, "It wasn't good."

"I didn't notice," Amber lies. "I had my hands full, too."

Amber's attention goes to the rail, scanning for Annie. When she makes eye contact, her trainer flashes a huge smile and a thumbs up, comforting Amber that she had a good ride. The positive impression is confirmed when, shortly after the announcer releases the class from the line-up, Dream Weaver is announced the winner.

After a long shower, Amber and Annie meet in the breakfast room of their hotel to share a large pizza.

Annie finishes most of a large pepperoni- and sausage-laden piece before saying, "You'll never guess who called me just now."

Amber's mouth is full, so she just shrugs and raises her eyebrows.

"Missy Phillips."

Amber coughs in surprise, and it takes a few moments to speak, "Really? What did she want?"

"To buy Dreamy."

Amber can feel her heart beat in her chest, but tries to act calm. "Did you sell her?"

"I told her that I hadn't put a price on her yet."

"Really?" Amber has completely stopped eating now, wondering if she will still have a horse to show in Louisville.

"After the kick-ass ride you had today, that mare's price went up again. And I'm not so sure it has peaked yet." Annie chews slowly, and then meets Amber's gaze. "But it's not just about the money. I can afford to make sure Dreamy has the very best home possible, and I just can't put her in the hands of the gal that is training Missy's horses now."

"I was so focused on my ride in the class that I wasn't paying attention to her, other than to try to stay away from her. What happened?"

"It was a train wreck. The horse wasn't ready for a class like that, and wasn't well enough conditioned to keep up. I think she's probably got talent, but she's held together with bubblegum and spit."

"That's too bad," Amber says, not really meaning it. "Missy is used to winning. I can't imagine her sticking with that trainer."

"That topic didn't come up. But I'd have to be sure Dreamy didn't end up in that barn."

"But Holly McNair has had a lot of success. What's going on?"

"I have no idea, but she should be embarrassed by what happened in that ring tonight."

CHAPTER 65

Kenny is putting a steaming platter of blueberry pancakes on the table when his phone rings.

"It can wait until after breakfast," Angela warns, shaking her head.

He glances at the caller ID. "Oh. Maybe it can't," he says, stepping quickly into the family room to answer the phone. "Hi Eileen, how are you?"

"I hope I'm not calling too early and I'm sorry to bother you on a Sunday."

His curiosity is piqued by the urgency in her voice. "It's not a problem. What can I do for you?"

"Holly called me last night. She was obviously drunk. She confessed that she has been skimming money from Spy Master's stud fees."

"Oh," he says carefully. "That must have been a shock. I'm sorry."

"Now that she told me, I understand that's what you were trying to tell me the last time we talked."

"I wasn't sure what was going on. I'm sorry. You must be angry."

"Not so much angry as disappointed. I trusted her like a daughter."

"So what will you do? Will you press charges?"

"If you had asked me last night, the answer would have been yes. But I've calmed down a little. I believe she is an alcoholic and she's ill. My dad was an alcoholic, so I know a little bit about it and I'd like to try to help her if I can. So I'd like to give her one last chance, but I need your help to do it."

"Oh? What can I do?"

"I am going to tell her that I won't press charges if she goes to rehab, starts attending meetings daily, and we make an agreement on how she will pay back the money she stole."

"That sounds generous. I'm sure she'll appreciate your willingness to work with her."

225

"Sending her to jail and giving her a felony record isn't going to help anyone," Eileen admits. "Even though last night, it was exactly what I wanted to do."

"I understand, but what do you need from me?"

"I am going to require that Holly go to rehab immediately, if she accepts this deal. So now I have horses entered in Louisville and no trainer."

Kenny starts to understand where the conversation is going. "I see."

"She doesn't have many horses entered. Just one of mine and two that belong to Missy Phillips." She hesitates now, and then blurts, "You told me that you were taking a couple to show. Is there any chance you would consider going early and taking over Holly's barn for a month? Just to get us through Louisville?" She doesn't give him a chance to respond, before rushing on. "I would pay you well and make sure it is worth your time. And I would continue to pay the grooms that she has. I'm just afraid that no other trainer is going to want to take new horses now. It's too close to Louisville. But I thought that you might be able to get us into the ring. I remember what a great job you did with Spy Master." Her voice trails off into silence.

"Wow. That's a surprise. I'm not sure. It's a busy time here at the ranch and I was already feeling bad about having to take the two weeks away. A month is a long time."

She interrupts quickly, "I understand if you don't want to do it, but you just need to name your price. I would be forever grateful if you'd consider it."

"Let me talk to my family and I'll call you back in a couple of hours."

"Thanks Kenny, I really appreciate your willingness to consider it."

He disconnects the call and returns to the kitchen, where his family is half-way through breakfast. "Did you leave any pancakes for me?" he jokes, eyeing Jeremy's heaping plate.

Emily hands him the platter, simultaneously biting down on a piece of crispy bacon. "You got here just in time, Dad. One more minute and all the bacon would be gone."

Angela's blue eyes meet his dark ones and she asks, "What was that about?"

Kenny sits and begins adding food to his plate. "That was Eileen Miller. She finally discovered that Holly is stealing from her."

Everyone stops eating at the same time, staring at him. Angela breaks the silence, "What's she going to do? Will she have Holly arrested?"

"She would like to avoid that, so she's willing to send Holly to rehab and give her time to pay off the debt, but only if she starts going to AA meetings and stays sober."

"So why did she call you?" Angela asks.

"She asked if I'd be willing to go out to Kentucky right away and run the barn for the 30 days that Holly will be gone. There are three show horses entered at Louisville and it's too late for Eileen to try to find a trainer to take her."

Jeremy is the first to react, "That would be awesome! Can I go?"

Kenny sees the look of displeasure on Angela's face and quickly quashes Jeremy's excitement. "Your mother and I need to talk about this. It would mean me leaving the ranch for a month, rather than the two weeks I was planning. If we decide to do this, I'd need you to stay home and run the ranch with your mom."

"Can I go?" Emily leans forward in her chair, her 13-year-old frame nearly vibrating with excitement. "I could groom for you and clean stalls."

"No one needs to get excited," Angela cautions, catching Kenny's eye. "Your dad and I have to talk about this before anything is decided. It was already going to be an expensive trip and making it twice as long would be difficult."

"That's the interesting part of it," Kenny replies. "She told me to name my price. Maybe we could ask for enough money to cover all of our expenses for the show."

"So you think we should consider it?"

"I'm just saying that we can set the price at something that makes it worth our while. She can always say no."

CHAPTER 66

Kenny turns the truck off and glances at his daughter. "Let me check out the stalls before we unload the horses so I'll know where we're putting them. Just hang out here, I'll be right back." Hoping she'll heed his instructions since he is uncertain about what he'll find in the barn, he climbs from the truck, gently shutting the door. Readjusting his ball cap, he enters the barn and hears voices from an open door near the center of the structure. He maneuvers around feed buckets and hoses that litter the aisle and past several empty stalls, finally reaching the open doorway.

Holly and Eileen are in the office and Holly is saying insistently, "I do appreciate all that you're doing. I'm just saying that I could go after the Fair."

Kenny clears his voice and knocks softly on the door jamb to alert them to his presence. "Sorry. Don't want to interrupt, but do you care which stalls I use?"

Holly jumps to her feet and Eileen smiles at him, "Welcome! I'm so very thankful that you came. You must be exhausted." She asks Holly, "Do you have any stalls bedded for Kenny's horses?"

Holly awkwardly stammers a hello, then points back towards the stalls Kenny just passed. "Uh, yeah. There are two clean stalls at the far end on the left. I thought you'd want to have them next to each other. You brought two, right?"

"Yep. Don't let me interrupt, I'll find the stalls," Kenny says, backing out of the office. As he walks down the aisle to locate the stalls and to make sure they are bedded, he can hear their conversation continuing.

"This isn't negotiable, Holly. I love you. I know from my experience with my dad that alcoholism is an equal opportunity disease. It isn't relegated to skid row bums that live in boxes and wear matted beards. They're people like you, and could easily be people like me. And it doesn't go away on its own. It takes hard work and commitment. So, either you get in the car with me in the morning and I take you to the airport, or I will have Kenny help me load my horses in his trailer and we will take them to another barn. You have until tomorrow morning to make your choice. If you decide to take the life line that I'm offering you, then you need to get busy and tell Kenny what he needs to know to fill in for you until you get back. He is doing this as an immense favor to me. Please don't make this harder than it needs to be." Eileen leaves the office, following Kenny up to the stalls.

"I'm sorry you had to hear that, Kenny. She's disappointed to be missing the show, but I'm not going to change my mind. She either goes for help now, or we're done."

"I'm sorry. This isn't fun for anyone."

"It isn't, but I believe she knows that she doesn't really have a choice. She has to go get some help." Eileen brightens her voice, deliberately changing the topic. "I saw Missy Phillips today and she said that you'd called her."

"I did. We talked about her horses and whether she wanted to leave them here, at least through the Fair. She's going to give me a couple of days with them and then come over and see how it's going. We had a good conversation and I'm happy that she's considering sticking with us. I want to do everything I can to give Holly a business to come home to."

Eileen smiles, "You're a good friend, Kenny. I hope you know how much it means to me. Holly might not be ready to show it, but there will be a day when she'll realize what you did for her. Did you bring that adorable daughter of yours like you promised? I haven't seen her since she was 5 or 6 years old, I don't think. I've made sure that the two extra bedrooms in Holly's house are ready for you two, and I hope that you'll be comfortable. I stocked the fridge and I'm guessing you're starving."

Kenny smiles, "Yes, I left Emily with the truck. I'll get her to help unload and we'll settle the horses in and get them fed and watered. Then I'll get instructions from Holly." He motions back towards Holly's office. "I need to get the lay of the land from Holly. Do you think she's up for that?"

"I think so. She's acting tough, but I know she loves these horses and the way to her heart is to help her understand that she needs to do this to benefit the horses and to be able to continue working with them." Eileen smiles sadly, "Why don't I take Emily into the house and get her something to eat? Why don't you get Holly to help you with the horses? That will give her something to do other than focus on herself."

"I'll try," Kenny replies doubtfully, "As long as you're sure she doesn't have any sharp weapons within her reach."

Eileen laughs softly, "If she had sharp weapons, I'd probably be bleeding right now, so I think you're safe."

He returns to the barn and finds Holly in her office, tears rolling down her face. Resisting the urge to turn around and give her privacy, he interrupts, "Hey Holly, I really need your help with these horses and I need you to help me figure things out around here so that I can hold down the fort and not screw things up too badly while you're away. I don't even know the names of any of these horses other than Spy Master. If you don't help me, I'm likely to try to put a harness on one of your gaited horses and make fools of both of us. That would provide these stuck-up Kentucky trainers enough stories about the Wyoming goofball to last a couple of years, I'd think."

Holly rewards his humor with a sad smile, brusquely wipes away her tears using her sleeve, sniffles, and follows him out to his trailer.

CHAPTER 67

Helen leans over Matthew's lap to see out the window of the airplane as it flies low over the Kentucky State Fairgrounds on its approach to the airport in Louisville. "Oh my gosh. Now I'm nervous," she says with a grimace. "Look at all those trucks and trailers. I think my heart rate just doubled!"

Matthew takes her hand. "That's just excitement. There's no reason to be nervous. You're going to be great."

"I wish I had your confidence," she says truthfully. "I've never driven a horse in a show this big."

"Well, in just three days, you'll be able to say that you have."

They're both silent as they feel the airplane's wheels contact the runway, and then Matthew says, "Don't be mad, but I ordered you a wheelchair. I know that we're going to head right over to the fairgrounds so you can get a practice drive in and I don't want you to be tired from walking through the airport."

"That was thoughtful, but I can probably walk. It'll just take me awhile."

"I know you can walk," he answers. "But if you take the wheelchair, you'll have more energy for driving Ninja once we get over to the fairgrounds."

She admits that this is true, and even with the assistance, it is more than an hour before they have gathered their luggage, found transportation, and made their way to the Mountain View stalls in the annex attached to Freedom Hall. Roger and Melody are relaxing in the sling back chairs in the lounge area in front of the stalls, leafing through the glossy show horse publications that are distributed to all exhibitors.

After greeting them with hugs and remarking on how nice the barn set-up looks, Helen asks, "How's our boy?"

"He's wonderful," Melody answers. "Even though it is his first time at a show this big, he's handling it like an old professional. We had to wake him up from his nap to get him ready for you. But more importantly, how do your fingers and feet feel?"

"Not terrible. The biggest problem is that I don't have any balance."

"I'm sorry that it's a bad day for your neuropathy. Would you rather have a practice drive tomorrow? We can certainly wait until you feel a little better."

"No. I'll be fine." Helen pulls a huge bag of peppermints from her oversized bag and laughs. "Just give me a few moments to sweeten him up a little before we get started so that he'll take it easy on me!"

"We won't work very hard. I just want to get you up and down Stopher Walk a couple of times and give you practice maneuvering in the warm-up area."

"I'm worried about going down the ramp into Freedom Hall. Can we practice that?"

"They've closed Freedom Hall, so we can't practice that, but it isn't going to be a big deal. We'll be there with you and the grooms will hold the buggy so that it doesn't push Ninja down the hill. I know you worry and over-analyze things, but don't spend a moment worrying about that."

CHAPTER 68

Kenny watches Missy slow gait down Stopher Walk on Secret Agent as she completes her warm up for the Junior Five-Gaited Mares class. "Good, Missy, good. Lower your hands just a little and lighten the curb." Then, "Perfect! That's it. Let's call that good." He walks quickly to where she is halted and motions for Emily to dry the sweat from the mare as he lets down her tail and makes final adjustments. "How does she feel?"

"She feels good. I'm glad we had time to get her shoes adjusted. I think the new shoes have improved her. She's nice and even. But I feel like she's easily distracted."

"I noticed that, too. You're going to have to keep entertaining her with the bridle. Just use small tweaks on the snaffle to keep her attention on you. Anytime she flicks an ear, use your body to communicate with her."

"Her slow gait feels solid," Missy remarks, patting the mare's neck.

"It looks nice and square. Try to resist getting your hands too high. If you feel like you need her to even out, raise just your inside hand and use your inside leg on the corners and then even them out for the straightaway. I think it will be easier to keep her balanced if you keep her close to the rail. It will reduce the distractions from everything going on around her. Just keep in mind that she hasn't really had that much ring experience." He has finished the tail and now straightens the skirt of Missy's riding coat. "She looks good, Missy. You're going to do fine in there. I'd recommend sitting the trot down the ramp so she doesn't try to catch a canter. And we'll wait to go in until towards the end. That will give her plenty of horses to follow and if it takes her a few strides to get comfortable it won't be so noticeable."

"I haven't thanked you properly," Missy says. "No matter what happens in there, you've done a phenomenal job in just three weeks. I'll be honest. I didn't even think this mare would be going to this show three weeks ago."

"She's talented," Kenny replies. "I certainly can't take credit for that. And I've worked a lot of Spy Master's foals. The adjustments we've made to her feed and her exercise program have really started to kick in."

"Well I appreciate your willingness to come out and take over while Holly is gone." She is interrupted from saying more when they hear the bugler calling their class to the ring.

Kenny jogs alongside Secret Agent as she descends the ramp into the ring, "Not too fast, Missy. And keep her focused on you!" His eyes remain glued on her as he works his way around the rail towards the left, finally finding a vacant spot from which he can watch the class and coach Missy. He finds himself standing next to a small, gray-haired woman that he has noticed in the warm-up area. It is soon apparent that she is coaching a dark-haired female rider on a chestnut mare.

"Good Amber. Good speed. Go off the rail on this next pass. Make 'em look!"

Kenny briefly glances at the horse and rider, admiring them as they trot around the end of the ring, and then shifts his attention back to Missy. "Good Missy. Use just a touch more curb. That's it!"

"You're coaching Missy Phillips?" the woman next to him asks, and then introduces herself. "I'm Annie Jessup. Missy was with me when she showed Josephine's Dream."

"No kidding?" Kenny answers, shaking her hand, and then says vaguely, "I'm just stepping in temporarily while her regular trainer is away."

"I see." Annie answers. "I hope it's nothing serious."

"No. She'll be back in a week or so." He quickly changes to subject, "That's a nice mare you have there. Do you own her?"

"I do. She's Josephine's Dream's first foal."

"That explains it," Kenny answers with a smile. "She looks like she has the same motor that her mama was known for."

Their conversation pauses as the announcer calls for the class to walk, and Kenny coaches Missy through the transition. "Don't get in a hurry, you have all the time in the world. Be gentle and use a lot of leg." He nods in satisfaction when the transition goes well, and then takes a moment to watch other horses in the class, noticing Annie's horse immediately as she demonstrates a masterful slow gait, hesitating slightly with her front feet at the top of each stride. He returns his attention to Missy, giving encouragement each time she is within ear shot as she completes all the gaits the first direction and the class reverses. As they work through the final gaits, Secret Agent uses her ears to show her frustration as Missy works hard to keep her balanced and square. By the time the announcer tells the class to slow gait, Kenny notices the mare is leaning into the bit. "Relax your fingers, don't give her anything to pull against," he coaches Missy.

Missy follows his instructions, and Secret Agent's gait becomes more regular, but she is going much too fast for a slow gait. Kenny glances at the judges, hoping they will call for the rack before noticing that Secret Agent is going too fast. His wish is granted when the announcer calls for the next gait and the rest of the class matches Missy's speed.

Annie catches his attention again as soon as Amber passes their spot on the rail going the second direction, "Show 'em what you've got, Amber." Annie says proudly as the young mare passes by her. "No sense in saving it!"

In response, Amber takes the inside track around the ring, passing the other four-year-olds easily, and looking completely comfortable. Her mare's headset is rock solid as they make their way around the ring, earning shouts and whistles from the appreciative crowd.

When the announcer tells the class to canter, Kenny focuses on Missy's transition until he is distracted by Annie saying softly, "Amber! Take your time! Come on, girl. Don't be stupid now."

He quickly glances at her and follows her line of sight to her rider, who still has not picked up a canter. In his peripheral vision, he can see Annie tensely leaning inward, both hands on the rail and he can hear her swearing under her breath. He glances back at Missy to confirm that she's still cantering, and then watches as Annie's rider fails to canter before the announcer tells the class to walk.

Kenny breathes a sign of relief when the class finally lines up, following Annie towards the gate to meet their riders after the class. She is shaking her head in disappointment and once they are standing next to each other at the gate, waiting for the announcer to call the winning numbers, he says gently, "Maybe all the judges didn't see it and she can come back in the championship."

Annie shakes her head, "There's no way they'll get a ribbon. She had it won. All she needed was one lousy canter. I have never seen that girl miss a canter. Not once. I can't believe it."

"It's disappointing," Kenny comforts, at a loss for something more to say. They wait tensely, and Kenny is completely pleased when Missy and Secret Agent are awarded sixth place.

On the way back to the barn, a smiling Missy says, "That went better than I expected. She was good the first direction but got really strong and stubborn the second direction. I'm glad I didn't have to go another round. I was completely losing her headset."

Kenny nods, "You did well. I think we might adjust her curb chain when she shows in the Championship on Thursday night so she'll respect it a bit more."

"Would you be willing to show her on Thursday night?" Missy asks. "I've seen you ride her and I think she'd do better. You ride with more authority than I do. Now that she's had a taste of the ring, I bet she'll have a full head of steam on Thursday."

"I can if you'd like me to do that," Kenny says. "But why don't you think about it a bit before deciding. You did a fine job. Holly will be proud."

CHAPTER 69

Melody is standing next to Helen's buggy, waiting for the gate to open for the Amateur Ladies Fine Harness class. They are parked near Sneaky Suspicion, and Helen notices her looking at the horse and driver that Kenny Rivers is coaching.

"Holy smokes! That woman looks so elegant." Helen says. "Is that Sneaky Suspicion?" Before Melody can affirm it, she continues, "The World Champion Harness Horse is in my class?"

Melody smiles, wondering why Helen hadn't realized that before this moment. "Yes, but she still puts her gown on one sleeve at a time," she jokes.

Helen laughs, "Ha! Or her Spanx one leg at a time?"

It's now Melody's turn to laugh, and Kenny must hear them because he looks over and says loudly, "Good luck Helen! Ninja looks great!"

"Thanks," Helen replies. "He was bred by some cowpoke from Wyoming." Their conversation is interrupted by the announcer in the warm-up ring, telling the class that the gate has opened.

Helen instantly tenses and Melody notices it immediately. "We'll give the others a chance to go in first. Don't forget to breathe, Helen," Melody reminds, as she adjusts Helen's black skirt and jacket. "How do you feel?"

"I feel great. My fingers are numb, but they don't hurt."

"Watch his ears so that you'll know if you're putting too much pressure on the reins. Pay attention to his signals and you'll do fine. We've got people spread all around the ring and there will be someone helping you with traffic. So just listen carefully and don't second guess. You had a great warm up and you look fantastic."

Helen smiles nervously, "I hope I don't embarrass you."

"There's no chance of that," Melody assures her. "Just stay calm and cool. Trust yourself and trust Ninja." She judges the traffic of the harness horses heading down the ramp to the ring and gently takes Ninja's rein. She looks over her shoulder at Helen, "Ready?"

Helen nods, readjusting her long whip slightly in her hand, "Let's do this thing."

Melody clucks gently at Ninja and they start jogging towards the gate, "Easy, easy, easy," she repeats as they begin the descent into the brightly lit show ring. Roger and the groom are at the rear of the buggy, holding it back so that it doesn't cause the horse to rush, and then Melody steps to the side as soon as she is sure the horse is aimed down the rail of the show ring.

She and Roger have pre-planned their positions around the ring, and have also stationed Matthew at the far end so that Helen will hear a familiar voice at every turn. Melody watches her client make her first pass, looking more tentative than the trainer would like, but completing the pass without any incident. She sees Matthew at the far end, step forward to tell Helen about the traffic behind her just like they've practiced, and is happy when Helen guides Ninja deep into the corner, allowing her to have a wide spot on the rail to herself for the next pass.

When Helen gets near her, Melody says, "Nicely done. Now step it up a notch Helen and go deep."

Helen clucks to Ninja and uses her reins to keep the gelding on the rail.

Melody notices that Roger must have given her the same message, as Helen gently touches the whip to Ninja's rump and the horse increases his animation and energy in response. Helen continues to improve with each pass, completing the class with only minor mistakes when she misjudges the speed of a horse in front of her during the reverse. When the announcer tells the class to line up, Roger jogs into the ring to stand at Ninja's head, and Matthew waits anxiously with Melody for the announcement of the awards.

"How do you think she did?" he asks.

"Really well. I think she did great." Melody's comments are cut short by the announcer's statement that Eileen Miller and Sneaky Suspicion have won the class, and watches Kenny Rivers as he follows Eileen's buggy to the far end of the ring to receive her awards.

It only takes a few minutes for the other ribbons to be announced, and Helen leaves the ring with a broad smile, a white

238

ribbon in her lap. "I got fourth!" she tells Melody unnecessarily when Melody meets her at the top of the ramp. "Can you believe it? I thought when I made that mistake on the reverse that I probably had messed up too badly to get a ribbon! I can't believe I got fourth! I think I was better the second direction than I was the first, don't you think?" Without waiting for a reply, she greets Matthew. "Look babe! We got fourth!"

Melody exchanges smiles with Roger as they escort their pleased client back to the barn area.

"Do you think I should show back?"

Melody looks at her in disbelief, "Yes I do. Are you joking? There's even room for you to move up. You're right that you were better the second direction. You had a lot more confidence and it translated to Ninja. If you show like that going the first way, you have a solid chance of getting a ribbon in the championship. You fit into the class well. We'll go through the video when they email it to us tonight and I'll show you what I mean. You looked great."

CHAPTER 70

9:00 PM August 22, Kentucky State Fairgrounds

"Tell me how it went!" Holly demands as soon as Eileen answers her phone.

"It went well. Sneaky Suspicion was fabulous. We won the class."

"Oh! I'm so glad. I can't believe they won't give me any access to internet. I had to cry before they'd even let me call you! Tell me everything!"

"She was great, Holly. She marched through that class as though she owned the green shavings. I'm so proud of her."

"Oh! That is great news. Congratulations! She loves that ring. I remember last year that when she got that blast of cool air in her face coming down the ramp she just lit up like a Christmas tree."

"That a great description," Eileen says. "She just strutted down the ring. She felt so confident."

"That's the best news I've had in a while. How did Missy do?" Holly asks.

"I'll let you talk to Kenny. I didn't get to see her class. I was back here at the stalls getting dressed for mine. But before I hand the phone to Kenny, tell me how you're doing."

"I'm good. I hated the therapy sessions at first. It seemed so intrusive and fake, but I guess I've gotten used to them because it isn't so bad now. The hardest part is that I feel so isolated. No TV, no internet, no phone. I've resorted to yoga to pass the time."

"That sounds like torture," Eileen jokes.

"No kidding. And they only feed us healthy stuff. I would kill for a cheeseburger and a bag of Doritos."

"I'll buy you both as soon as you get home," Eileen promises. "How do you feel?"

"Disgustingly healthy. And all kidding aside, I'm learning a lot about myself and what triggers my desire for alcohol."

"That self-awareness is key for avoiding a relapse."

"I know. But some of the triggers are hard to avoid. Like loneliness. I need to find a way to make friends and I think I'll get a dog. But being stressed out about money is a trigger, too. And that's harder to avoid."

240

"I'll help. We'll figure it out, Holly." Eileen catches Kenny's eyes. "Kenny wants to talk to you though before they make you end the call." She hands the phone to Kenny.

"Hey there," he says quietly.

"Hey. I'm sorry I was such a bitch to you. I know that you're doing me a big favor."

"No problem. I need to talk to you about Secret Agent." He tells her about the class, ending with "She got sixth, but I'm not sure we deserved that good of a ribbon. She was good the first direction, but started to fall apart the second direction. She just got more and more stubborn, leaning on the bridle and refusing to sit back on her hind end. She was a freight train. Missy has suggested that maybe I should show her back in the championship but I'm not at all sure that I could ride her any better than Missy. Do you think I should try another bit?"

"It will probably help if you change her snaffle and either raise or lower her noseband by a notch. I used to change her bit really often, every couple of weeks or so. I kept thinking that I couldn't find one she liked, but maybe she just likes change." Holly pauses, obviously thinking through the problem "I've experienced exactly what you describe, though. Typically, when a horse is leaning on the bit, we'd fix it by lightening up the hands and strengthening the seat and legs, but Missy has great hands, so I don't think that's going to be the key here. The only thing I've found that works other than the bit change is to make the mare wait on the transitions and not let her step forward until all of her weight is on her hind end."

"What do you mean by that?"

"It's almost like she's easily bored, and if you get too predictable, she finds ways to entertain herself and usually that includes just going faster and faster."

Kenny thinks through this, "You might have something there. When I first started working her, she was an angel. It seems like the longer I work with her, she gets to be more and more of a renegade."

"Yeah. Exactly. You really have to use your body with her. You might have better luck than Missy just because you're heavier and stronger. I'd also put on a little spur to distract her and give her something else to think about."

"Thanks Holly. I'll give those things a try. She's a nice mare, she's just got kind of a stinky attitude."

"They're telling me They're telling me that I have to hang up," Holly says hurriedly. "Congrats on the win tonight. I wish I was there."

"I do too, but you have to be where you are. Get well and get back to the barn before I screw up all the hard work you've done."

After he hangs up, he hands Eileen's phone back to her. "She sounds good."

"She does, but I worry about what will happen if she has to step back into the barn and pick up where she left off. She'll be just as isolated and stressed as before she left. What's to keep her from falling back into the habits?"

"A good sponsor and regular meetings?" Kenny suggests.

"I'm sure that will help, but I'm not sure it will be enough." Eileen looks upset. "Is there any chance you would consider moving back to Kentucky and helping with the barn?"

Kenny sighs, "I love our life in Wyoming. I like working with the cattle as much as the horses, and I think it is good for our family. I know how difficult it is to be a horse trainer in Kentucky, and especially in Shelby County. I certainly don't mind stepping in for the few weeks that Holly is going to be gone, but I don't really have any desire to come back to this life."

"I understand. I just thought I'd ask."

"Maybe Holly would consider finding a partner or being an assistant at a barn. She's a great trainer and there are some barns around that could use her. My old boss at Kiplenan Stables is looking for an assistant. He's very calm and they don't have a lot of outside clients. That might be a really good place for Holly and for your horses as well. He stands a couple of his own stallions, but I imagine he'd consider taking in Spy Master. Do you want me to arrange a meeting?"

CHAPTER 71

"I'm so sorry Annie. I don't know what happened. I couldn't get her to pick up that second canter. And when I couldn't get it the first two times, I panicked. It's all my fault. I can't believe I did that." Amber's voice trails off.

Despite her own disappointment, Annie comforts the young woman sitting beside her in the lounge area for Big View Farm. "These things happen. I wish our entire industry didn't put so much stock into this one show. The pressure causes even the most experienced of us to make mistakes. I once saw a reigning world champion road pony come into the ring and go the wrong direction."

Amber puts her head in her hands, "I feel like I blew Dreamy's chance to get the ribbon she deserves."

"Yes. I really thought you had it won." Annie sighs and leans back in her chair, running her hands through her gray hair. "Well, it's over. There isn't anything we can do about it. We need to work a few horses for tomorrow and try to get some sleep. Tomorrow is another day. The championship for the four-year-olds is open, so she didn't need a ribbon to show back. But after watching the stallions go, I'm convinced the first-place ribbon is locked up and I think it will be hard for the judges to give Dreamy a great ribbon, even if you have a perfect ride. I think we should just sit out the championship class."

Amber's eyes well with tears of disappointment. She sniffles once and asks, "Annie, did you scratch Dreamy from the Amateur class? Did you remember that we double-entered her because we weren't sure which path would be best?"

"I remember that, and I didn't scratch her. I should have, though. Remind me to stop by the office in the morning."

"I know this is a crazy idea, but would you consider letting me show Dreamy in the Amateur Five-Gaited qualifier?"

"Absolutely not. That class is the second class tomorrow night. It's only a few hours away. That is far too much to ask from a four-year-old. We just have to take our licks and accept it."

243

"I know it's a lot to ask, but I could take it easy on her. We only need an eighth-place ribbon to qualify for the championship. Then, she would get to rest until Saturday night."

"That young mare doesn't know how to take it easy," Annie's frustration comes through in her voice, but she stands and begins to pace, thinking about Amber's idea.

"Please give me a chance to redeem myself, Annie. I messed up. It was my fault. I've gotten a million canters in my life and I can't believe that I missed the most important one of Dreamy's career."

"That's overly dramatic, Amber. She'll have other chances. She's young. She has a long career ahead."

"I know I'm being dramatic, but please let me try to fix this. I won't screw up again."

"It's a crazy idea. We shouldn't even be considering it," Annie says quietly. "I know that on the county fair circuit, people show gaited horses two nights in a row all the time. But they're usually seasoned horses and she's only four."

Amber leans forward in her chair, watching Annie closely as the trainer paces around the small lounge area.

Finally, Annie stops and looks at Amber, "This is probably a really bad idea so I need to think about it. I'm willing to consider it. Let's see how she looks in the morning. If she looks good, then maybe we'll see how she warms up. If she looks tired or off in any way, we don't go into the class."

"Oh my gosh. Thank you. I promise that if I get another chance, I will not screw up again."

"I think you'd better go hand-walk her and then give her another liniment rub down. Then we'll let her rest and see how she is tomorrow."

CHAPTER 72

Annie is waiting at the top of the ramp when Amber trots Dreamy from the ring after the Amateur Five-Gaited Mares qualifier, waving a fifth-place ribbon and smiling.

"She was good, Annie. I could tell she was tired, so I did my best to shorten her class by not taking an extra pass when I could have. But she was wonderful. She wasn't irritated and she stayed completely square."

As they walk back down Stopher Walk to return to the stalls, Annie pats Dreamy's neck in appreciation. "She looked good. I could tell that she wasn't as strong as last night. That second rack was about 70% as fast as she usually goes. I'm glad she has four days to rest before we ask anything of her again."

"I'll give her another liniment bath tonight and massage her legs before I wrap them. Do you think we could maybe get her a massage tomorrow? I know someone that might come do it for us."

"That's a good idea. She might really like that. Let's do the liniment rub, wrap her legs, give her electrolytes, and then hand-walk her just to relax her. Try to get a massage scheduled for late tomorrow morning. Then we'll just give her some light exercise before letting her have the rest of the day off."

"Thanks for letting me show her tonight. I know that you weren't very comfortable with it."

"I wasn't, I'll admit. But she's a big, strong, young mare and she showed a lot of maturity tonight. She kept her head and did her job. I'm really proud of her." Annie looks up at Amber and shrugs, "I still don't know if she has enough starch to win on Saturday night against the rest of the amateurs. The top couple of horses are going to be tough. But that's the track we're on now, so there's no sense in second-guessing it."

CHAPTER 73

"I'm so proud of you Blair! You rode Texas Debutaunt like a boss!" Blair, Bobby, and Jennifer have all returned to the stalls after Blair's win on Texas Debutaunt in the Amateur Five-Gaited Mares qualifier. A groom leads Debbie into her stall, and Blair smiles broadly.

"She was so good. Her rack was like sitting on a cloud. It was so smooth!"

"She was good from the first step. I've never seen you come into the ring like that. The judges couldn't take their eyes off you!" Jennifer gives Blair a hug and then hands her the championship ribbon so she can pose for photos.

"I just knew you would win," Marianne's triumphant voice sounds from the end of the aisle. "I just can't believe it wasn't unanimous."

"Have you seen the judge's cards?" Bobby asks curiously.

"I have. That judge from Texas gave her a fourth. Either he's blind or else he has some sort of bone to pick with you, Bobby. I don't know how he could possibly have thought she was fourth."

Bobby and Jennifer make eye contact, and Bobby gently says, "No, I've never met him and I'm sure that he didn't give Blair a fourth for some sort of personal reason. There were a lot of nice horses in there and he must have seen something that we didn't see."

Marianne expels an indignant breath, "Well, I've no doubt that those other judges will get him in line before the finals on Saturday night." She exchanges air kisses with her daughter.

Turning to Bobby she continues, "You must have been happy to see that Missy got last place on War Paint."

Blair rolls her eyes, "Mother, you know that she didn't get last place. There were 21 horses in the class."

"Well, she got the last ribbon, which is the same thing, really."

"Mother, it isn't the same thing at all."

"She had a lot of trouble on her last canter transition," Jennifer says quietly. "It was going pretty well until then."

246

"Were you watching her instead of Blair?" Marianne's tone is accusatory and Jennifer can't resist the bait.

"No, Marianne. I was watching Blair and all of her competition because that's what I do."

Bobby recognizes the flash of anger in Jennifer's voice and quickly steps forward to diffuse the situation, "I just can't say enough about how proud I am of Blair. She rode liked she owned that ring. Very smart ride. Good ring management and she trusted her horse."

"I've already engaged a caterer for the victory party here on Saturday night, so will you make sure that you have adequate tables available?" Marianne is talking while she looks at her phone, oblivious to the surprised looks being exchanged by everyone else.

"Mother! You're going to jinx it! What if I don't win?"

Marianne doesn't even look up from her phone, "Fiddlesticks, Blair. You're a beautiful rider. There's no doubt you'll win another World Championship."

CHAPTER 74

"I'm glad we aren't showing Dreamy in the Junior Gaited Class tonight," Amber greets Annie. "It's so hot out. Tomorrow and Saturday are supposed to be much cooler. Dreamy will be fresh as a daisy for the Amateur class. I'm dying to see how that Rebel Leader looks in the Junior Gaited class tonight.

"It's not the way I planned it, but ending up in the Amateur class might turn out to be serendipitous. Dreamy has recovered well and from everything I can tell, that colt could win the Junior class if he only had three legs. He's going to be the next great gaited horse in our industry, I believe. And we might as well benefit from you maintaining your amateur status this year. You must be ready to start earning some money."

"Yes, my savings from selling Texas Debutaunt are running low. I hope that I can make it all worth the sacrifice by getting a nice ribbon with Dreamy on Saturday."

Amber, I have to tell you something," Annie says gently.

Sensing immediately that something is wrong, Amber apprehensively asks, "What is it?"

"I sold Dreamy this afternoon."

"What?" Amber is sure she hasn't heard Annie correctly, "I didn't even know that you had shown her to anyone."

"I didn't. They bought her without riding her."

"Who? Who bought her?" Amber tries to keep her voice calm, but her chest and throat are tight and her voice comes out an octave above its usual level.

"Missy Phillips."

"Oh no." Amber's disappointment is evident and she sinks into one of Annie's sling-back chairs.

"I'm sorry, Amber. I know that you love her, but we're in this business to make money."

"I really thought Dreamy had a chance to help me win the Amateur gaited class this year. Is Missy going to try to show her?"

"Well, that's the good news. She still wants you to show Dreamy on Saturday night."

"No kidding?" Amber studies Annie's face, trying to figure out if she's sincere.

"No kidding. We aren't going to complete the sale until after the class. So please don't have a big wreck in the ring. I don't care if you hurt yourself, just please don't let Dreamy get injured." She is obviously trying to make a joke, but Amber doesn't even smile, so she goes on. "I was thinking that maybe you could transition to professional status as soon as the class is over, assuming you still want the life of a horse trainer."

"Yes, that was my plan."

"Then I'll split Dreamy's commission with you."

"Really? You don't have to do that."

"I know that I don't have to, but it's only fair. I would say that you've earned it, but that would be illegal. Since you're an amateur, you actually can't earn anything."

"Wow. That's so generous. Thank you."

"So there's one other thing."

Amber's smile fades, "Oh? What's that?"

"Missy said that she'd pay a bonus if you won the Amateur class on Saturday night."

"She's going to pay a bonus? Isn't she going to show in that class?"

"Yep. She's showing War Paint and she's going to reward us for beating her."

"That's awesome," Amber says, brightening considerably. "I'll do my best to make that happen."

CHAPTER 75

"Oh my gosh, Helen! You look beautiful!" Melody gawks in astonishment at her glamorous-looking client.

Helen ducks her head in embarrassment. "You don't think it's too much? Matthew set up an appointment for a makeover this afternoon. But I'm a little worried that it's too much."

"I made her promise to show you before she washed it off." Matthew interrupts his wife, "I think she's gorgeous."

"Everyone's staring at me, though."

"Helen! Everyone's staring because you look like a movie star!" Melody adds, "Don't change a thing! You're stunning. And that dress fits you perfectly." She calls over her shoulder, "Roger! Come look at Helen!"

Roger emerges from the tack room and does an obvious double-take when he sees Helen. Her hair is piled on her head and she has sparkly earrings in her ears. Her navy blue sequined jacket and skirt hug her body, and are accentuated by jeweled ballet flats. He gives a long, low, admiring whistle. "You look like a million bucks, Helen."

"You do!" Melody agrees. "You look like you are ready to win the Amateur Fine Harness class tonight. How do you feel?"

"I feel great. I've been keeping on top of my pain today. The numbness is always there, but I don't hurt at all."

"That's wonderful news," Roger looks relieved. "You have a little time before you need to get in the buggy, so let's talk through your drive."

Matthew helps Helen settle carefully into a chair, and Roger starts talking. "We're going to warm up a little differently than we did on Monday night. We'll start a little early so that we can work gradually and we'll use the big practice ring out behind the barns. We'll put you in the buggy out there when the class before yours goes in. That will give you time to trot around once each direction."

"Won't I get to trot up and down Stopher Walk before the class?"

"Not tonight. I want Ninja to be really bright when he hits the ring, and I think that we'll try to time it so that we can start trotting at the end of Stopher Walk and then take a big gentle turn and keep going right into the ring."

A look of concern crosses her face, and Roger hurries on. "You're a good driver. You can handle this and I'll be right beside you. The grooms will be behind the buggy. I want you to hit the ring with a big, bold trot this time. On Monday, we kind of pussy-footed around the ring the first direction. Tonight, I want you to hit the ring and let everyone in Freedom Hall know that you came to win."

At her uncertain nod, he continues. "You're good enough, Helen. And you owe it to Ninja to help him do his thing. I've watched your video over and over. You were stellar the second direction on Monday night. If you had looked like that the first direction, you'd have given that lady from California a run for her money."

"I messed up the reverse," Helen reminds him.

"I've watched it a dozen times and only one judge even saw that, and he didn't make any annotations on his card. I'm completely convinced that didn't have anything at all to do with your placing." Roger takes a deep breath, "You look like a winner, Helen. I'm not just blowing smoke at you. You have a real shot at this. You just need to believe it yourself."

Helen is quiet for several moments, obviously digesting Roger's words. "Okay. I'm in it to win it."

"That's the spirit," Melody agrees with a smile.

Thirty minutes later, Roger helps Helen into the black-lacquered fine harness buggy, and he and Melody adjust her clothes.

"Take a deep breath," Melody advises, studying the tense look on Helen's face. "Be tough. Be confident. Take control and show everyone that you deserve to win this."

"You guys give the best pep talks, ever!" Helen says weakly.

"We wouldn't say it if we didn't believe it," Melody quickly retorts, then in a calmer tone she goes through a last-minute list of reminders. "Sit up straight. Relax your shoulders. Keep them right over your hips to stay stable. Widen your feet a little so that you feel well-balanced. Don't forget to use your voice to let Ninja know that you're watching out for him. Watch his ears so you'll know what he's paying attention to. If his ears aren't pricked forward, change something so they are."

"Let's do this thing," Helen answers, looking determined as she clucks to Ninja and trots down Stopher Walk to Freedom Hall.

Fifteen minutes later, Helen is in the line-up with Roger at Ninja's head. She shrugs at him and raises her eyebrows, pantomiming her curiosity about how he thought the class went.

He smiles broadly at her and gives her two thumbs up. "You two were on fire," he says quietly. "It's like you were on a different planet from the drives I've seen you make before."

Helen says, "I don't even remember most of it. I just concentrated on letting Ninja do his thing."

"You were good," Roger confirms confidently. "Really good."

"Do you think I'll get a ribbon?" she asks quietly, glancing over her shoulder to make sure the judges aren't in ear shot, and noticing that they've already returned to the kiosk in center ring.

"Hell, yeah, I think you'll get a ribbon," he answers.

Helen mentally crosses her fingers and tries to wait patiently for the announcer to finish introducing the presenters and to announce the ribbon winners.

"We have a number of firsts in this class," he begins. "We have a first-time winner."

When he pauses dramatically, Helen looks around at the other drivers around her to see who might be celebrating.

He continues with "And this is the first time we've had a World Champion born and bred in the state of Wyoming."

He keeps talking, but Helen can only hear roaring in her ears. She is so surprised she drops her whip and her mouth falls open in shock.

"Yeah BOY!" Roger yells, leading Ninja out of the line up and towards the end of the ring where a small crowd has gathered with their arms full of awards.

It takes the entire distance to the end of the ring for Helen to begin to recover from her surprise and to replace the shock on her face with a beaming smile.

After the awards, photos, and her victory pass, the entire team from Mountain Ridge Stables jogs back up Stopher Walk with championship ribbons streaming from both sides of Ninja's bridle and a blanket of yellow roses covering Helen's lap. There are tears streaming from under her clear goggles, making tracks in her makeup as they flow down her face. Her smile dominates her face, and everyone they pass smiles and yells their congratulations as she repeats, "Oh my gosh. What just happened?"

"You just won a World Grand Championship, babe!" Matthew is jogging alongside the harness buggy with the others, laughing and breathless. When they finally stop in front of the stalls, they're met by Kenny, Emily, and Eileen, who is holding her Reserve Grand Champion ribbon and a bottle of champagne.

Kenny steps forward to help hold Ninja and repeatedly pats the horse on the neck. "Congratulations!" he calls. "We tried to give you a run for the roses, but you were too much for us tonight. Holy cow, Helen. Where did that drive come from?"

She laughs, "Would you believe that I don't even remember most of it?"

"You were definitely in the zone, Helen. I've never seen anyone concentrate that hard. You were focused like a laser. I wasn't even sure you heard me when you came by," Melody says. "But it didn't matter, because I just wanted you to keep doing what you were doing!"

Roger shakes Kenny's hand, "Congratulations, friend. You just bred, raised, and trained a World Grand Champion!"

After they help her out of the buggy, Eileen extends a hand to Helen, "Congratulations! We haven't ever met but I wanted to come over and say how happy I am for you! Kenny says that you folks are the nicest people on earth, and I'm really happy for you." Helen bypasses the hand shake and hugs Eileen, while asking Emily to take pictures.

As everyone is posing with Ninja and the ribbons, Roger mentions to Kenny. "I'm sorry you missed that award ceremony,

Kenny. They mentioned that was the first time a World Grand Champion had been bred, born, and raised in Wyoming!"

"That's awesome!" Kenny responds. "But we didn't do so bad. Eileen got second place. That's the second time I've been part of a Reserve World Championship. The first time was with Spy Master in the Gaited Stake many years ago. It's not as good as winning, I'm sure, but I'm happy with it."

"I have a feeling that you'll have more chances," Roger nods towards Emily. "You must know that you made the biggest mistake of your life bringing Emily to Kentucky for the last month."

Kenny looks proudly at his young daughter, who is still taking photos of the happy group. "I'm really glad that I brought her. She's been a ton of help at the barn, and now she wants to show gaited horses."

Roger laughs, "She's lucky to have a dad that breeds nice horses. It makes them a lot easier to afford."

CHAPTER 76

"Well, that was disappointing, but we did the right thing," Missy remarks, watching Kenny dismount from Secret Agent. "The warm-up was a disaster and I don't think the class would have been any better. I'd rather step back and not enter the ring, than go in and give her a bad experience."

"I'm sorry, Missy. I think you made the right choice. I would have been willing to try it, but if she were my horse, I would have made the choice you did. She's just not mature enough to handle this show, yet. I'm convinced she'll get there, but it almost never pays off to hurry one. In my experience, you're much better off to step back and be patient."

"I was watching all the horses in the warm up ring and she might not have gotten a ribbon, even on her best day. The four-year-old crop this year is really strong."

"I'll have Emily help me put her away. Why don't you watch the rest of the class on the monitor? I'd like to know if Rebel Leader wins it unanimously. He's about all anyone can talk about at this show."

"Yes," Missy agrees. "I wonder if he's going to show up in the Amateur division next year."

"It's hard to say, but it takes a very special stallion to have the temperament for that. They're pretty rare." Kenny leads Secret Agent into her stall and gently removes her bridle, slipping on her halter and attaching the cross ties. He leaves Emily to remove Secret Agent's tack and joins Missy in front of the monitor that is showing the final rack from the Junior Five-Gaited Championship. The camera, which typically moves from horse to horse as they make their passes, is fixed on Rebel Leader. The display shows the liver chestnut four-year-old with the big blaze and four white legs as he makes an entire circuit of the ring, effortlessly passing horses. The crowd roars as he passes, with many spectators out of their seats watching the exciting young stud dominate the class. By the time they finally announce the winner, it is a foregone conclusion that a new and exciting young horse has taken the sport by storm.

"He looks like he could win the Gaited Stake this year," Missy says, marveling at his talent.

Kenny agrees. "It will be interesting to watch him in the future. The owners have some difficult choices to make. They could win everything on him, or they could send him to the breeding shed and introduce an alternative that could rival Spy Master."

"Or maybe they could do a bit of both," Missy muses. "Imagine what a stud like that might do crossed with something like Annie Jessup's mare."

CHAPTER 77

"Is Vendome ready?" Jennifer asks Bobby. "Can I do anything to help?"

"Yep, he's all ready to go," Bobby answers, rubbing the gelding's gleaming neck. "I sure love this horse."

"I know you do. I've never had to compete with a woman for your affection, but I know that I've met my match with Vendome Copper. If he left the barn for some reason, I wouldn't be surprised if you went with him."

"We meet a lot of horses in this business, and there aren't that many that make a lasting impression. This boy changed my life. He is the reason that I stayed in this business when Johnnie Stuart fired me. Louise Clancy-Mellon moved all her horses over to Kiplenan Saddlebreds and recommended that Clark Benton hire me as an assistant. He's the reason that I met you, when you brought Blair and Marianne over to try him out. When they bought him from Clark, I came with the package."

"And the rest is history," she finishes, leaning in to kiss her husband.

"I'm glad that Blair and her mother didn't sell him when they bought Texas Debutaunt."

"It's the first time in the many years that I've known her when Blair has stood up to her mother," Jennifer says, petting the horse's nose. "I think she loves him almost as much as you do. What do you think his chances are tonight?"

"I think it depends on how Blair rides him," Bobby says, lowering his voice so they won't be overheard by their clients. "He's a professional show horse. He'll do what she asks of him. No more, no less. If she rides as well as she rode Debbie the other day, we'll be fine. But if she rides him like she did in his qualifier, it could be a struggle. I need to go give her a pep talk."

"Yeah. I'll wait with him if you want to do that now." Jennifer takes Bobby's place at Vendome's neck, using a comb to make sure his mane is laying perfectly flat.

Bobby finds Blair pacing nervously in the aisle. "Let's talk about your ride for a minute, alright?"

She nods. "I need to redeem myself after my ride on him in the qualifier. I sucked."

"That's overstating it a bit, Blair. You got fourth. That isn't sucking. But I would agree that you can do better."

"I saw on Facebook that someone said Vendome Copper was over the hill because I got fourth. I hate that I'm not doing him justice."

"By now, you should know better than to listen to people on social media. That platform is full of people that think they know more than they do. The last time I checked, there was at least one Five-Gaited stakes winner that was 15. Many of them were 11 or older. Vendome is only 13, and he's totally sound and healthy. There isn't any reason at all that he won't show another three years or so."

"It's hard not to listen to their chatter. It gets under my skin."

"That's actually what I wanted to talk to you about before your ride tonight. I want you to ride Vendome with the same intensity you rode Debbie with the other night. Even though you're comfortable on him and you've been showing him for a long time, you need to focus on every single step. Pay attention every single moment. You have a tendency to make a good pass and then let your guard down. The competition is too fierce for that. You have to show the judges that you want to win more than anyone else in the class. Resist the tendency to look perfect. It's a horse show. Not a riding competition."

She smiles slightly, "Surely you're not suggesting that I usually look perfect."

He laughs, lightening the mood. "I want to see you come out of there with sweat dripping down your face. Even better if you're sweating through your suit coat." He glances up, listening to the announcer on the closed-circuit television in the corner. "That's our cue. Let's go out and beat somebody."

In just ten short minutes, Blair and Vendome are ready to enter Freedom Hall for the last class of the evening, the Amateur Ladies Five-Gaited Championship.

"Remember what we talked about. The key to this is going to be to focus on your ride and your signals to your horse. Work hard to keep him elevated. Not too fast down the ramp, but then use your legs to push him on."

Blair takes a deep breath, clucks once, and rides into Freedom Hall.

Bobby hurries to the rail, checking the opposite side to make sure that Jennifer is already in position, and then switches his attention to Blair and Vendome. They are almost halfway through the first pass and look good. Vendome's ears are pricked forward and his knees are popping up well above level with every stride. He takes a moment to compare her speed to the horses around her and waits for her to trot by. "Lower your post a tad and more leg. Step it up a notch."

He watches her trot around the end and is pleased when she raises her inside hand slightly to reset his head for the next pass. He can see Jennifer lean forward and say something as Blair passes, and notices that Blair drops her hands a fraction of an inch in response. This brings Vendome's head up slightly, improving the overall picture and enabling him to drive more powerfully from his hind quarters. Bobby continues watching and sees the ring master motion to the announcer to ask the horses to walk, so he moves further toward the end of the ring so that he will be next to Blair when she asks Vendome to slow gait.

He judges it perfectly and as Blair walks toward him, he says, "Don't get in a hurry. Just widen your hands, keep them low, sit deep, and keep using your legs." He watches her anxiously when the announcer asks for the slow gait, and Vendome makes the transition effortlessly. Bobby notices two judges writing her number down as she passes them and she is next to him on the rail when the announcer tells the class to rack.

"Set him up in the corner, then GO!" He almost shouts the last word to be sure she hears him as she goes by, and he can hear Jennifer's voice on the other side of the ring, "Good, good, good, keep that!"

The class racks two full circuits around the ring before the announcer calls for a walk. Blair is near Jennifer when it is time to make the canter transition, and it goes perfectly. She halts Vendome, Bobby can see her lower her right hipbone slightly and very subtly shortens her right rein. He takes the canter cue immediately and Bobby breathes a sigh of relief.

When she canters by him, he tells her, "You're doing great. On the reverse, cut through the middle and make them look at you."

The class is on the opposite end of the ring when the announcer calls for the walk and he can see Blair looking over her shoulder to judge the traffic. When the announcer tells the class to reverse, she hesitates until she has a clear path past the judge, then sits the trot for a couple of paces before turning Vendome in a large arc towards the center of the ring. He watches her adjust her reins and lower her post, and trot past the judge that hasn't yet appeared to notice her. Bobby watches with satisfaction as the judge cranes his neck to read her number and makes a note on his card.

The next time she trots by, Bobby says, "Show him your whip before the next pass." He watches carefully as she makes the next turn and waves her whip once over Vendome's inside shoulder. Her horse increases his animation and speed, and she passes two horses in front of the judges on the next pass.

During the next gait change, Bobby can see that Blair is tired. Her face is red and he can see she is breathing through her mouth. "Keep breathing," he coaches. "Take your time. Keep your hands low. You're doing great."

He watches her complete the class without any incident, and after the horses line up, he and Jennifer join the other trainers and grooms that jog into the ring to remove the saddles for the conformation judging. Blair has halted at the far end of the ring and as they jog up the green shavings, Bobby asks Jennifer, "What do you think?"

"It was the best ride she's had in her life," Jennifer answers with a grin.

He grins back, "It wasn't just me then?"

"Nope. Let's not screw it up now." Jennifer breathes hard, reaching their rider first and holding Vendome while Blair dismounts.

"I know that you halted as far away as you could just to make us run farther than anyone else, right?" Bobby teases, breathing hard as well.

"I figured that if I was going to sweat, you might as well do the same," Blair responds. "What do you think?" standing back from Vendome as her trainers quickly remove the saddle and begin wiping the sweat from him with clean towels.

"You did everything you needed to do. I'm proud of you," Bobby says over his shoulder, adding, "Let us know when the judges are three horses away."

They work furiously to make Vendome shine and to set him up while the judges quickly look at his conformation, making annotation on their cards before turning away. They quickly re-saddle him and Jennifer holds Vendome while Bobby gives Blair a leg up to mount. Jennifer leads Vendome in a small circle, making sure that Blair has her reins adjusted and is secure before releasing the bit.

Bobby pats Blair on the leg before they gather their towels and leave the ring, only to return a few moments later when Blair and Vendome Copper are announced the winners of the Amateur Ladies Five-Gaited Championship.

CHAPTER 78

As is their custom, Lee Kiplenan and his best friend Michael Vine are seated next to each other, sipping bourbon and watching the final classes of the World Championships.

"My favorite class is this next one," Michael says. "I'd rather watch the Amateur Five-Gaited Championship than the open class with all the professionals in it."

"I prefer it as well. It's always a huge class," Lee agrees. "And you get to see several of the same horses each year."

"And a lot of these amateurs can ride as well as the professionals."

"They can." Lee mentions casually, "We're going to have a new stallion at the barn this next breeding season."

Michael looks at him in surprise. "Did you buy a new stallion? Or is it one you raised?"

"Neither, actually. It's an outside stallion."

"Really? I've never known you to do that."

"This opportunity was too good to refuse. I get to use him myself."

"Who is it? Anyone familiar?" Michael asks, sipping from his bourbon.

"Spy Master," Lee answers, trying to keep the grin from his face.

Michael begins coughing, obviously struggling to keep from shooting bourbon through his nose. "Spy Master? The leading Saddlebred stallion for the last two years?"

"Yep. That's him. I made the deal last night. Eileen Miller is moving her horses over to Kiplenan and her trainer, Holly McNair will be Clark's new assistant."

"Wow. That's an interesting change."

"I'm looking forward to introducing Spy Master's line into my blood lines. I think it could be pretty interesting. And Holly is young and talented. She is willing to ride the young horses that Clark doesn't want to ride any more. It could work out pretty well."

262

"I heard a rumor that Holly might have an alcohol problem. Clark is such a strait-laced teetotaler that they'll either be a perfect match or it will be dreadful."

Lee smiles, "I've never known Clark to have a real conflict with anyone. But yes, she's in California right now in some sort of alcohol treatment center. He talked to her on the phone and he seems really excited about having her join the Kiplenan team."

Their conversation is interrupted by the first amateur gaited horses, trotting through the gate into Freedom Hall. They watch quietly for a few moments, consulting their programs to figure out who the riders and horses are that they don't recognize.

"Damn. Check out that horse Amber Gianelli is riding," Michael says. "Didn't she ride for Clark a few years ago?"

"She did. She rode Emoticon for Louise the year she won the three-year-old gaited class. And the year before that, she rode Louise's mare Texas Beauty Queen. She got third."

"Oh yeah, that's right. Didn't she show in the Four-Year-Old Gaited Mare qualifier?"

Lee checks his program to be sure. "That's Dream Weaver, a foal out of Annie Jessup's great gaited mare, Josephine's Dream. She missed the second canter and didn't get a ribbon, but she came back the next night and rode the Amateur Mare qualifier."

"They were lucky she was double-entered and that's a risky move but it looks like a smart decision," Michael says. "She's putting those older horses to shame right now. And I saw that Junior Gaited Championship. That stud colt from California kicked everyone's ass. It sure bodes well for the young horses in our sport."

"It does," Lee agrees, keeping his attention on the class in the ring. "I wouldn't count the others out just yet in this class. Blair Durant is riding Texas Beauty Queen's foal, Texas Debutaunt. I watched her win the Mare qualifier. She won it easily. There wasn't a horse in there that even came close."

"I'm surprised about that. Missy Phillips is showing War Paint. That mare got second place in this class last year."

"She did, but that was when she was still at Beech Tree. She hasn't had a great year. She moved to Holly McNair's barn and that didn't seem to help. I'm not sure what's up with her."

They're both quiet, watching the class work at the slow gait, rack, and canter. Lee finally says, "Well, I don't see anything wrong with War Paint tonight. It looks like Missy is doing well. To me, it looks like a three-horse race."

"Let me guess," Michael says. "Missy's horse, Blair's horse, and that horse that Annie Jessup owns."

"That's what I see. Of course, the judges and I don't always see things the same way."

"They always say that the perspective is so much different from the middle of the ring."

"That may be true, but politics certainly play into it." Lee lowers his voice, "In a community this small, people are naturally going to have loyalties and friendships that will cause a judge to look more favorably or critically than they would if the entire thing was anonymous. I've thought and thought about this problem and have never come up with a good idea that would erase that."

"It makes it hard for the unknowns to compete against the famous and the monied," Michael agrees.

"It does. I truly admire all the people that stay in this sport in spite of the politics."

"If they didn't, there wouldn't be anyone to sell horses to."

"You're absolutely right about that."

"So if Holly McNair isn't here, who put Missy in the ring?"

"Do you remember Kenny Rivers? He was an assistant to Clark for a while. He came off a horse and got hurt and he kind of limped along with his own barn for a few years. Then he moved to Wyoming and has been running his family's cattle ranch. He's still breeding and training some Saddlebreds."

"Wow. That must be a unique sight in Wyoming. Is he the only Saddlebred trainer in the whole state?"

"Probably. He's turning out some nice horses though. The Amateur Fine Harness class was won by a gelding he bred. It's by Spy Master.

By now the class has reversed. Michael leans forward, "Okay Lee, let's make this interesting. I'll bet a bottle of Pappy Van Winkle that Blair Durant wins this class on Texas Debutaunt. Her slow gait is going to put her over the top. There isn't a horse in this class that can do that gait as well as Texas Debutaunt."

Lee watches the class carefully, "Okay, I'll take that bet. I think the four-year-old Amber is riding is going to win it."

"A four-year-old may have the talent, but does she have the strength and stamina to hang with these older, professional show horses?" Michael asks.

"We're going to find out."

CHAPTER 79

In the line-up, Amber and Missy happen to be next to each other. After dismounting and standing back while Kenny unsaddles War Paint and Emily holds the mare's bridle, Missy edges over towards where Amber is standing and asks, "How was your ride?"

"It was bittersweet," Amber replies. "I understand congratulations are in order. You're buying a wonderful young mare."

"Thanks. I would have mentioned it sooner but I wasn't sure you knew."

"Annie told me on Thursday. It makes me sad, actually. I love this horse and I'm really going to miss her."

"What do you mean? I thought Annie told me that you were going to be her assistant next year," Missy quickly glances from Amber to Annie.

"I am, I just meant that I'll miss Dreamy. She's my favorite horse in the barn."

"But I don't intend to move her. I thought Annie knew that."

It's obvious that Annie has overheard their conversation and she stares at Missy in surprise. "No! I just assumed you would move her to Kentucky."

Missy laughs, "Not if you don't make me! I had one of my most successful years when I was at your place. You'll take me back, won't you? I hope I'm not being too presumptuous."

Their conversation is interrupted when the judges come close, and Missy quickly steps back in front of War Paint, turning so that the judges can see the number on her back. Amber also turns, unable to suppress the grin that on her face.

Once the class is remounted and the trainers and grooms have left the ring, the announcer releases the class while the results are tabulated. Amber jogs Dreamy to where Annie is standing on the rail, and says, "What do you think my chances are?"

"Not sure. I was watching you and not paying too much attention to everyone else. I thought she did well. She kept her composure. I'm glad they didn't have to go any longer. I think she's going to sleep well tonight."

"I can't believe she's staying at Big View. I spent the last two days moping around for nothing."

Annie smiles, "You and me both. The money is great, but there was a part of me that was regretting it."

She is interrupted by the announcer, "This was a very strong Amateur Five-Gaited Championship, and we welcome Josephine's Dream to the winner circle!"

Amber's mouth falls open in surprise and she leans down to give Dreamy a big pat on the neck, waiting for Annie to enter the ring before racking to the end for the awards presentation.

CHAPTER 80

"We were robbed," Marianne tells Jennifer bitterly, looking over the catered spread in the aisle by Beech Tree's stalls in disgust.

Jennifer deliberately misunderstands her, saying "I think it looks delicious! There's more food here than we'll ever eat."

Marianne looks confused for a moment and then snorts, "I don't mean the food. I mean the second-place ribbon. I can't believe that horse from North Carolina beat us. Blair was a much prettier rider."

"Mom! It's not a riding competition, it's a horse show." Blair makes eye contact with Bobby and he has to turn away to hide his amusement. "And most people don't call it a second-place ribbon. It's a Reserve World Championship."

"That mare that won is out of Josephine's Dream," Jennifer says. "She's a very nice horse."

"From what I hear, we're probably going to see her again, too," Bobby adds.

"What do you mean?"

"I heard that Missy Phillips bought her."

Marianne's halts her inspection of the lavish cheese plate, "What? When did that happen?"

"I don't know. I just heard it on the rail tonight."

"I guess that explains why she looked so happy even though she got some low ribbon. I think it was fifth or worse. I stop paying attention after third." Her tone is derisive and she goes on, "I should have known that she wouldn't be able to stand Blair beating her this year. You're not going to let her come back to Beech Tree, are you?"

"She hasn't asked," Jennifer admits. "I'm not sure what her plans are. And I was really glad she got a ribbon tonight. War Paint was a lot better than when she showed at Shelbyville. That guy that stepped in for Holly McNair made a difference.

"I'm putting you two on notice," Marianne's gaze sweeps from Bobby to Jennifer and back. "You'd better find a way to win at Kansas City. I won't tolerate second place twice in a row."

268

"Mother! Stop it! I can't believe how rude you're being."
Jennifer, Bobby and Marianne all stare at Blair in shock.

"I mean it!" Blair's voice is tight. "You're ruining what should be a great celebration. I got a Reserve World Championship on Debbie and a World Championship on Vendome, and all you can do is obsess about Missy Phillips. It's rude and disrespectful to the hard work that Jennifer and Bobby do for us. We should be drinking champagne and taking pictures and celebrating. If you can't do that, then you should go home so that the rest of us can have some fun. You're spoiling what ought to be a pretty good party."

An awkward silence descends, and Marianne gawks at her daughter. "Well!" she finally huffs, looking embarrassed. "You're all taking me too seriously. Don't be so sensitive. I do appreciate everyone's hard work. I just have high expectations and I'm trying to keep you all from getting complacent. You're right that it was a successful show. And if I'm supposed to be celebrating, I don't know why no one has poured me a glass of champagne."